MURDER IN CHELSEA

Center Point
Large Print

Also by Victoria Thompson and available from Center Point Large Print:

Murder on Bank Street

This Large Print Book carries the Seal of Approval of N.A.V.H.

MURDER IN CHELSEA

⇀ A GASLIGHT MYSTERY ↼

Victoria Thompson

CENTER POINT LARGE PRINT
THORNDIKE, MAINE

This Center Point Large Print edition is published
in the year 2013 by arrangement with
The Berkley Penguin Group (USA) Inc.

The text of this Large Print edition is unabridged.
In other aspects, this book may
vary from the original edition.
Printed in the United States of America on permanent paper.
Set in 16-point Times New Roman type.

ISBN: 978-1-61173-854-4

Library of Congress Cataloging-in-Publication Data

Thompson, Victoria (Victoria E.)
Murder in Chelsea : a gaslight mystery / Victoria Thompson.
—Center Point Large Print edition.
pages ; cm.
ISBN 978-1-61173-854-4 (library binding : alk. paper)
1. Brandt, Sarah (Fictitious character)—Fiction.
    2. Women detectives—New York (State)—New York—Fiction.
    3. Nannies—Crimes against—Fiction.
    4. Malloy, Frank (Fictitious character)—Fiction.
    5. Police—New York (State)—New York—Fiction.
    6. Abandoned children—Fiction.
    7. New York (N.Y.)—19th century—Fiction.
    8. Large type books. I. Title.
PS3570.H6442M863 2013b
813'.54—dc23

2013012355

MURDER IN CHELSEA

To the real David Wilbanks,
thanks for saving the day!

Sarah hurried down Mulberry Street, dodging running children, housewives bartering vigorously with the street vendors, and the occasional stray dog. Mrs. Keller wasn't expecting her at any particular time, but her note had hinted at something ominous, something to do with Sarah's daughter, Catherine. And her note had arrived two days ago. Sarah had left the child with her nursemaid, Maeve, and her own sense of urgency spurred her on. She volunteered at the Daughters of Hope Mission as often as her midwife duties allowed, but the trip from her home on Bank Street to the Mission had never seemed longer.

At last she saw the ramshackle Dutch colonial house and managed not to actually run up the front steps. She knocked on the door and stared at the familiar sign that offered girls in need a chance to seek refuge at the Mission. Maeve had been one of those girls. After what seemed an eternity but was really only a couple of minutes, a girl answered. She wore the plain gingham dress and apron that passed as a uniform for the residents. She smiled in welcome.

"Mrs. Brandt, how nice to see you." She stepped back to allow Sarah to enter. "I didn't know this was your day to come."

"It's not. Mrs. Keller sent for me. Is she here?"

"Oh, yes, and she'll be that glad to see you, I'm sure. Do you want to wait in the parlor?"

"No, I'll . . . Is she in her office?"

"I think so."

"Then I'll just go on back. Thank you, Claire."

Sarah found Mrs. Keller's office door open. The woman who served as housemother to the girls had claimed the former butler's pantry as her own. The tiny room was spotlessly clean and neat as a pin. Mrs. Keller, a widow in her forties, sat at the battered desk. She looked up from a list she was making. "Mrs. Brandt, I'm so glad to finally see you."

"I just got your note this morning. I was out on a difficult delivery and was gone for two days."

"Oh, yes, I should have guessed that." She rose and closed the door.

Sarah's concern deepened. "Your note frightened me."

"I'm sure it did. Please, have a seat." Sarah perched on one of two mismatched kitchen chairs taking up most of the extra space in the room. Mrs. Keller took the other. "You haven't been able to adopt Catherine, have you?"

"No. A single woman can't adopt." Sarah's husband, Tom, had died almost five years earlier.

"That's what I thought, which is why I knew I had to contact you immediately. Someone came to the Mission the other day, looking for Catherine."

Terror twisted her heart. "Who? Her mother? Her family?"

"No, a woman named Anne Murphy. She said she was Catherine's nursemaid."

Sarah could only stare back in surprise. "A family who could afford a nursemaid would not have abandoned a child. That doesn't make any sense."

"I know, and I . . . Forgive me, I've been trying to remember exactly how Catherine came to be at the Mission. It was before my time here, and I've forgotten the details."

"She'd already arrived when I first discovered this place, but I understand they'd found her sleeping on the doorstep one morning. She had nothing but the clothes on her back."

Mrs. Keller nodded. "And of course she couldn't tell anyone where she came from because she couldn't speak."

"That's right. She didn't say more than a word or two until months after she'd come to live with me."

"Did you ever find out why she wouldn't speak for so long?"

"We took her to a doctor, and he believes

she'd been badly frightened by something."

"And now that she's started talking again, has she ever told you anything about her past?"

"She . . . she occasionally has a frightening memory, but nothing that makes any sense. Whatever it was, I don't think she remembers completely, and I'm not sure I want her to."

"I can understand that."

"So tell me more about this woman who came to see you."

"I have to say, I didn't want to believe her, but she has a very interesting story."

Sarah braced herself. "What did she tell you?"

"She said she lived with Catherine and her mother in a cottage in the country somewhere north of the city. Harlem, I think she said. Catherine's father would come to visit them from time to time. Miss Murphy knew him only as Mr. Smith, but she understood this was not his real name. He was quite wealthy, and he kept Catherine's mother as his mistress."

Stories like this were much too common, and Sarah knew they rarely ended well for the women involved. "Did she tell you how Catherine ended up here?"

"She said Catherine's mother believed her life to be in danger, so she asked Miss Murphy to take Catherine away and keep her safe."

Sarah gasped. "So this Anne Murphy abandoned her to strangers?"

12

"I was as appalled as you, but Miss Murphy pointed out that she did not know Mr. Smith's true identity or how extensive his power might be. She didn't even know if Mr. Smith himself wanted Catherine's mother dead or if it was someone else. With no idea who her enemies were, she decided to hide Catherine someplace she'd be safe and then disappear herself. She'd hoped to come back for the child later."

"It's been almost a year!"

"I know. I pointed that out and asked her where she'd been all this time. She said she'd found work and waited for Catherine's mother to get in touch with her, but she never did. She decided that since no one had come asking about the child in all this time that it must be safe, so she'd returned to claim her."

This was the most ridiculous story Sarah had ever heard. "Did you believe her?"

Mrs. Keller sighed. "Not entirely, no. There may be some truth to her story, but I had no way of judging which part or how much."

"What did you tell her?"

"I told her Catherine had left the Mission. That upset her, as you can imagine. She obviously cares for the child."

"How much could she really care if she just left her here all this time?"

"Oddly, that is the one part of the story I did believe. She is still genuinely frightened of

13

something or someone, even now. When I told her Catherine had gone, she feared the people who wanted to kill her mother had somehow gotten the child as well. I assured her that Catherine was safe and sound and very happy, but she refused to believe me. She demanded to see her."

"Oh, dear, Catherine is home alone with Maeve. What if she shows up while I'm gone?"

"I didn't tell her about you, Mrs. Brandt. You must believe I would never betray your confidence."

Relief surged through her. "Thank you, Mrs. Keller. I shouldn't have doubted you."

Mrs. Keller waved away her apology. "As I said, I didn't believe her story, or rather, I didn't know what part of her story to believe, so I decided I should tell you what happened and let you decide what to do."

Sarah had no idea what to do. She had a thousand questions, and she wasn't sure she wanted any of them answered. Was Catherine's mother still alive? Still in danger? Who had wanted her dead and why? Was Catherine in danger from the same people? Did her mother want Catherine back? And what about her father, the elusive Mr. Smith? Did he want his child or did he want her dead? Why had this Anne Murphy suddenly come looking for Catherine after all these months? Did she really care for the child or was she working for someone who wished Catherine ill? And if any of these people had a claim on the child, how on God's green earth could she bear to lose her? Sarah raised a hand to her throbbing temple, surprised to see it tremble. She closed her fingers into a fist.

"How did you leave matters with this Miss Murphy?" she asked.

"I told her I would pass her request along to the family who had Catherine. I said 'family' so she wouldn't know you're a woman alone. She gave me the address of a rooming house in Chelsea. I promised someone would contact her there. If you don't wish to see her, I'll send her a note and tell her you refused."

"I couldn't possibly refuse. I can't imagine she'd give up so easily, and she might cause you trouble here."

"I'm sure we could handle anything she might try."

Sarah smiled grimly. "I'm sure you could, but you know as well as I that we can't afford any more scandals here. Our donors have just begun to give again after the last trouble. They might decide to stop supporting us once and for all if there's more, and heaven knows, you barely make ends meet here as it is."

"Do you really think your mother and her friends would stop donating?"

"Not my mother, but I can't speak for her friends. Society women are . . . Well, their values are so different than ours."

Mrs. Keller smiled. *"Ours?* Didn't you used to be one of them?"

Sarah smiled back. "No. I fought them every step of the way, and then I eloped with a poor doctor and never looked back."

Mrs. Keller's smile faded. "This isn't getting us any closer to a decision, is it?"

"Yes, it is. I can't allow this Miss Murphy to cause trouble for the Mission, so I will go to see her and find out what she really wants."

"Do you think that's wise? Or even safe? Perhaps you should ask Mr. Malloy to go with you."

Sarah shook her head. "I can just imagine what he would say if I asked him."

"And he would be right. But if he knows you're going to meet with this woman no matter what he says, he'd accompany you, I'm sure."

He would, too. Detective Sergeant Frank Malloy of the New York City Police would *insist* on accompanying her. So she wasn't going to tell him anything at all.

"What's wrong, Mama?" Catherine asked.

Sarah had just tucked her into bed, glad beyond reason that no one had summoned her to a birth today so she could spend the whole evening with the little girl who had become so precious to her. "Nothing's wrong, my darling." She tried to smile.

Catherine's big, brown eyes missed nothing. "You look sad."

"How could I be sad when I'm with you?" She stroked the fine wisps of hair from the child's forehead and kissed her. She smelled sweet. Sarah fought the urge to wrap her arms around her and never let go. "I love you very much."

Catherine smiled. "I love you, too. I'm glad you're my mama."

Sarah blinked hard to keep her tears at bay. "I'm glad I am, too. Catherine, do you remember anything about where you lived before you came to the Mission?"

Catherine's smile vanished, and her chocolate eyes clouded. She shook her head.

"It's all right if you don't," Sarah said quickly. "I was just wondering."

"I want to stay with you."

This time Sarah did wrap her arms around her and held her close, burying her face in Catherine's gossamer hair and inhaling her little-girl scent. "That's what I want, too."

This was all she could promise at the moment.

A few minutes and many kisses later, the clouds had passed from Catherine's eyes and Sarah could finally leave her to fall peacefully asleep.

She went downstairs to Maeve, who had waited for her in the kitchen through the bedtime routine. Sarah watched the lamplight play on her coppery hair as she told her everything Mrs. Keller had said.

"I'm going with you," Maeve said, her dark eyes as clouded as Catherine's had been.

"You can't go with me. Who will stay with Catherine?"

"Mrs. Ellsworth would be thrilled to take her for a few hours, and you know it."

"We can't take advantage of her," Sarah tried, but Maeve rolled her eyes at such a ridiculous excuse. They both knew Sarah's neighbor would love having Catherine all to herself for a few hours.

"Tomorrow is Sunday, and she'll be over here right after Sunday dinner anyway. We'll ask her to take Catherine home with her. If you won't tell Mr. Malloy about this and something happens, I'm not going to be left behind to explain why I let you go off by yourself."

Sarah couldn't help smiling at that. Besides, deep down, she knew Maeve was right. She shouldn't see Miss Murphy alone. Most people wouldn't consider a seventeen-year-old girl a suitable companion for a potentially dangerous task, but Maeve was no ordinary girl. Only a few months ago, she'd helped find the man who had murdered Sarah's husband, Tom. "All right, but you have to promise to let me do all the talking."

She half expected Maeve to roll her eyes again, but she just grinned, pleased with her victory. "You know she's lying, don't you?"

"Of course she is, but at least some of her story

may be true. Mrs. Keller thought so, at least."

"Mrs. Keller is a nice lady, but she doesn't know about people like this Anne Murphy. Everything she said could be a lie."

Sarah knew Maeve's grifter grandfather had trained her to recognize the weaknesses of others. "I know it's hard for you to trust people, Maeve, but not everyone is a liar."

"I know that!" she said. "I may come from a long line of liars and thieves, but I've learned there are *some* good people in the world, like you and Mr. Malloy and Mrs. Ellsworth."

"Thank you for that."

"But I also know there aren't *many* of you. This Anne Murphy, she might never have even set eyes on Catherine. Maybe somebody hired her to make up a story to get her away from the Mission."

"Mrs. Keller said she seemed genuinely frightened of something."

"Maybe she's afraid whoever hired her will hurt her if she fails. You can't be too trusting, Mrs. Brandt."

"I hope nobody can ever say I was too trusting."

"My grandfather would've eaten you for breakfast," Maeve said in dismay. "And I can't promise not to say a word. What if I need to warn you about something?"

"Then pinch me."

Maeve rolled her eyes again. "That's a good idea. She'll never notice that."

"All right, you can speak, but try not to offend her, at least until we find out everything we can about Catherine's parents."

"If she even knows anything about Catherine's parents."

"Maeve . . ."

"All right, I'll be polite, but you have to promise me you won't give her any money."

"I don't have any money to give her."

"Your parents do, and she probably knows that."

"I told you, Mrs. Keller didn't tell her anything about me."

"Maybe she found out about you some other way. It's not a secret that you took Catherine from the Mission. Any of the girls who live there could have told her. She might've talked to any of them before she came to see Mrs. Keller."

Sarah hadn't thought of that. Maeve was probably right about her being too trusting. She just hoped Anne Murphy didn't eat her for breakfast.

Anne Murphy's rooming house was like hundreds of others in the city, a large old house the owners could no longer maintain, so they rented rooms. The Chelsea neighborhood varied between tenements and rooming houses where immigrants and their offspring found cheap lodging near their jobs on the waterfront. On this Sunday afternoon, the neighborhood seemed to doze in the wintry sunshine.

The slatternly woman who answered their knock looked the two women up and down with silent approval. "We're full, but if you're looking for a room, I might have an opening soon."

"We're looking for Miss Anne Murphy," Sarah said.

The woman's eyes widened. "Now what would you be wanting with her?"

"Is that your business?" Maeve asked, already breaking her promise to keep quiet.

Sarah shot her a warning look, then smiled at the affronted landlady. "Please excuse my sister. We were in the neighborhood and thought we would stop by to say hello to Miss Murphy. Is she in?"

"I ain't sure." She glared at Maeve.

"Maybe we could come in and wait while you check," Sarah said with her best finishing school charm.

The landlady reluctantly admitted them, offering them the meager comforts of the sparsely furnished parlor while she went in search of her boarder.

"Maeve . . ."

"You don't need to remind me," she whispered. "And by the way, nobody will believe I'm your sister."

She was probably right about that. With her red hair, Maeve could never pass for anything but

Irish, while Sarah's honey gold hair and practiced bearing marked her as one of the upper classes, no matter how unfashionable her clothing might be.

Sarah swallowed her reply as Anne Murphy stepped into the room. A woman of middle age with a trim figure and a handsome face, she clutched her hands in front of her. She glanced over her shoulder, then back at them. "Who are you?"

"Mrs. Keller sent us," Sarah said, not ready to reveal her name just yet.

Miss Murphy stiffened. "I see." She glanced over her shoulder again. "Let's go up to my room so we won't be . . . overheard."

Sarah turned to Maeve for guidance, and the girl shrugged and nodded. They followed Miss Murphy up the stairs and down the hall, close enough for Sarah to notice the worn heels on her once stylish shoes. Her clean shirtwaist showed wear, and she wore her auburn hair in a simple bun. Whatever work she'd found during the past year had not been lucrative.

Like the parlor, her room was sparsely furnished, with an iron bedstead, a dresser, a washstand, and two straight-backed chairs.

"Sit down," Miss Murphy said, indicating the chairs. She closed the door behind them after checking the hallway one last time. Then she perched on the edge of the bed. "The landlady is nosy. I didn't think you'd want her listening in. Now, who are you?"

"You don't need to know my name just yet." This had been Maeve's suggestion, and Sarah thought it a good one. If Miss Murphy didn't know who she was, she couldn't find her later. "Mrs. Keller told me you're the one who left Catherine at the Mission."

"Her mother told me to take her someplace where she'd be safe."

Sarah almost winced. She'd come to think of herself as Catherine's mother. "How could you know she'd be safe there?"

"It's a place where they take care of girls, isn't it? And I couldn't keep her with me, could I? They'd've found us for sure."

"Who is this 'they' you're so frightened of?"

She pressed her lips together, and for a moment Sarah thought she wouldn't answer. "I don't know."

"You expect us to believe that?" Maeve asked.

Sarah shot her another look, but she didn't see it. She was too busy trying to stare down Miss Murphy, who proved to be no match for her.

"I don't know *for sure*. It could've been a couple of different people, couldn't it? All I know is Miss Emma told me to pack up and get away as fast as I could and take Catherine someplace safe and she'd find us."

"Miss Emma? Is that Catherine's mother?" Sarah asked.

Miss Murphy clapped a hand over her mouth.

Sarah let it pass. "How would she find you?"

"She said she'd write to me at . . . at this place we both knew."

"And did she?"

"A few weeks ago, finally. I thought . . . I'd started to think she was dead, didn't I?"

"What did she tell you?"

"She said it was safe to bring the girl back. I'm to meet her in a few days."

"Then you haven't actually seen her?" Maeve asked. Sarah didn't give her a look this time.

"I told you, we're going to meet soon."

"How do you know she was the one who wrote the letter then?" Maeve asked. "Maybe she is dead and whoever killed her wants to get his hands on Catherine now."

"I . . . I know her handwriting."

Maeve glared at her the way they'd both seen Malloy glare at people he didn't believe. "Do you?"

Miss Murphy suddenly squared her shoulders. "No need to be rude now. I don't have to talk to you at all, do I?"

"You do if you want to find Catherine," Maeve said.

Sarah silenced her with a gesture. This was getting them nowhere. "If Catherine's mother is alive, of course we want to see them reunited," Sarah said, even though the words almost stuck in

24

her throat. "But we aren't going to put the child in danger. Now I want you to tell me everything you know about Catherine's mother and father and why you think someone is trying to kill this woman, Emma."

"And why should I?" Miss Murphy asked.

"Because if you don't, I'll walk out of here and you'll never see me or Catherine again."

Miss Murphy's shoulders slumped in silent defeat. "All right, I'll tell you, but how do I know you aren't trying to find the child yourself?"

"Because I'm the one Mrs. Keller told about your visit to her, and I'm the one who has Catherine. Now stop acting like a goose and tell me everything."

Miss Murphy glanced at Maeve as if expecting her to weigh in, too, but this time Maeve wisely said nothing. "I don't know what Mrs. Keller told you . . ."

"Start at the beginning."

She sighed. "Miss Emma and I were friends for a long time. Well, not friends exactly, but I knew her. From the theater."

"What theater?"

"Not just one. I mean she was *in* the theater. An actress. She sang, too. Real pretty. All the men was wild for her. She got flowers every night from somebody. Then Mr. Smith come along."

"Catherine's father," Sarah said.

"That came later, of course. At first, he just sent

her flowers. I never thought anything about it, but then he stopped by to see her after the show one night. I didn't want to let him in, but when she saw how fine he looked in his expensive clothes and how he was older than most of the other men who sent her flowers, she told me it was all right."

"Were you an actress, too?" Maeve asked.

"No, I . . . I worked backstage, helping the girls dress and such."

"Go on."

"He invited her out to supper that night, and then he started coming for her every night after the show. He gave her things, jewelry and such. She told me his name wasn't really Smith, that the waiter where he took her to eat called him something else, but she never told what. She knew he was rich, though, rich as a king. The girls in the chorus don't get paid much, you know, so she liked that he gave her things. She even started thinking maybe he would invest in a show for her or something, so she could be the star. But then she found out she was going to have a baby."

"How did Mr. Smith react to that?" Sarah asked.

"She didn't want to tell him, but she had to do something about it, and she didn't have money for anything like that, so she had to. He was happy about the baby, though. He wouldn't let her get rid of it. Said he'd get her a house and keep her in style. He did, too, and she hired me to look after her and take care of the place. Cute little house, too."

"Where was it?" Sarah asked.

"Way up in Harlem. Miss Emma, she didn't like being out in the country like that, but I did. So pretty and quiet, and we had flowers. They grew in the yard. Somebody'd planted them before we came, and they'd come up every year. All kinds and colors."

Sarah remembered Maeve and Catherine cutting the last of the summer flowers in her yard last fall. Catherine had suddenly started screaming about some bad people taking the pretty lady away. She'd thought then that it must be a memory of her previous life. Could the flowers have triggered the memory of the garden in Harlem? And what had frightened her so badly? "Then what happened?"

"Catherine came, and Mr. Smith, he doted on her. He would've been happy to keep things just like they was, with us living in that little house and him coming to see us a day or two a week."

"But I'll bet Miss Emma got bored, didn't she?" Maeve said.

"How'd you know that?" Miss Murphy asked.

Maeve shrugged.

"She would have gotten very bored after all those years," Sarah said. "How many was it? We aren't quite sure how old Catherine is."

"She'd be almost five now, I guess. She was born in July, on the fifth. I remember because we could see fireworks out the window while Miss Emma was in labor."

"So Emma was stuck out there in Harlem for over four years, first waiting for Catherine to be born and then watching her grow up," Sarah said.

"Oh, it wasn't that long because she went back to the theater."

"How did she do that?"

"Mr. Smith, he knew people and got her some jobs. She told him she wasn't going to sit around a parlor mending socks for the rest of her life, and he didn't want her to take Catherine and disappear, so he let her go back to acting. Well, singing it was, mostly. She never was real good at acting, but she could hold her own in the chorus."

"Did she make the trip into the city every day?" Maeve asked.

"Heavens, no. Even on the train, it's too far. She'd get a room and live there during the run of the show, and when it closed, she'd come back home until the next one."

"And you stayed with Catherine?"

"Yes, it was just her and me most of the time. We got along fine, we did. She was a sweet little mite."

"So she'll remember you," Sarah said.

Miss Murphy frowned. "I expect she will, but you know how it is with wee ones. They forget you if you stay away too long. Sometimes, Catherine cried when her mother came home because she didn't know who she was."

Sarah exchanged a glance with Maeve. Was

Miss Murphy trying to explain in advance why Catherine wouldn't recognize her? How easy it would be to send Miss Murphy packing if Catherine didn't know her. "Your life sounds idyllic. What happened to change it?"

"I don't know exactly. I know when Mr. Smith came one day, he and Emma had a terrible row. I took Catherine out for a walk, so I don't know what it was about, but after that, things was never the same between them."

"How soon was it after this before she told you to take Catherine away?"

"Just a few days, but not before some other people came to the house."

Sarah leaned forward. "Who?"

"Mr. Smith's son was one of them. I knew he was because when I opened the door, he looks me up and down and says, 'So this is Father's little whore. Kind of long in the tooth, aren't you?' I almost slammed the door in his face, but Miss Emma come running and told me to leave her alone with him."

"Do you know what they talked about?"

"I know Miss Emma didn't think much of him. He tried to scare her, I think, but she wasn't worried, at least not at first. Mr. Smith was that mad when he found out, and I'll tell you, I never expected the young man would ever come back, but he did, and the next time he really scared Miss Emma."

"What did he do?" Sarah asked.

"He brought another man with him, a friend of his, I guess. I never did get the straight of it, but the two of them come barging in, wanting to see Miss Emma, and when they found her, they laid hands on her. Didn't hurt her really, but the son, he grabbed her and shook her like she was a doll."

Gooseflesh rose on Sarah's arms. "Where did this happen?"

"At the house I told you about—"

"No, I mean where in the house?"

"Well, it wasn't *in* the house at all. It was in the garden. Miss Emma was cutting flowers, and—"

"And Catherine was watching her," Sarah finished.

Miss Murphy gaped at her. "How did you know?"

She knew because watching Maeve cut flowers had reminded Catherine of that day and frightened her so badly she'd started screaming a year later. "Then what happened?"

"The son threatened her. She wouldn't tell me what all he said, but I heard enough to know he wasn't teasing. Seems like Mr. Smith had put Catherine in his will or something, and the son didn't like that one bit. He wanted everything for himself."

"In his will?"

"Yes. I didn't know what that meant, but Miss Emma said it meant when Mr. Smith died,

30

Catherine would get some of his money. I thought that was a nice thing for him to do for the child, but it just scared Miss Emma. That's when she told me to take Catherine someplace safe. She didn't want to know where we went so they couldn't make her say."

"And what happened to Emma?"

"I . . . I'm not sure."

"But you have an idea," Maeve said.

Miss Murphy frowned at her, but she said, "I do at that."

"Are you going to tell us what it is?" Maeve asked.

"Maeve," Sarah tried, but Maeve ignored her.

"Are you?"

"I think she went on tour."

"On tour?" Sarah frowned, thinking of the European tours people like her parents took. "She went on a holiday?"

"Not a holiday. She went on tour with a show. They're always putting together touring companies of shows that start out here, and they travel all over, doing the show in different places. They don't get the first-class actors to go because nobody wants to be away from the city that long. People forget you, you know. And it's a hard life, traveling all day and doing a show in some dirty little theater and then moving on to the next place in the morning. She never would've done it otherwise, but if she was desperate enough, it

31

was a way to go someplace Mr. Smith's son couldn't find her."

"Wouldn't Mr. Smith have protected her?" Maeve asked.

"I don't know why she didn't try that. Maybe she did. Maybe he wouldn't believe no evil of his son. Some men are like that. And I don't know for sure that's what happened, you see. It's just what I hope happened. What I pray happened, because if it didn't . . ." Her voice broke and she dropped her eyes.

"Because if it didn't . . ."

"Well, maybe Mr. Smith's son found her and killed her like she was afraid he would."

2

"She's probably right, you know," Detective Sergeant Frank Malloy said, glaring at Sarah across her kitchen table. "This Emma woman is probably dead, and you're lucky you and Maeve didn't join her. What were you thinking?"

A telegram sent to Malloy's flat had probably terrified his mother—telegrams never bring good news—but it had brought him to her doorstep that evening without alerting anyone at Police Headquarters that she was looking for him. Malloy took enough teasing about her as it was.

"I was thinking I wanted to hear her story before I decided what to do next."

She hadn't often seen him quite this furious. "I thought Mrs. Keller already told you somebody wanted to kill Catherine. How much more of the story did you need to hear before you thought about calling in the police?"

"If they wanted Catherine, they aren't likely to harm me until they find her, now are they?" Sarah was getting a little angry herself.

"You couldn't be sure of that."

"Will you stop being unreasonable and help me figure out what to do next?"

"I'm not being unreasonable!"

"You most certainly are!"

"Stop it, the both of you!" Maeve said, stomping into the kitchen in her wrapper. Her auburn hair hung over her shoulder in a braid.

"I told you to go to bed," Malloy said.

"How can I sleep with the two of you shouting like that? You're lucky Catherine didn't wake up."

That silenced both of them. Malloy contented himself with a murderous glare, which Sarah ignored. "Maeve and I didn't get ourselves murdered, and I'm asking for your help *now,* Malloy. Will you give it?"

"Of course I'll give it. And I won't let this Anne Murphy off as easy as you did either."

"What will you do to her?" Maeve asked with way too much interest.

"Never you mind, but she'll tell me this Mr. Smith's real name and who this Emma woman is and where she's been hiding all this time." He turned back to Sarah. "Are you sure nobody followed you when you left her place?"

"I wouldn't have even thought to check, but Maeve did, and she was sure."

Malloy glanced at Maeve, who flipped her copper-colored braid over her shoulder and grinned. "I made her get on the El and ride around

34

for a while. First south for a bit. Then off and a few blocks of wandering. Then back north. If anybody followed us, we lost them."

Sarah couldn't see how anyone could have kept up with them in the crowded city streets, in any case. "If you've calmed down, can we talk about what to do next?"

Malloy rubbed a hand over his face, and Sarah felt a pang of guilt. He'd had a long day, and now she was saddling him with her problems.

"This can wait until tomorrow if you're tired."

"I don't dare let it wait until tomorrow. There's no telling what the two of you will get up to in the meantime. And don't start telling me you weren't in any danger again, because you know you were. That's why you didn't tell me about this before you went. You knew I wouldn't let you go see this woman by yourself."

Sarah saw no point in arguing since he was absolutely right. "So you'll go with me tomorrow?"

He looked at her as if he'd never seen her before. "No, I will *not* go with you tomorrow," he said with exaggerated care, "because *you* are not going anywhere tomorrow. I will go and see this woman myself and find out what you couldn't."

"And then you'll come straight here and tell us?" Maeve said.

Malloy narrowed his eyes at her. "Didn't I tell you to go to bed?"

"If you're going to start yelling again, I won't be able to sleep."

"Maeve," Sarah said.

"All right, but you know we'll be worried. Don't make us wait too long," she said before flouncing away.

Malloy shook his head. "We never should've let that girl get involved with those Pinkertons."

"We didn't exactly *let* her," Sarah reminded him. "Besides, she made a very good detective."

He just shook his head again and pulled a small notebook out of his pocket. "Give me the address of this woman's rooming house." He wrote it down and tucked the notebook back in his pocket.

"Thank you, Malloy."

"For what? I'm just as fond of Catherine as you are."

"Thank you for being as fond of Catherine as I am." She smiled then, and he smiled back, a lopsided half grin that made her heart flutter a bit. For a second, she thought . . .

But he cleared his throat and stood up. "It's late. I'd better go."

Knowing she had no right to be disappointed, she followed him out through the front room that served as her office, the room that had been her husband's office when he'd been alive and practicing medicine. Malloy gathered his hat and coat from where she'd hung them earlier in the front hallway.

"Malloy, you never told me what you and my father talked about when you went to see him."

He hesitated just an instant as he buttoned his coat, hardly enough to notice but enough to tell her she'd touched a nerve.

"He just wanted to thank me."

She could hear the strain in his voice, the uneasiness he felt about her father. She still wondered if her father had offered him a "reward" for helping him solve the murder of one of his fellow club members. Such things were common practice in the city, of course. The police rarely solved crimes unless such rewards were paid, but she also knew Malloy's pride chafed at having her father acknowledge it. "He *should* thank you. Did you talk about anything else?"

Malloy's dark eyes twinkled just a bit. "Why don't you ask your father? Good night, Mrs. Brandt. I'll stop by tomorrow when I have some news for you."

Sarah was gritting her teeth as she locked the front door behind him. Ask her father indeed. He'd be more tight-lipped than Malloy about whatever business they had together. She knew someone who might be able to find out, though.

If anyone stood a chance, it was her mother.

Malloy figured he'd be sure to catch Anne Murphy in first thing the next morning. If he went before reporting to Headquarters, he also

37

wouldn't have to worry about being called out on an investigation and getting tied up all day. He wanted to get this settled as soon as possible—before Sarah and Maeve could get themselves any more involved with this Murphy woman.

He found the address easily enough among the ramshackle houses crowded in between the looming factories and warehouses in Chelsea. He was surprised to find the front door ajar on this wintry morning. Even if the weather had been pleasant, nobody in this neighborhood left the front door hanging open. He rapped on the jam and called out, "Hello? Anybody home?"

He pushed the door open and peered into the gloom of the entrance hall.

He blinked, letting his eyes adjust, and then the shadow at the foot of the stairs became a woman's body sprawled at an awkward angle. "Hello? Anybody here? Hello?" he shouted. Surely, a boardinghouse would have more than one resident.

The woman didn't stir at the sound of his voice or when he knelt beside her. "Miss? Are you hurt? Can you hear me?"

She lay facedown, her head turned to one side. He touched her cheek. Still warm. He started to turn her, but stopped. Blood had soaked the front of her shirtwaist, but there was no pool of it on the floor or the stairs around her. He fumbled for her wrist, searching for a pulse even though he already knew. Only dead people did not bleed.

The sound of footsteps on the porch brought him to his feet. He turned to find a woman in the doorway staring at him in surprise. "Jesus, Mary, and Joseph!" She pulled her overflowing market basket closer to her worn coat. "Who might you be and what're you doing in my house?"

"I'm Detective Sergeant Frank Malloy of the New York City Police Department, and who might you be?"

"I might be the Queen of Sheba, for all it is to you. I don't allow men in my house, and I especially don't allow police in my house, so . . ." Her gaze drifted past him to the figure on the stairs. "Hello, what's that? What's going on here?" She pushed past him, glared down at the body, then back up at Frank. "What've you done?"

"I haven't done anything."

"The devil you say!" She slammed him with her basket. "Look at her. Annie? What has he done to you, Annie?"

"Is that Anne Murphy?"

"Of course it's Anne Murphy, as if you didn't know. What've you done to her? Killed her, most likely. Dear heaven, is that blood on her?"

"It seems to be."

"Murder! You've done murder!" She dropped her basket and ran out the front door, screaming . . . Well, screaming bloody murder.

Frank sighed. It was going to be a very long morning.

• • •

Sarah knew it was going to be a long morning and maybe a long afternoon as well, if Malloy couldn't get back to them. She almost wished someone would summon her to a birth, just so she'd have something to help pass the time, but of course no one did. Babies never came when she wanted them to.

Luckily her neighbor Mrs. Ellsworth came over to help the girls make a pot roast. The cooking lesson kept Catherine busy and distracted. It also kept Sarah from pulling the child into her arms and never letting her go. How would she bear it if some stranger returned to claim her?

At least she now knew Catherine's real age and her birth date. But would she still be here to celebrate her birthday in July? Sarah couldn't stop the ugly thoughts from plaguing her as she watched Mrs. Ellsworth and the girls at their work.

When the pot roast was in the oven, Maeve and Catherine went upstairs to play, and Mrs. Ellsworth turned to where Sarah sat at the kitchen table. "Mrs. Brandt, you look troubled."

"Is it so obvious?"

Mrs. Ellsworth pulled off her apron and hung it up. "I hope you aren't stewing over a difficult birth or something."

"No, I . . . Well, I shouldn't worry you with my troubles, but a woman went to the Mission the other day, asking about Catherine."

"Oh, dear! Who was she?" Mrs. Ellsworth asked, pulling out a chair for herself.

Sarah told her what she and Maeve had learned about Anne Murphy.

"I knew it," Mrs. Ellsworth said.

"You knew about this woman?"

"Oh, no, not about her exactly, but I knew something bad was going to happen. I saw an owl yesterday morning, in the tree out back. It's very bad luck to see an owl in the daylight."

Sarah managed not to roll her eyes. At least the girls weren't there. They were fascinated by Mrs. Ellsworth's superstitions, and she always seemed to have one for every occasion. Sarah didn't mention that she'd heard the owl hooting last night. Heaven only knew what that meant.

"Mr. Malloy was right," Mrs. Ellsworth said. "You should never have gone to see this woman without him. You don't know who her cohorts might be."

"I'm afraid I didn't think about her having cohorts or anything else, for that matter. I just wanted to find out if she really has any claim on Catherine."

"I remember that day last fall when we were outside and Catherine had that . . . Well, I don't know what to call it."

"I know, I don't either, but she was so frightened. I can't help thinking that the 'pretty lady' she was remembering was her mother."

"I suppose I always half believed that myself,

41

even without having heard this woman's story. What kind of a woman sends her child off heaven knows where and doesn't even inquire after her for a year?"

Sarah sighed. "A woman who fears for her own life, perhaps, or that of her child."

"Mrs. Brandt, you're picturing Catherine's mother as some angelic creature who sent her child to safety, but I don't think that's necessarily accurate."

"I don't think she's angelic," Sarah protested.

"Maybe not, but you do think she's like you, at least."

"Like me?"

"Yes. You're trying to picture her as a respectable person who loved Catherine above everything else, but the story this Miss Murphy told suggests otherwise."

"You mean because she was an actress?"

"I mean because she thought nothing of going off and leaving the child for weeks at a time while she carried on in the city. Oh, I know she'd hired this Murphy woman to take care of the child," she added when Sarah would have protested again, "and if she needed to work to support herself and her child, I could applaud her devotion. But she didn't need to. This Mr. Smith supported her."

Sarah had to admit she had a point. "I suppose she really loved acting and didn't want to give it up."

"Even for her child?"

Sarah frowned. "I hate to say it, but she wasn't very happy about having a child. Miss Murphy said Emma originally asked Mr. Smith for money for an abortionist, but he convinced her to have the baby instead. He promised to take care of them, and it sounds as if he kept that promise."

"At least for a while."

"Miss Murphy said Emma and Mr. Smith had an argument shortly before Miss Murphy left with Catherine. I hadn't thought about it, but maybe he told her he was tired of her and was going to turn her out."

"If he wasn't going to keep them anymore, that would explain why she sent Miss Murphy and the child away," Mrs. Ellsworth said.

"But Miss Murphy said he doted on Catherine. Surely, he wouldn't punish her just because he was tired of her mother."

"Men do strange things," Mrs. Ellsworth reminded her. "Maybe he had come to believe the child wasn't his. Maybe he wasn't as fond of Catherine as Miss Murphy thought. Or maybe he lost all his money and couldn't afford to keep them anymore."

Sarah rubbed her temples, more than tired of trying to figure out why people she'd never set eyes on had done what they'd done. To her relief, someone rang her doorbell. Maybe it was Malloy.

• • •

Frank stood in the doorway, watching the orderlies carry Anne Murphy's body out to the waiting ambulance.

Doc Haynes, the medical examiner, said, "I'll do an autopsy, but I doubt I'll find anything surprising. She was stabbed in the chest with an ordinary kitchen knife. The blade probably nicked her heart or a major blood vessel. From the trail of blood, she was stabbed upstairs in her room and managed to get to the stairs, probably trying to get help or maybe running away from her attacker. At some point she died and fell the rest of the way down the stairs."

This was pretty much what Frank had determined before Haynes ever got there, while he'd been taking a look around and waiting for the hysterical landlady to get back with a beat cop in tow. She'd expected the cop to arrest Frank, but instead he'd obeyed Frank's orders to summon the medical examiner. "If you could tell me who stabbed her and why, I'd be very grateful, Doc."

Haynes grinned. "Ask me after the autopsy."

When he was gone, Frank closed the door and turned to the beat cop who'd been waiting around in case he was needed. "How's the landlady doing?"

"Fine once she broke out her gin. After a glass or two, she settled right down. She didn't want to believe you was a copper, you know. She thought for sure you killed that woman."

"Thanks for looking after her."

"Like I said, she was no trouble after she had herself a nip or two. She's in the kitchen."

Frank found her sitting at the table, staring at an empty glass. "Mrs. Jukes?"

She scowled. "Are you still here?"

"I need to ask you some questions."

"I don't have no idea who done for her, if that's what you want to know."

Frank was glad to note she didn't seem too drunk. "How long has Miss Murphy lived here?"

"Less than a month. Leastways, she paid for a month, and the rent's not due for a few more weeks."

"What did she tell you about herself?"

She sighed. "If a woman's got the price of a room and she don't look or act like a tart, I take her. I don't ask for no references, if that's what you mean."

"I don't expect you do. I meant did she tell you anything about herself? Did she have any visitors? Did she have a job?"

"She didn't have a job. My other boarders, they do, though. That's why she was here alone this morning."

"If she didn't have a job, how did she pay the rent?"

"She had the cash. I don't do charity work, if that's what you're thinking."

Frank hadn't thought that for a minute. "She didn't mention where she got her money if she didn't work?"

"What do I care where she got it? She could've stole it from the U.S. Mint for all I know. It's nothing to me as long as I get paid."

Frank didn't sigh. "When did you last see her?"

"She come down to breakfast early, with the rest. If you want to eat, you're here when I serve it. Then she went back up to her room. I never saw her again until I got back from the market and . . ." She shook her head.

"What time did you leave the house?"

"How do I know? A little after eight, I imagine."

Frank had arrived a little after nine, so he'd probably just missed the killer. "Did you see the knife Miss Murphy was stabbed with?"

She winced. "Yeah."

"Is it from your kitchen?"

"Not that I know of."

"Do you know if Miss Murphy had it in her room?"

She frowned at this. "How would I know? Boarders, they have all kinds of things in their rooms."

"So you never saw it before?"

"No, I never."

"What about visitors? Did anybody come to see her while she lived here?"

"Not that I ever saw, until yesterday. Two

women come to visit. Ladies, they was. I don't know what they wanted with her."

Sarah and Maeve. Maeve would be flattered to have been thought a lady. "Nobody else?"

"Like I said, not that I ever saw, but I'm not here all the time, am I? Like today. Jesus, Mary, and Joseph, if I'd been here, I might be dead, too."

"I think whoever killed her waited until she was alone."

"How can you know that? How do you know they won't be back and kill all of us in our beds?"

"Because Miss Murphy was involved in something dangerous. That's why I came to see her today, to question her about it, so you don't have to worry. Whoever killed her was only interested in her."

"What do you know about it? You didn't know a thing about her or why would you be asking me?"

Frank again managed not to sigh. "And you're sure she didn't have any other visitors?"

She glared at him again.

"Was she friendly with any of your other boarders?"

"Not likely. Kept herself to herself, that one. But if she wanted to see somebody, she didn't have to do it here. She went out most afternoons."

"Where did she go?"

"She wasn't likely to tell me, now was she? And what did I care? It's not like she was out all night and coming in drunk. She went out in the

47

afternoon and come back in time for supper. It's included with the room, and she never missed but once or twice."

So whoever had contacted her about Catherine must have met her someplace else. "I'll need to search her room and pack up her belongings."

This got her attention. "Pack them up for what?"

"To take as evidence."

"Evidence? Evidence of what, I ask you? Her clothes didn't stab her."

"What do you care about her belongings?"

"Somebody might come for them."

"You said she didn't have any friends."

"How do I know who she had? Her family might want her things."

"Then they can get them from the police."

Mrs. Jukes frowned. "I might need to sell them to get my rent money."

"You said she was paid up for a month."

She had no answer for that and had to content herself with another glare. "Just don't make a mess. It's bad enough there's blood everywhere. Them stains'll never come out of the floor-boards."

Frank made his way back up the stairs, following the blood drops to Anne Murphy's room. It looked like a thousand other rooms in cheap lodging houses, where people with little money and less hope found a place to live and some human companionship. Only the overturned chair and the blood splashes on the floor betrayed the violent death the room's occupant had suffered.

Miss Murphy's meager wardrobe hung on pegs on the wall, an extra skirt, a woolen cape, a jacket that matched the skirt. The drawers in the washstand held her extra linen. A brush and some stray hairpins lay on the stand beside the bowl and pitcher. A battered carpetbag sat in one corner.

He searched every inch of the room, fingering each article of clothing for anything hidden in pockets or seams. He pulled out the drawers and turned them upside down in case something had been stuck underneath. The carpetbag was empty with no secret pockets. He checked under the sagging iron bed, then he pulled off the bed-clothes and shook each piece.

Finally, he flipped the mattress up off the bed and there it was, a thin packet of letters placed squarely in the middle, so someone tucking in a sheet or blanket wouldn't accidentally discover them. They'd been tied into a bundle with string. The envelopes were addressed to Anne Murphy but at an address a little farther north, in the Theater District.

Frank righted the chair overturned in Anne Murphy's final struggle and sat down. The oldest letter, dated about five weeks ago in January, instructed Anne to find a boardinghouse where no one would know her and wait there for further word. It was signed, "Emma."

The next letter, dated two weeks ago, told her Emma would be returning to the city soon, and she would meet Catherine and Miss Murphy and they would leave the city together. Anne was to write to her, care of General Delivery in Philadelphia, and tell her where she was living. Anne Murphy must have panicked when she realized she couldn't locate Catherine. Emma would have been furious to find the child missing.

The letters had no return addresses, and the postmark on the oldest one was Indianapolis and the most recent was Altoona, Pennsylvania. Miss Murphy's theory about Emma touring was probably correct. The last letter, the most interesting one, had been sealed and addressed —in a different handwriting—to a Mr. David Wilbanks on Seventy-second Street on the Upper West Side. Frank ripped it open and found a letter from Miss Murphy, telling him that Emma would soon be returning to the city to reclaim Catherine and take her away. It also indicated that Miss Murphy would be happy to tell this man where to find Catherine, if he paid for the information. She didn't say it right out, of course, but her meaning was clear. So Miss Murphy did know the real name of Catherine's father, and his address, too.

Frank decided he would leave Anne Murphy's belongings for Mrs. Jukes to dispose of. All he needed were these letters. And he'd deliver one of them to Mr. David Wilbanks himself.

• • •

"Oh, Sarah, what were you thinking? I come by to spend time with our darling Catherine and you tell me you put your life in danger!" her mother asked when Sarah had finished telling her tale. "Mr. Malloy was right. What if this Miss Murphy had attacked you?"

"I think Maeve and I could have adequately defended ourselves. I'm not the one in danger, in any case."

"Of course you're not, my dear, but they might have tried to force you into telling them where Catherine was."

"I think you're reading too many novels, Mother. Things like that don't happen in real life."

"Of course they do. Where do you think novelists get their ideas?"

Sarah decided not to answer that question. "And there is no 'they' to force me to do anything. There is just Miss Murphy."

"You're forgetting this woman who is supposed to be Catherine's mother. She's the most dangerous of all, because if she's telling the truth, she actually has a claim on the child." Her eyes filled with tears, and Sarah felt the sting of tears herself. She reached across the kitchen table and clasped her mother's hand. "I don't even want to think about that. I hardly slept all night for worrying."

"I suppose we should take comfort in knowing

51

your father will never allow anyone to take Catherine from you."

Sarah's jaw dropped open, and she didn't bother to close it. "I can't imagine Father would involve himself in this."

"Can't you? Sarah, dear, surely you know you are the most important thing in the world to him, to both of us. Your happiness is all that matters, so no one will ever take Catherine away from you."

Sarah shook her head, trying to make sense of this. "Mother, I know you're fond of Catherine . . ."

"*Fond?* Don't be coy, dear. You know how much I love her. I love her as much as you do. You can't possibly think I would stand idly by while someone snatches her away from us as if she were a rag doll to be passed from hand to hand whenever someone gets bored with her."

Sarah could hardly believe her senses, but she recovered quickly. "You're right, of course. I do know how much you love her, but if this woman really is Catherine's mother, how can we, in good conscience, keep her from her own child? If our situations were reversed, I'd be moving heaven and earth to get her back."

"Oh, please, be reasonable. You would never have let your child go in the first place. What kind of a woman does that?"

Mrs. Ellsworth had said the same thing. "She might have had a very good reason."

"I can't believe you're defending her."

"I'm not defending her. I'm just trying to withhold judgment until I hear all the facts. And I also want to think the best of Catherine's mother, whoever she might be, for Catherine's sake."

"That's honorable of you, darling, but you also need to think about what is best for Catherine. Would she be better off with you or with some flighty actress who disappears from her life for weeks and months and even years at a time?"

Sarah couldn't be sure if her mother's argument really made sense or if she just wanted it to. "I didn't say I was going to turn Catherine over to her, even if she is her mother. I just want to reserve judgment."

"Fair enough, but remember that your father has enough power and influence in the city to ensure that these women never so much as set eyes on our Catherine again."

"Thank you for reminding me of that," Sarah said with some asperity.

"You're welcome. Now, I came here to play with Catherine, and that's exactly what I'm going to do." In another moment, Sarah sat alone in the kitchen with her fears.

Frank knew the Upper West Side well. He'd visited too many of the fancy town houses with their marble steps and their velvet draperies and their dreary furniture. He'd listened to too many rich people make the pettiest complaints and give the paltriest excuses for committing murder. He did not expect today would be much different.

The maid who answered his knock at Mr. Wilbanks's house looked him up and down and stuck her nose in the air. "Tradesmen use the rear," she said and started to slam the door in his face.

Frank gave it a shove and sent her staggering back. Before she could recover, he stepped inside and closed it behind him.

"I'll scream," she said, her eyes wide.

"Don't bother. Just announce me to Mr. Wilbanks. Tell him I have a message from Miss Anne Murphy."

"I shouldn't've let you in. He'll give me the devil."

"Not if you tell him what I said. He'll want to hear news of the child."

"What child?"

"Just tell him. Tell him I have a message and tell him I know where the child is."

Frank wasn't as confident as he let on, of course, but he'd convinced the maid. Or maybe she was just anxious to get away from him. She scurried up the stairs, leaving him to kick his heels. Or at least he might've kicked his heels if she'd invited him to sit, but since she hadn't, he had to content himself with pacing around the unfurnished hallway and admiring the portraits of generations

54

of Wilbanks ancestors. If they really were Wilbanks ancestors, of course. Frank had heard that "new money" families sometimes purchased portraits of other people's relatives and passed them off as their own. Was Wilbanks "new money"? Maybe he should have consulted Felix Decker before coming all the way over here. On the other hand, Sarah hadn't said anything about involving her father in this, so he didn't want to go behind her back.

He turned at the sound of a throat clearing on the stairs. The maid, nose still in the air and now out of joint, glared down at him from the fifth step. "Mr. Wilbanks will see you."

Without being instructed to, he followed her upstairs and over to the door to what had to be a parlor. She stopped suddenly and turned to face him. He almost stumbled in his effort not to run into her.

"What is your name? I need to announce you."

"Detective Sergeant Frank Malloy of the New York City Police."

"Well, I never," she muttered and started on her way again. She threw open the parlor door and repeated it.

A middle-aged man in a velvet smoking jacket rose slowly from an overstuffed chair. "Good heavens, Gabby, why didn't you tell me he was from the police?"

3

Both men waited for the maid to leave, using the time to take each other's measure. Wilbanks was probably in his fifties, a tall, slender man confident of his place in the world. He still had his hair and a luxurious mustache into the bargain. Frank tried to imagine a woman of Sarah's age finding him attractive, but perhaps his money alone would be enough for a penniless actress.

"Gabby said you know where the child is."

Frank winced inwardly. The child was the most important thing to him, which meant he'd do whatever it took to get her back. Frank would have to be very careful. "I do."

"Where is she? Take me to her."

"Why should I?"

Wilbanks obviously wasn't used to being thwarted. The blood rushed to his face, turning him a dangerous shade of crimson. "If you're here, then you know I'm her father. What is it you want? Money? Name your price, but you're not getting a penny until I see her."

"Aren't you at all interested to know why a police detective is here to see you?"

Frank watched the emotions play across his face. Confusion replaced the anger, then changed rapidly to concern, and finally, fear. The color drained from his face. "Dear God, has something happened to her?" His knees appeared to buckle, and he grabbed the arm of the chair where he'd been sitting and lowered himself into it. When he looked up, he seemed almost frantic. "Answer me, damn you!"

"No, nothing's happened to her. She's perfectly fine and in a safe place."

His eyes narrowed. "What does that mean?"

"Just what I said. She's fine."

"I don't . . ." His words strangled in a wracking cough torn from his chest. He fumbled in the pocket of his dressing gown for a handkerchief and pressed it to his lips. It barely muffled the painful hacking that shook his slender frame. The coughing went on much longer than Frank would have thought possible, and when Wilbanks finally pulled the cloth away from his mouth, Frank saw it was spotted with blood. Still gasping, Wilbanks said, "Water," and indicated a tray beside his chair.

Frank hurried to him and filled the glass sitting there from the carafe and pressed it into Wilbanks's trembling hands. As he watched Wilbanks sip the water, he saw what he had failed to notice before. The man was not merely thin, but gaunt, his skin sallow and his eyes shadowed from illness. Frank instinctively took a step back, realizing he shouldn't be so close.

When Wilbanks had recovered, he looked up at Frank. He must have read something on his face, because he said, "It's not what you think."

"Pardon?"

"It's not consumption, so you don't have to worry. You can't catch what I've got."

"And what have you got?"

"Cancer, which means I don't have time to waste. Now, who are you, and what are you doing here?"

Frank hesitated only a moment. "May I?" he asked, indicating a nearby chair. He sat without waiting for an answer. "I'm here because of Anne Murphy."

"Anne? What about her?"

Frank removed the letter he'd found from his pocket and handed it to Wilbanks.

He frowned when he saw it had been opened, but Frank didn't feel any need to explain. As he read, the color returned to his face. All of this anger probably wasn't good for a man as sick as Wilbanks, but there was nothing Frank could do about that.

"Where did you get this?" he asked when he'd finished.

"From Miss Murphy."

"You're in league with her then."

"No, I'm not. I'm investigating a crime."

"What crime?"

"Murder."

He blanched again. "Murder? Dear God, not Catherine!"

"No, I told you, she's fine."

"Who then? Emma?" The thought did not upset him nearly as much as Frank would have expected.

"No, although I don't know where she is, so I can't say for sure that she's all right."

"Emma is like a cat. She always lands on her feet."

Now wasn't that interesting? "Anne Murphy."

"Anne? Yes, you said you got this letter from her."

"Not from her. I found it in her room, after she was murdered."

The news caused another coughing fit. This time Frank poured the water without being asked and waited patiently for Wilbanks to recover. This time he seemed shrunken, as if the news of Anne Murphy's death had sapped him somehow. "Who killed her?" he asked hoarsely when he could speak again. At least Frank was now pretty sure Wilbanks had not been involved.

"I don't know yet. I went to question her this morning, and I found her already dead."

"Question her about what?"

"That's really none of your business, Mr. Wilbanks. I only came here because I found the letter addressed to you. I thought you might be involved somehow."

He smiled grimly. "You thought I might have killed Anne? I can hardly swat a fly these days, as you can see."

"Or that you might have an idea who did."

"For who might've killed Anne? Not any at all. Now if you'd said Emma was murdered, I could give you a list, but not for Anne. She never hurt a soul. But you said you don't know where Emma is, and if Anne's dead, who's looking after Catherine?"

"I told you she's safe. She's been living with a family."

"What family? Who are they?"

"Mr. Wilbanks, you can't expect me to tell you anything until you've answered a few questions."

"I most certainly can. Catherine is my daughter, and I have every right to her."

"And I have every right to protect her until I find out what's going on. A woman is dead, Mr. Wilbanks. Until I know why, I don't know that Catherine isn't in danger, too, and neither do you."

"She's in no danger from me!"

"And you're in no condition to protect her from anybody else."

That seemed to do the trick. All of Wilbanks's bluster evaporated. He rubbed a hand over his face. "You're right, of course. Forgive me, Mr. . . . Malloy, is it? What do you need to know?"

"Tell me everything you know about this Anne Murphy. When did you first meet her?"

He drew a breath, as if testing himself, and when he didn't start coughing again, he said, "I met her at the same time I met Emma. Emma Hardy, Catherine's mother. She was an actress. It was over six years ago now. My wife . . . My wife was an invalid, Mr. Malloy. She'd been ill for years and unable to . . . to perform her wifely duties. I was faithful to her all that time, I assure you. I put my energies into making money, and as you can see, I was very successful. But even making money pales after a while. You're a man, Mr. Malloy. You can understand. I went to the theater one evening, and Emma caught my eye. She was just in the chorus, but something about her . . ."

"So you made her acquaintance and started seeing her," Frank said when he hesitated. "And that's when you met Miss Murphy."

"Yes. Anne was a dresser."

"A dresser?"

"She helped the girls get into their costumes, kept the backstage area clean, that sort of thing. When Emma . . . When she found out she was with child, I got her a house. She needed help with the housework and when the baby came, so at Emma's suggestion, I hired Anne to take care of her."

"Do you know anything about her? Does she have any family? Anyone who might wish her harm?"

"I don't think she had any family. She was from the city, I think. She'd never been married, of course. She was grateful for the position I gave her, I know. She loved living in the country, and she adored Catherine."

"What happened last year, when they disappeared?"

Wilbanks frowned. "How do you know about that?"

"I'm investigating her murder. I've learned a little about her."

He didn't look like he believed that, but he said, "I really don't know what happened. I went out to visit one day, as I usually did, and they were gone."

"Miss Hardy didn't leave a note?"

"She didn't leave anything at all except the furniture, which I assume was too cumbersome to carry away with her."

"Did you look for her?"

"Of course I looked for her! She had Catherine, and whatever my feelings for Emma, I love my daughter, Mr. Malloy. I would have moved heaven and earth to find her, but I had to settle for hiring a private investigator. He could find no trace of them, however."

Frank wondered how hard the fellow had tried,

but he didn't want to upset Mr. Wilbanks again, so he didn't wonder it out loud. "Do you think she left because of the argument you had with her?"

Wilbanks gaped at him. "How do you know about that?"

"Just assume I know everything about your affair with Miss Hardy. What did you argue about?"

"I thought you knew everything."

"I want to compare your version with the one I heard."

Wilbanks snorted his disbelief. "I don't know whose version you heard, but I'm sure it was a lie. I asked Emma to marry me. That's what we quarreled about."

Frank blinked in surprise. He could usually tell a lie when he heard one, and this sounded like a whopper, but Wilbanks wasn't lying. Frank would've staked a month's pay on it. "First of all, I thought you were already married."

"I was. I was married when I met Emma, but my wife passed away a little over a year ago. I was then free to marry whomever I chose, and I asked Emma to be my wife."

"And you're saying this is why you quarreled?"

"Yes. Emma did not want to marry me."

This made no sense at all. "Why on earth not?"

"You flatter me, Mr. Malloy, although I'm afraid you may assume my main attraction is my ability to support a family in a certain amount of luxury.

Emma did not find that ability irresistible, however. By then, she'd returned to her career as an actress, if you can call it that. She was still a chorus girl and never likely to be anything more, but she liked being on the stage. She did not like being stuck at a house in the country with a young child, and she most definitely did not want to be stuck in a large house in the city with a young child and an aging husband, no matter how much money he might have."

Frank scratched his head in confusion. "She doesn't sound like she would've made a good wife, Mr. Wilbanks. Why were you so eager to marry her?"

"I wasn't."

Now he was really confused. "Then why did you ask her?"

"Because I wanted to legitimize my daughter's birth, Mr. Malloy. I wanted to raise her in respectability. I made a terrible mistake when I took up with Emma Hardy, but Catherine was an innocent and did not deserve to be tainted by my mistakes. Marrying her mother was the only way to give her the life I wanted for her."

"So you're saying that after she refused your marriage proposal, Miss Hardy packed up Catherine and Miss Murphy and disappeared."

"Shortly after that, yes."

"Did you tell her to get out if she wouldn't marry you?"

"Of course not. I still wanted to be able to see my daughter."

"If she wouldn't marry you, why not just take the child and cut Emma loose?"

"I might have done just that eventually. As I said, I wanted Catherine to be legitimate, and marrying Emma was the easiest way to do that, but my son-in-law was still investigating my other legal options when Emma disappeared. He's an attorney."

So far, Frank was pretty sure Wilbanks had been honest with him. Now it was time to test him. "Maybe your son had something to do with Emma leaving town."

"My son? What does Oswald have to do with this?"

"He went to see Miss Hardy shortly before she disappeared."

"That's impossible! He knew nothing about her."

"You're wrong about that. He visited her at least twice and frightened her pretty badly, from what I understand."

Wilbanks straightened in his chair, his eyes blazing. "Who are you getting your information from?"

"From Anne Murphy."

"You said she was already dead when you found her."

"She told her story to someone else the day before she died. Miss Murphy didn't know what passed between Miss Hardy and your son, but it wasn't pleasant, and you said yourself, she left town shortly after that. Maybe he found out you wanted to marry her, and he didn't like the idea of sharing the family fortune with his father's mistress and bastard child. Maybe he threatened her."

He'd expected Wilbanks to explode at that, but to his surprise, he sank back into his chair and covered his face with both hands.

"Mr. Wilbanks? Are you all right?"

When he lowered his hands, his face was white, his eyes blazing. "I've told you everything I know about Anne Murphy, Mr. Malloy. Now when can I see Catherine?"

"That isn't my decision."

"Then whose decision is it? And don't toy with me. I can have your job."

"You wouldn't like my job, Mr. Wilbanks," Frank said, knowing he was foolish to taunt a man as powerful as Wilbanks but unwilling to be bullied all the same. "And I have to consider what's best for Catherine."

Wilbanks was furious, but he knew how to control it. His eyes narrowed. "You speak as if you care about her."

"I do. I've known her for almost a year."

"You said she lives with a family. Is it your family?"

Frank could only wish. "No, but I know them well."

"How did they get her?"

"When Miss Hardy and Miss Murphy ran away, they separated. Miss Murphy took Catherine, and Miss Hardy told her to hide and that she would contact her when it was safe."

"Safe from what?"

"She didn't tell Miss Murphy, but Miss Murphy thought she feared for her life. At any rate, Miss Murphy was afraid to keep Catherine with her in case whoever was after Miss Hardy were to find them, too. So she dropped Catherine off at a settlement house here in the city."

"Good God!"

"She thought Catherine would be safe there, and as it turned out, she was right. Eventually, one of the women who volunteer there took Catherine to live with her. The first anyone knew anything about Catherine's background was when Miss Murphy went to the settlement house the other day looking for her."

"And how did you get involved in all of this?"

"The matron at the settlement house refused to tell Miss Murphy where Catherine was. She wanted to check with Catherine's guardian first. The guardian asked me to speak with Miss Murphy and find out if she really did have a claim on the child. She cares for Catherine very much and has no intention of turning her over to a total stranger."

"I am not a total stranger, Mr. Malloy. I'm her

father. This guardian, as you call her, can turn her over to me with a clear conscience."

"Do you think that's a good idea?"

"Of course it's a good idea. She's my daughter!"

"Anne Murphy went looking for Catherine, and a few days later someone murdered her."

"That has nothing to do with Catherine."

"Are you sure? I'm not. And until I am, I'm not going to risk her life." Frank waited, watching Wilbanks's anger flare and then die as Frank's words sank in.

"Mr. Malloy, as you can see, I'm quite ill. My doctors give me a few months at the most. I want to spend them with my child, and I will do whatever is necessary to make that happen."

Frank thought about stopping by to see Sarah. She'd be worried sick, but the news he had to give her would upset her even more, so he was in no hurry to deliver it. Besides, if he waited until this evening, Catherine would be asleep, and they'd be able to speak freely. He decided to find the address on the letters Emma Hardy had sent to Anne Murphy.

It was an old house just off Broadway. A wealthy family had built it long ago when this had been a fashionable part of town. Now it was a boardinghouse, like so many others in the city. A young woman answered his knock, striking a pose in the doorway. She looked him up and down and grinned a little too boldly to be a maid. "And what would you be wanting?"

"I'd like to speak to the landlady."

"Would you now? And what if the landlady is busy?"

"Then tell her Detective Sergeant Frank Malloy of the New York City Police is here to see her."

Her grin vanished. "What is it? What's happened?"

"I need to speak to the landlady."

She started away, then caught herself. "Come in," she called back and hurried down the hall toward the back of the house. Frank stepped into the foyer and closed the door behind him. The place looked like all the other boardinghouses he'd ever seen except this one seemed a little brighter somehow. Maybe it was the garish yellow wallpaper.

Two young women peered at him from the parlor.

"Are you a copper?" one asked.

"Detective sergeant."

They exchanged a knowing look. "Who're you here to pinch?" the other one asked.

"Who do you think?"

They grinned at that, flirting a little. They were bold, but not like whores. And their clothes were a little too flashy, but not that way. He couldn't put his finger on it at first, and then . . .

"Are you actresses?"

"Of course," the first one said, as if insulted he had to ask.

"Mrs. Dugan only rents to actresses."

"Chorus girls," an older woman said as she came down the hall toward him. "Get in the kitchen, you two, and help Maggie or there won't be no dinner tonight," she said to the girls, who hurried off.

"You must be Mrs. Dugan," Frank said.

She'd been a handsome woman in her youth, probably a chorus girl herself, and age had dimmed her only slightly. "Nell Dugan, and what would you be wanting with us, Mr. Detective Sergeant?"

"Can we talk in private?"

Alarm flickered over her face, but she said, "In here." She directed him to the parlor where the two girls had been and closed the door behind them. "Is one of my girls in trouble?"

"Do you know Emma Hardy?"

"Emma?" She looked relieved. She apparently had no love for Emma Hardy. "Is that who you're looking for?"

"You know her?"

"Yes, I know her. I know a lot of girls who work in the theater."

"You mostly rent to actresses? Chorus girls, I mean."

That made her grin. "Yes. I used to be in the chorus myself. Married an actor, which I don't

70

ever recommend. He left me, like they all do, and when I got too old for the stage, I managed to get this house. The girls don't always pay their rent, but they keep me young. What do you want with Emma?"

Frank pulled two letters from his pocket. "She sent these to Anne Murphy at this address."

"Did she? I guess Anne did get some letters while she was here."

"She was living here, then?"

"For a few months. The better part of a year, I guess."

"When did she leave?"

"A couple weeks, maybe. I don't know. Time goes so fast nowadays. Oh, wait. She was here just the other day, to get her mail, she said. I thought it was a joke." Mrs. Dugan glanced at the letters. "Is she the one in trouble?"

"Anne Murphy is dead, Mrs. Dugan."

She gave a little cry, then hastily crossed herself. "Merciful Mother of God."

"I'm sorry."

"You should be, coming in here like this and telling me somebody I've known most of my life is dead."

"I'm not the one who killed her."

The blood drained from her face. "*Killed,* did you say? Don't tell me she was killed!"

Frank grabbed her arm and steered her to the closest chair.

When she was safely seated, she glared up at him. "Who killed her?"

"I don't know. That's why I'm here."

"Nobody here did, I can tell you that. Everybody loved Anne."

"I'm sure they did, but I thought you might be able to tell me more about her so I can figure out who might have wished her harm."

"Not a soul on this earth." She crossed herself again, and tears flooded her eyes. "I can't believe it."

"Why did she leave here?"

"What?"

"You said she'd been living here for almost a year, and then she left. Did she say where she was going or why she was leaving?"

"She . . . I don't know. She had some story about a job, I think. She was leaving the city, she said. I don't remember. People in the theater are always coming and going. I didn't pay much attention. Maybe the other girls can tell you. But I guess she didn't leave the city, did she, if she's dead? Ingrid knew her the best."

"Who's Ingrid?"

"Ingrid Cordova. One of the girls who was just here. She can tell you what there is to know. I'll get her."

In a few minutes, Mrs. Dugan was back with the pretty, dark-haired girl who'd been insulted that Frank didn't know she was an actress. She was protesting vigorously until she reached the parlor. Then she just dug in her heels. "I don't know what he wants to see me about. I ain't done nothing wrong."

"I told you, he has to ask you some questions. About Anne."

"Anne? Why would he want to know anything about Anne?"

Mrs. Dugan gave him a pleading look. Obviously, she hadn't broken the news.

Frank sighed. "Miss Cordova, Anne Murphy was murdered this morning."

Ingrid's pretty face registered her struggle to deny his words. She turned to Mrs. Dugan, outraged. "What's he saying?"

"Annie's dead, God rest her soul, and he's trying to find out who killed her."

"Killed?" she said, as if she'd never heard the word before.

This time Mrs. Dugan helped Ingrid sit down and produced a handkerchief when the girl started sobbing. They waited until she'd recovered herself. Finally, she looked up at Frank. "I just saw her the other day." As if that proved she couldn't be dead today.

"Mrs. Dugan said she came by to pick up her mail."

"She did. It was funny, you know? None of us gets letters, but she said Emma Hardy wrote to her." She turned to where Mrs. Dugan hovered at her elbow. "I didn't believe her. I didn't know Emma hardly at all, but I'd guess she never wrote a letter in her life. But sure enough, there was a letter here for her."

"Do you remember what day this was?"

"I don't know. A week or so ago, I think."

"Did she say anything about the letter, what it said?"

Ingrid frowned. "No. She just tucked it in her pocket and then we talked a little."

"What did you talk about?"

"I don't remember."

"Try. It could be important."

Tears flooded her eyes again, but she took a minute to think. "I asked her what happened to the job she was getting out of town. She said it didn't start yet, but she'd be going soon."

"Did she say what the job was?" Frank asked.

"Said she'd be taking care of Emma Hardy's little girl again. Emma had been on tour, you know," she added, glancing at Mrs. Dugan as if for confirmation. "That's why Anne came back here last year."

"Anne left the city years ago to look after Emma Hardy and her kid," Mrs. Dugan said. "But maybe you already knew that."

"Did Emma Hardy live here, too?"

Mrs. Dugan frowned. "What do you mean?"

"You obviously know her. Did she ever live here?"

For some reason, she needed a few seconds to consider her reply. "Back before she had the baby, yes. Years ago, that was."

"And had you seen her lately?"

Another hesitation. "Well, then she had a room here for a few years, for the times when she was in a show."

"She did?" Ingrid asked.

"Hush, you don't know anything about it." Mrs. Dugan turned back to Frank. "Her gentleman friend paid me to keep one for her." She didn't look like she'd been too happy about that arrangement.

At least this part of the story made some sense. Emma Hardy and Anne Murphy had both lived in this rooming house, so they must have agreed Emma could contact Anne here. That would explain why the most recent letter to Anne was addressed here, even though Emma had instructed her to find another place to live. "Did Miss Murphy seem upset about anything when you saw her the other day?"

Ingrid thought about this for a moment. "No, she was real happy, in fact. Said she couldn't wait to see the little girl again."

"Did she say where the girl was?" Frank wondered what story she'd given out.

"She was with Emma."

"Did she say that?"

Ingrid opened her mouth to reply, then hesitated. "I . . . I don't know if she did or not. Maybe

I just thought that's where she was. But where else would she be?"

Where else, indeed. "Do you know of anybody who might want to harm Miss Murphy?"

Ingrid's eyes flooded again. "I can't believe she's gone. No. No, I don't know of a soul who'd want to hurt her. Do you really think it was somebody who knew her? Sometimes people get killed by strangers, you know. Lots of bad things happen in the city."

Frank knew that very well. He wasn't going to explain Anne Murphy's death to them, though. They were upset enough. "Thank you for your help, Miss Cordova. If you think of anything else, let me know." He gave Mrs. Dugan his card.

The sky was still light when he left the boardinghouse. The days were getting longer, and winter's chill had left the air. These pleasant weeks between winter's frigid blasts and summer's searing heat were too few. Too bad he never had a chance to really enjoy them. He'd get something to eat, and then head over to Sarah's house. He'd put off telling her about Anne Murphy long enough.

Sarah and Maeve still sat at the kitchen table, trying to decide whether to go to bed or wait a little longer for Malloy, when they heard the knock. Hoping it wasn't an expectant father come to summon her for a delivery, Sarah hurried to the front door.

"Malloy," she said in relief. She took his coat and tried not to read anything into his grim expression. "Are you hungry?"

"No, but I could use some coffee."

He followed her into the kitchen. Maeve greeted him.

"I thought you'd be in bed by now," he teased, taking a seat opposite her at the table.

"And how would you expect me to sleep without knowing what you found out? And where you've been all day, too."

Sarah stoked the fire and put the coffee on to heat. "I've been wondering that myself," Sarah said, trying not to sound as annoyed as she felt that he'd made them wait so long for the news.

Then she noticed Malloy's expression, and her annoyance evaporated. "What is it? What's happened?"

"Anne Murphy is dead."

Sarah needed a minute for the truth of it to sink in. When it did, she managed to lower herself into a chair before her knees gave way. "What did she die of?"

"Somebody stabbed her."

"Dear heaven," Maeve murmured.

Sarah still could not make sense of it. "Who? Why?"

"I don't know that yet. I went to see her first

thing this morning, and I found her dead. She was alone in the house, and whoever killed her had probably just left."

Sarah glanced at Maeve. Her face was white, her eyes wide with shock. Guilt tore at her. "You were right," she told Malloy. "We should never have gone to see her alone."

He waved away her contrition. "It's too late to argue about that now. There's more, a lot more, and none of it is good news. I found Catherine's father."

Sarah's breath felt like a shard of glass in her chest. How could she bear this? "Who is he?"

"His name is David Wilbanks. Does that mean anything to you?"

Sarah shook her head. "No. Miss Murphy said he was a wealthy man. I thought I might know him, but I don't think I've ever heard that name before."

"Maybe your father knows him, or at least knows of him. He wants Catherine."

Sarah covered her mouth to hold back a sob, and Maeve threw an arm over her shoulder.

"We won't let him have her," the girl said, tears spilling down her cheeks.

But Sarah could only shake her head. He was Catherine's father. How could she keep his child from him? Fighting her own tears, Sarah said, "How did you find him?"

"Anne Murphy had written him a letter. I found it in her room."

"So she did know who he was," Sarah said, grasping on to anger like a lifeline to keep her from slipping into despair. "What did the letter say?"

"She was offering to tell Wilbanks where Catherine was if he was willing to pay her for the information. I'm not sure why she wrote it but hadn't mailed it. Maybe she would have sent it if Emma didn't show up or something. We'll probably never know, but it led me right to Wilbanks."

Fury swelled in her chest. "Did you tell him where Catherine was?"

"Of course not, but he's her father. He has a right to at least see her. And he's dying."

"Dying? What do you mean?"

"He's got cancer, he said. He told me he only has a few months to live."

Sarah wanted to feel pity for this unknown man who could destroy her world, but instead she hated herself for feeling relief that he might not live to do so. "But he still wants Catherine."

"He told me he wanted to marry Emma Hardy so he could raise Catherine to be a respectable young lady."

"I thought he was already married," Maeve said.

"His wife died over a year ago. Remember Miss Murphy said that Emma and Wilbanks had an argument right before Emma ran away? Wilbanks said it was because she didn't want to marry him."

"But that doesn't make sense," Sarah said.

"None of this makes any sense," Maeve said. "And why would somebody want to kill Miss Murphy, of all people?"

Sarah didn't know, and right now, all she could think about was losing her daughter. "How did you leave it with Wilbanks?"

"I told him that until I find out who killed Miss Murphy and why she thought Catherine might be in danger, too, I wasn't going to tell anyone where she is."

"And he agreed to that?"

"He did. He wasn't happy about it, but he doesn't want any harm to come to her either."

Tears stung Sarah's eyes. How could she hate a man who loved Catherine that much? "But if he's dying . . ."

"I know. He won't wait very long."

"So what do we do now?"

"We find out who killed Miss Murphy," Maeve said.

Malloy gave her a half grin. "That's a good idea, but first, Sarah, I think we need to speak to your father."

4

Sarah had suggested Malloy meet her at her parents' house, but he came to fetch her that morning in a hansom cab. They would have made faster progress if they'd walked to the elevated train station and ridden it uptown, but Sarah didn't mention this. She suspected Malloy wanted to deliver her to her parents' house in the best possible style.

Whatever his reasoning, Sarah leaned back in the cozy confines of the vehicle and sighed, grateful for the opportunity to spend some time with Malloy before facing her parents.

"Are you all right?" he asked when they were on their way.

Sarah had seen the dark circles under her eyes this morning, so she wasn't insulted by his concern. "I haven't been sleeping very well. At first I was worried about Catherine's mother taking her away, and now I'm worried about her father."

"I wish I could tell you not to worry."

She smiled. "I know you do. Do you think there's anything my father can do to help?"

This time Malloy sighed and not with contentment. "It's been my experience that money and power can solve an awful lot of problems."

"But this time both sides have money and power, so whose problems will be solved?"

Malloy's dark eyes held no answers.

"What kind of a man is Wilbanks?" she asked after a moment.

"Are you asking if he's ruthless? I'm sure he is when he needs to be. You don't get rich by being kind to other people."

Sarah wished she could disagree with him. "Could he have sent someone to kill Anne Murphy?"

"Of course, but I don't think he did. He was too surprised to find out she was dead. Besides, why would he kill someone who could help him find Catherine?"

"I suppose you're right. The question is, who would?"

"I know, and I don't like any of the answers."

"Like Wilbanks's son?" she said.

"If he killed Anne Murphy to keep her from producing Catherine . . ."

He didn't have to finish that thought. Sarah squeezed her eyes shut to hold back the tears.

To her surprise, Malloy took her hand in his. "It's too soon to give up, Sarah."

Suddenly, she didn't feel like crying anymore. "You're right. It is."

By the time they reached her parents' town house, Sarah had regained her courage. Surprised to see visitors so early in the day, the flustered maid escorted them to the rear parlor—the family parlor—to wait. Sarah took a seat on the sofa while Malloy prowled the room restlessly.

In a remarkably short time, her parents came in together. Her mother, she could tell, had dressed in haste, not even taking the time to let her maid do her hair. It still hung down her back, tied with a ribbon. She went immediately to Sarah and took both her hands. "Do you have news?"

"Were you expecting this visit, Elizabeth?" her father asked with an unmistakable hint of annoyance.

"I was hoping for it, yes," she said. "I'm so glad to see you, Mr. Malloy."

"And you told me nothing about it?" her father said.

"No. I thought you should hear it all from Sarah. Shall we sit down?"

Even in her distracted state, Sarah thought her father was behaving strangely. Then again, she'd never brought Malloy with her on a visit before either. She resumed her seat on the sofa, and her mother sat beside her. Malloy, she noted, took a chair at a respectable distance from her, leaving her father the nearer one.

"What is all this about?" her father asked when they were settled.

Even though he had addressed the question to Malloy, Sarah said, "It's about Catherine."

Her father frowned. "Catherine? The little girl?"

Sarah wanted to say, "*My* little girl," but she knew this was no longer true. "Yes, the other day a woman went to the Mission looking for her. She claimed she was the child's nursemaid and was returning to claim her."

Her father considered this information for a moment, then turned back to Malloy. "I thought perhaps you were here because you'd changed your mind."

Changed his mind about what? Sarah wondered, but before she could ask, her father said, "Elizabeth, we'll discuss why you chose to keep this information from me at a later time. For now, I think you had better tell me everything, Sarah."

Sarah did, beginning with her meeting with Mrs. Keller up to her and Maeve's visit with Anne Murphy. He listened patiently to that point, then turned to Malloy, furious. "And you permitted her to see this woman alone?"

Malloy never batted an eye. "What makes you think I have any more control over her than you do?"

Her mother made a strange little choking sound that might have been a smothered laugh and which Sarah refused to acknowledge.

"Malloy didn't know about it," Sarah said. "I didn't tell him anything at all until I'd already met with Miss Murphy."

This had the desired effect of drawing her father's ire back to her. Ignoring his scowling disapproval, she continued the story, telling him everything she had learned from Anne Murphy. "That was when I decided to ask Mr. Malloy for assistance."

Her father seemed almost relieved. "And what have you done about this woman?" he asked Malloy.

"I went to see her yesterday."

"And?"

Malloy glanced apologetically at her mother. "She was dead. Somebody had murdered her."

Sarah had underestimated the horror her parents would feel at this news. They naturally assumed that Sarah had come perilously close to meeting the same fate with her reckless disregard for her own safety in visiting Miss Murphy unprotected. She had to allow them to be furious with her for several minutes before they could continue.

"You're absolutely right, I should never have done it," she said at last, "and Mr. Malloy has already taken me to task for it. However, I was not murdered along with Miss Murphy, and along with the question of who murdered her, I still have the problem of Catherine's parents wanting to claim her."

"Parents?" her father said. "I thought it was just her mother."

Malloy picked up the story from there and told them about finding the letters and going to meet David Wilbanks. "Do you know him?" he asked her parents.

Her mother shook her head. Her father said, "I've heard of him."

"Good things or bad?" Sarah asked.

"Business things. I don't know the man himself, but I will by tonight. I suppose he wants Catherine back."

"He does, but he also told me he's dying. He has cancer, and he said he only has a few months to live."

Sarah could actually see her father registering this weakness as something to use to their advantage. "He can't possibly imagine he can take care of a young child then."

Malloy explained Wilbanks's plan to marry Emma Hardy and give Catherine a life of privilege.

"I'm afraid we must admire him for that," her mother said.

"If we can admire a man who broke his marriage vows with a strumpet, then I suppose we must," her father said. "Mr. Malloy, will you be the one to investigate this woman's murder?"

"I've gotten myself assigned to the case, yes. No one else is interested in it, so I'm not sure how long they'll let me work on it, but I'll have a few days, at least."

"I don't suppose this Wilbanks would use his influence." This, Sarah knew, was a polite way of asking if Wilbanks would pay the necessary bribes to ensure police department cooperation.

"He didn't offer," Malloy said.

"Perhaps he doesn't understand his responsibility in the matter. I'll explain it to him."

"Father! You're not going to see this man, are you?"

"Of course I am."

"Then he'll know where Catherine is."

"Mr. Malloy said he'd already hired a private investigator to find her once, and now he knows Mr. Malloy's connection to her. Even the most incompetent operative would be able to learn of his friendship with you and that you have a foster daughter. I imagine someone will be at your door tomorrow to claim her."

Instinctively, Sarah jumped to her feet. "I've got to get home!"

"Of course you do, dear," her mother said. "I'll go with you."

"And you'll bring Catherine back here," her father said. "That girl who takes care of her, too."

"Her name is Maeve," Sarah said, furious at him for taking over her life and especially for being right to do so.

"Yes, Maeve. They'll be safe here, and your mother will love having them."

"I certainly will."

"I will go to my club and find out who knows this Wilbanks fellow, and Mr. Malloy will find out who killed this Murphy woman. Does that plan meet with your approval, Mr. Malloy?"

Sarah glanced at Malloy and caught a momentary flash of surprise at her father's demonstration of confidence, but he recovered instantly. "Yes, sir, it does."

"You must call upon me for whatever you need. Elizabeth, go finish dressing. I'll have the carriage brought around for you and Sarah. Mr. Malloy, I'm sure you will want to be on your way, so we won't keep you any longer."

"Wait!" her mother said when Malloy would have taken his leave. They all looked at her in surprise. "There's one thing about this that doesn't make any sense."

"Just *one* thing?" her father asked.

"Oh, most of it is very strange, to be sure, but one thing struck me as completely unbelievable. Why wouldn't this Emma person marry Mr. Wilbanks after his wife died?"

"I wondered about that myself," Sarah said. "I guess I forgot about it with everything else, though. Did Mr. Wilbanks know why she refused?"

Malloy shook his head. "He thought she didn't

want to give up acting to be tied down with an old husband and a child."

"Nonsense!" her mother said. "No woman in her right mind would refuse an offer like that."

"Maybe she didn't love him, Mother," Sarah argued.

"He was the father of her child and rich into the bargain, and women marry men they don't love every day. What kind of a life did she have to look forward to? She wasn't a great actress, just a chorus girl, and she was already getting close to the end of that career."

"How can you know that?" her father asked.

"Think about it. She'd taken up with Wilbanks at least six years ago. When she went back to it a few years later, she was still only in the chorus. Now we think she's in a touring company, where you only find the actors who can't get work in the city. How would she support herself and her child when she's too old to kick up her heels anymore? And who would choose that over a life of luxury with a rich husband, no matter how old he is?"

"His being old would actually be an advantage," Sarah realized. "She'd figure to outlive him by many years."

"Exactly!" her mother said.

The two men exchanged a horrified glance.

"So you see, she must have had a very good reason for refusing him," her mother said. "One she didn't want to share with Wilbanks."

Her father still looked skeptical, but Malloy said, "She's right."

Now they all turned to him in surprise.

"I just remembered something Mrs. Dugan said."

"Who's Mrs. Dugan?" her mother asked.

"The landlady at the boardinghouse where Emma and Anne Murphy lived at different times through the years. I went there after I saw Wilbanks. Remember Anne Murphy told you that when Emma went back into the theater, she would stay in the city during the week? I asked Mrs. Dugan if she stayed at her boardinghouse. She told me that Wilbanks paid her to keep a room for her, but she never actually answered my question about her living there."

"But if she had a room there . . ." her father said.

"That's what I thought, too, but now I remember another woman who lives there said she hardly knew Emma. If Emma had lived there for several years, even if she didn't stay there all the time, the other people in the house would have known her well."

"Maybe this woman didn't move in until after Emma ran away from Wilbanks," Sarah said.

"Or maybe this Emma was staying someplace else entirely when she came to the city," her mother said, earning a surprised look from her husband and an admiring one from Malloy.

"That's what I was thinking, too, Mrs. Decker,"

Malloy said. "Maybe she just wanted Wilbanks to think she stayed there."

"But where else would she have stayed?" her father asked.

"Oh, Felix, use your imagination. She had a lover! She probably told Wilbanks she wanted to go back to acting so she'd have an excuse to come to the city to see him. She could have stayed with *him* when she was here."

"Because no respectable boardinghouse would allow her to entertain a man there," Sarah said.

Her mother nodded. "And she didn't want to marry Wilbanks because then she would be living with him all the time and would no longer have had the freedom to see her lover. She wanted Wilbanks to support her, but she couldn't marry him without giving up the man she really loved."

Her father was looking at her mother as if he had never seen her before, but she didn't notice. She was too busy grinning at Malloy, who was grinning right back.

"And that man might not have wanted Emma to be reunited with her child because that could have gotten her back with Wilbanks, too. Thank you, Mrs. Decker. I'm going back to see Mrs. Dugan right now."

This time her father said, "Wait!" when Malloy would have taken his leave. "We need to meet this evening to share information."

"Come to my house," Sarah said.

"Why not here?" her mother asked. "Won't you be coming here with Maeve and Catherine?"

"No, I think I should stay at my house in case someone needs to find me. I also don't want to take a chance of Catherine finding out what's going on. She's already noticed that I'm not myself, and I don't want her to be frightened."

"All right. We'll meet at your house at eight o'clock," her father said and rang for the maid to show Malloy out and order the carriage.

For the first time in days, Sarah felt the tiniest bit hopeful.

On his way back to Mrs. Dugan's boardinghouse, Frank reviewed his earlier conversation with her. She had been very careful to mislead him without lying, he realized, but why? Not to protect Emma Hardy, of that he was certain. She despised Emma. In fact, Anne Murphy was the only person in the whole bunch who seemed to have cared for her at all. In Frank's experience, the only person most people really wanted to protect was themselves. When he asked himself why Mrs. Dugan would need to protect herself, the answer was easy: She'd taken money from Wilbanks for years for rent on a room Emma Hardy had never—or rarely—used. She wouldn't want him to find that out.

Could it be that simple?

Mrs. Dugan frowned when she opened the door

to him. "I didn't expect to see you back again."

"I just need to ask you a few more questions."

With obvious reluctance, she let him in and led him to the deserted parlor. "The girls are all still asleep, so try to keep your voice down." She was doing her best to seem at ease, but her hands betrayed her, clutching each other in a white-knuckled bunch.

"How long has Ingrid Cordova lived here?"

"What does that have to do with anything?"

"Just answer my questions. The sooner you do, the sooner I'll be gone."

She sighed unhappily. "A couple years, I guess."

"So she lived here at least part of the time when Emma Hardy's protector rented a room for her here."

"I . . . I suppose so, yes."

"And yet she said she hardly knew Emma."

Mrs. Dugan stiffened. "Emma kept to herself."

"Or maybe Miss Cordova didn't know her well because Emma didn't really live here."

"She had a room here, I tell you. Mr. Wilbanks paid me every month. He wanted to know she had a safe place to stay when she was in a show, he said."

"I know she had a room here, but she didn't really stay in it, did she?"

"I don't know what you're talking about."

"Don't you? I'm not going to tell Wilbanks, so you don't have to worry about that. I just want to know where she did stay and who she stayed with."

The color bloomed in her cheeks. "What do you mean?"

"You know what I mean. She had a lover, didn't she? That's where she stayed when she was in a show. Oh, she might've spent a night or two here sometimes, but most of the time she was with him. That's right, isn't it?"

"What possible difference does that make now? She's been gone for a year, and for all I know, she isn't coming back."

"Oh, she's coming back. That's what she wrote to tell Anne Murphy, and she expects Anne to have her daughter."

"Anne? Anne never had the child."

"Yes, she did. Emma left her with Anne, but Anne hid her someplace she thought would be safe. Then someone killed Anne before she could get the girl back."

Mrs. Dugan reached out and grabbed the back of a nearby chair for support. "And you think it was him?"

"Emma's lover? I don't know, but I'd like to find him and ask him. Do you know who he is?"

Her eyes blazed. "He's an actor. I warned her about him. I was married to an actor. Did I tell you?"

He nodded.

"A nasty lot, all of them. She wouldn't listen, though. Oh, she left him a dozen times, but she always took him back. I thought when she took up with Wilbanks, that would be the end of it. I thought his pride would never stand for her to be with another man, but I should've known better. He liked Wilbanks's money as much as she did. She half supported him with what Wilbanks gave her."

"And Wilbanks never suspected?"

"Why should he? Emma was always there when he came to see her."

"Didn't he come to see her here?"

"I don't allow men in the house. Emma would let him visit her at the theater and take her to dinner afterwards, but she couldn't have him here, so he never knew she didn't really live here."

"Where did she live?"

"Different places. He wasn't as good about paying the rent as Wilbanks was. Sometimes she'd come here for a while because they'd been thrown out of a place and she didn't want to be on the street with him. Did that make her think, though? No, she never blamed him for anything."

"What is his name?"

"Parnell Vaughn," she said, as if saying it left a bad taste in her mouth.

"Fancy name."

"Fancy name for a fancy man. And no, I don't have no idea where he might be. I haven't heard a peep about him since Emma left town. I expect he went with her. He'd been living off her for years, so he's not likely to let her out of his sight now, is he?"

"Do you know anything else about him besides that he's an actor?"

"Yes, he drinks."

Frank didn't think that would help him much.

"And you think he killed Annie?" she asked again.

"Do you think he could have?"

"I wouldn't put anything past him, but killing somebody . . . Why would he do it?"

"I'll be sure and ask him when I find him. Mrs. Dugan, Emma might come here looking for Anne Murphy and her daughter. When she does, would you ask her to come and see me?"

"Emma ain't likely to want to see a copper."

Frank had figured that. "Just tell her I know where her daughter is, and I'm the only one who does."

"Do you really know?"

"Yes, I do."

"Poor little mite. She didn't deserve none of this."

"No, she didn't, but she's safe, and I want to keep her that way."

He left her another of his cards and got her promise to pass it to Emma, should she show herself. Now he had to figure out how to find an actor.

As always, Catherine was thrilled to see Sarah's mother.

"Catherine, I have a surprise for you. I begged and begged, and your mama has agreed to let you come to visit me at my house for a few days."

Catherine's eyes widened. "Can I, Mama?"

"Of course, darling," Sarah said, fighting the urge to weep at the thought of losing her forever.

Catherine turned back to Sarah's mother. "Can Maeve come, too?"

"Of course she can. We'll have so much fun. You can sleep in the room where your mama used to sleep when she was a little girl. Let's go up and pack your things."

When her mother and Catherine were upstairs, Sarah turned to Maeve. "You don't mind, do you? We thought it would be safer."

"Of course I don't mind. I won't have to lift a finger or worry about Catherine either. I've been afraid all morning that someone would come to the door and I wouldn't know whether to answer it. Are you coming, too?"

"No. I don't want Catherine to see how worried I am or overhear me talking about her, and if someone needs me, this is the first place they'll look."

"Are you sure? You might not be safe here alone."

"If someone wants Catherine, they're not going to hurt the person who can take them to her."

"They hurt Anne Murphy. You could at least spend the night at Mrs. Ellsworth's."

"Let's see how it goes today. Now go get your things together. The carriage is waiting."

Only after she had kissed Catherine good-bye and seen them off in her mother's carriage did Sarah realize that her father had neglected to assign her something to do that afternoon.

Frank stopped off at Police Headquarters to report on his progress and see if anyone there could advise him on locating an actor. He also found a message from an attorney named Michael Hicks who wanted to meet him that afternoon at his home, an address in Lenox Hill, which was a section of the city with large comfortable homes full of wealthy people. As a general rule, Frank avoided dealing with attorneys at all costs, but the message also said the matter concerned David Wilbanks. Catherine's father had worked very quickly.

He still had a few hours before his appointment with Hicks, so he went upstairs to see who was in the detective offices who might have some knowledge of the theater. A few minutes later, he left Headquarters, heading to Broadway in search of a theatrical agent.

The first few he consulted each sent him to agents in progressively seedier buildings until he found the right one. He climbed the unswept stairs to the second floor, where he located a door with the right name stenciled on the glass. The outer office contained a desk of ancient vintage at which no one sat. Aging posters of shows long closed covered the walls, and the scent of cheap cigars hung in the air. The door to the inner office stood half-open, and Frank heard the unmistakable sound of snoring coming from within. He walked over and pushed the door, letting it swing wide. He saw another desk, equally old and battered and covered with papers. Behind it sat a middle-aged man in a checked suit. His feet rested on the desktop, displaying a fairly good-sized hole in the sole, and he leaned so far back in his chair that Frank wondered why it hadn't toppled over. His mouth hung open, allowing the snores to escape.

Frank rapped loudly on the doorjamb, startling the fellow awake and almost causing him to upset his chair. Scrambling, he swung his feet to the floor and stood, looking around wildly to see who had disturbed his peace. His bleary gaze finally settled on Frank. He cleared his throat and straightened his jacket, in a vain attempt to regain some dignity. "May I help you, sir?"

"Are you Ralph Nathan?"

"Ralph Nathan, agent extraordinaire, at your service. And who might you be, my man?"

"Detective Sergeant Frank Malloy of the New York City Police."

Nathan's bloodshot eyes widened with alarm. "I can assure you that nothing illegal is going on in this office."

Frank could plainly see that nothing at all was going on in this office. "I just need some information from you. I need to find some actors."

This appeared to confuse him, but only for a moment. "For a production? Are the police entering show business now?"

"Uh . . ."

"You have come to the right place, Mr. Malloy. The Ralph Nathan Agency represents only the finest thespians to have ever trod the boards. If you tell me more about the show, I'll be better able to assist you."

"You misunderstand, Mr. Nathan. There's no show. I just need to locate an actress. I think she's on tour. It's about her daughter."

"Her daughter? Is the girl in some trouble?"

"No, she's very young," Frank said, using just the necessary mix of truth and lies to get Nathan to cooperate. "She's been staying with some friends while the mother is on tour, but they can't keep her anymore. They asked me to find her so they can send the child to her."

"Oh, well, why didn't you say so? We always want to help out when we can. I often tell actresses they shouldn't have children for this very reason, but do they ever listen? Of course they don't."

"Can you find this actress?"

"I'll certainly try. Do you think she's with one of my touring companies?"

"That's what I was told. Her name is Emma Hardy."

"Emma? Why didn't you say so? Of course, of course. She's touring with *Saints and Sinners*. That's the name of the show, you know, not a commentary on her traveling companions, although now that I think of it, it very well could be that, too." He chuckled at his own joke.

"Do you know where they are now?"

Nathan frowned. "I . . . Wait a minute. I think . . ." He shuffled through one of the many piles of papers on his desk and found the page he was looking for. "They finished up in Philadelphia a week ago."

"A week ago? Are you sure?"

"Yes, indeed. They should have been back in the city by now. I haven't heard from any of the actors yet. They usually try to get a show in town after being on the road. They hardly ever do, but they always try. It's no fun playing a different town every night for months at a time. I expect to see them straggle in next week, wanting to know what I've got for them. Say, I wonder why Emma hasn't gone to get her kid by now."

Frank was wondering the same thing. But maybe she had. Maybe she'd found Anne Murphy and gotten upset when she found out Anne had lost track of Catherine. "The, uh, the family had to move. Maybe she can't find them. Look, let me give you my card, and if she comes by looking for work, you can tell her I know where her daughter is."

Nathan took the card, although his expression said he was starting to doubt Frank's story. "Certainly, certainly, always happy to help the police."

Frank thanked him and started to leave, then pretended to remember something else. "Say, can you tell me if my old friend Parnell Vaughn was in the play with Emma?"

Nathan's placating smile vanished. "What do you want with him?"

"Nothing. Just thought I'd say hello."

But Nathan shook his head. "Parnell never made friends with no police detective. You might want to say a few things to him, but none of them would be 'hello.' "

Frank tried a placating smile of his own. "I know he's a troublemaker. I was just wondering if Emma had gotten shed of him yet."

"Not likely. Seems like he's got some kind of spell on that girl. Don't know how many people have told her to kick him out, but she says she loves him. Oh, he's a good enough actor when he's sober and even most of the time when he's drunk, but he's pretty worthless otherwise."

"So he was on tour with her?"

"He was with the company when they left here, and nobody ever wired for me to send a replacement. That's about all I can say."

That meant he was probably still with Emma, roaming the city somewhere, maybe in search of Catherine and maybe not, and maybe they'd found Anne Murphy and maybe not, and if they had found her, maybe one of them had stabbed her and maybe not.

But if they had stabbed her, Frank figured they weren't likely to contact him about finding Catherine. He thanked Mr. Nathan and left the dingy office in the rundown building and then stood on the sidewalk out front, considering what to do next.

If Emma and Vaughn had indeed found Anne Murphy, even if they weren't the ones who stabbed her, she might have confessed to leaving Catherine at the Mission. Would they go there looking for her? Frank pulled out his watch. He still had several hours until his meeting with Wilbanks's attorney. He should probably stop by the Mission and at least warn Mrs. Keller that Anne Murphy was dead and Catherine's mother might come looking for her. He didn't think she'd tell anyone where Catherine was, but one of the girls might. Of course, Catherine was no longer at Sarah's house, but Sarah was, and he didn't want them anywhere near her.

He headed back to Police Headquarters. The Mission was only a couple blocks from there. He had just turned onto Mulberry Street when he caught sight of a familiar figure half a block ahead of him. He quickened his pace, catching up to her with no trouble.

"Sarah," he said when he'd reached her.

She looked up in surprise. "Malloy, what are you doing here?"

He loved the way she said his name and the way she always smiled when she said it. "I could ask you the same question. I thought you were going home."

"I think that's what my father intended. Did you notice he gave everybody else a task to accomplish today but me?"

Malloy wasn't going to admit any such thing. "Did he?"

"Yes, I had to make one for myself."

"So you're going to the Mission."

"Of course. I suddenly realized that we should tell Mrs. Keller what we've learned in case someone else comes looking for Catherine. Were you going there, too?"

"Yes, I just found out that Emma Hardy does have a lover, a man named Parnell Vaughn."

"What a charming name. He must be an actor."

"He is, but just in case you're interested, I have it on good authority that actors make terrible husbands."

"I will certainly keep that in mind," she said with a grin.

It was good to see her smile, but her eyes were still shadowed with worry. He wished he didn't have to add to it. "I also found out that Emma and this Vaughn character were on tour, just like Anne Murphy thought, but the show ended in Philadelphia a week ago."

"A week ago? Then they could be in the city now."

"They could have been in the city six days ago. That's the main reason I was going to the Mission. I wanted to be sure everyone there knows not to tell anyone who you are or where you live."

Sarah smiled grimly. "If they haven't already."

5

"Dear me, how horrible," Mrs. Keller said when Sarah had told her about Anne Murphy's death. "Do you have any idea who could have done it?"

They were crowded into Mrs. Keller's tiny office in hopes of keeping the tragic news from being overheard and frightening the girls at the Mission.

"Not yet," Malloy said, "but we do know that Catherine's mother and her . . . uh . . ."

"Paramour," Sarah supplied.

Malloy flashed her a grateful look. ". . . her *paramour* have been in the city for nearly a week. We don't know if they saw Anne Murphy or know she brought Catherine here, but we wanted to warn you in case they show up."

"Oh, Mrs. Brandt, I'm so sorry this happened. And now that poor woman is dead."

"You don't need to apologize. It wasn't your fault, Mrs. Keller."

She didn't look convinced. "I want you to know that I spoke with all the girls to find out if anyone had been asking about Catherine. I didn't want to alarm them because if they thought they'd done something wrong, they might not want to admit it, so I just asked if anyone had come by when I wasn't here. I said I'd been expecting someone and didn't want to miss them. No one admitted to it, at least, and I think they would have. I gave them no reason to deny it."

"That was very wise of you, Mrs. Keller," Malloy said. "But now I think you'd better warn them, just in case."

"Of course. Perhaps you could speak to them yourself, Mr. Malloy. They hold you in very high regard, and I think your warning would carry more weight. It's almost time for them to come down to eat. You both are welcome to join us. I think the girls would enjoy that."

"Thank you," Sarah said. "That's a good idea."

Malloy didn't look like he thought it was a good idea. He didn't seem to enjoy being the center of attention of a bunch of giggling girls as much as Sarah enjoyed watching it. "I can't stay long. I have an appointment this afternoon," he said.

Mrs. Keller smiled knowingly at his flimsy excuse. "The girls will be heartbroken, I'm sure. I'll go let cook know you'll be joining us."

When they were alone, Sarah said, "Do you really have an appointment?"

He raised his eyebrows, as if he were offended that she doubted him. "Yes, I do."

"With who?"

"Wilbanks's lawyer wants to see me."

"Oh, dear."

"I know. He probably has some legal paper he thinks will force me to tell him where Catherine is."

"Thank heaven we took her to my parents. Where is his office?"

"I don't know. I'm supposed to meet him at his house."

"His house? That's strange."

"Wilbanks told me his son-in-law is an attorney. Maybe he's doing this because he's family."

"I'm going with you."

"What?"

"You heard me. I'm going with you."

"Why would you do that?"

"Because I'm tired of sitting at home waiting for you to come and tell me what you did."

He looked like he sympathized, but he said, "Sarah, I can't let you put yourself in danger."

"How could I be in danger in an attorney's house?"

"I don't know. For all we know, the message is a fake and this Hicks fellow is the one who killed Miss Murphy. I'm not going to take you."

Sarah sighed. "Then I'll just have to follow you."

"No, you won't."

"Or I can look this fellow up in the City Directory. Hicks, you say? There can't be too many attorneys by that name."

Malloy looked like he might start shouting, but Mrs. Keller returned at that moment. "Cook is just putting out our dinner. I already told the girls you'd be joining us, and they're very excited."

Felix Decker had spent a productive morning at his club, learning almost everything he needed to learn about David Wilbanks. He knew his business dealings, his approximate net worth, his family connections, his social standing, and his tailor. Rumors abounded that his health was failing, and he had not been seen around town in weeks. Everyone believed his son, Oswald, would run through his fortune in less than five years after he died.

Decker located Wilbanks's address and took a cab to his house. The maid showed him to the small room where unexpected visitors were relegated until the servants could determine if they were welcome or not and then took his message to Wilbanks. As he had expected, Wilbanks did not keep him waiting long. The maid escorted him into the well-appointed parlor where a man about his own age sat in an overstuffed chair beside a roaring fire.

"Mr. Decker, welcome to my home. Forgive me for not getting up, but I have not been well."

Decker shook the man's hand and realized that Wilbanks had probably not exaggerated his illness to Malloy. The skin stretched tightly over his once-handsome face, and his sunken eyes held a resignation he had seen more than once in those whom doctors had failed to help.

"Thank you for seeing me," Decker said.

Wilbanks smiled slightly. "Did you really think I would refuse after you told me you wanted to discuss my daughter?" He didn't wait for a reply. "Please, sit down and tell me why you're here."

Decker took the nearest chair, although it was unnecessarily close to the fire. The room, he'd noticed, was too warm, but even still, Wilbanks wore a quilted dressing gown and had a lap robe thrown over his legs. He felt almost guilty taking advantage of a man so weak, but he wouldn't let that stop him. "I don't believe we've ever met, Mr. Wilbanks."

"No, but of course I know who you are. The only thing I don't know is why you've taken a sudden interest in me and my family affairs."

"Because they are also *my* family affairs."

Wilbanks considered this information for a moment. "I had a visitor yesterday who told me Catherine has been living with a family. Is it your family?"

"My daughter's."

"I see. Can you tell me how this came about?"

"Did Mr. Malloy tell you how the nursemaid dropped Catherine off at a settlement house here in the city?"

Wilbanks's pain-filled eyes widened. "Malloy? Does he work for you?"

"You flatter me, Mr. Wilbanks. Although I have some minor sources of influence in the city, I do not control the Police Department. Even if I did, I do not believe Mr. Malloy is controlled by anyone." Decker did not have to feign his annoyance at this fact.

"And yet he reports to you."

"As a favor only."

"He told me he knows the family who has Catherine. He knows your daughter?" His surprise that Decker's daughter would know a policeman was plain.

"My daughter has always been a bit rebellious. She married against my will, and she has a rather unconventional circle of friends."

"I should say. Malloy told me Catherine's guardian was a volunteer at the settlement house."

"That is how my daughter met her, yes. Catherine is much younger than the girls who usually go there. I believe their main purpose is to keep girls from turning to prostitution out of desperation."

"Prostitution!" Wilbanks nearly choked on the word, and he turned scarlet. For a second Decker feared he might keel over with apoplexy.

"The Mission *successfully* keeps them from turning to it," he hastily explained. "But the girls there are much older than Catherine. My daughter thought she needed a real home."

"Of course she does, and I have a real home right here for her. I've contacted my son-in-law, who is an attorney. I believe he is meeting with Mr. Malloy today to discuss the legalities of the situation."

"Mr. Wilbanks, I understand how you must feel—"

"Do you? Have you ever lost a daughter, Mr. Decker?"

The question was like a physical blow, the pain as fresh as the day it had happened. "Yes, I have. But *your* daughter isn't dead, Wilbanks. She's well and happy."

Somewhat taken aback, Wilbanks still did not give an inch. "I only have your word for that."

"If you know anything about me at all, you know my word is good."

"That's cold comfort to a dying man."

"Suppose I do tell you where your daughter is? What then?"

"My son-in-law assures me he will have that information for me in a matter of days with no assistance from you."

"Does he have an investigator working on it?"

"Of course."

"The same one who failed to find her the first time?"

Wilbanks's eyes narrowed. "Why did you come here, Decker? Just to torture me? Are you one of those holier-than-thou do-gooders who thinks I should be punished for my immorality?"

"Of course not," Decker said, pushing aside his personal distaste for Wilbanks's moral failings. "I came to see if we could work out a compromise that would be in Catherine's best interest."

"Catherine's best interest is to be with her father."

"Is that the only solution you'll accept?"

"Why should I accept any other?"

"Because you're dying, Wilbanks. Even if you manage to live another year or two, Catherine will still be very young. What will become of her when you're gone?"

"I'll leave her with a fortune. She'll never want for anything."

"And who will manage that fortune for her? Who can be trusted not to squander it all before she comes of age? Or cheat her out of it in some other way? And if someone did murder the nursemaid because they didn't want you to find Catherine, what's to stop them from murdering a child to keep her from collecting her inheritance?"

The color had drained from Wilbanks's face, and he reached blindly for a carafe sitting on the table beside him. He knocked a book onto the floor and nearly toppled the carafe. Decker caught it just in time and poured some water into a glass for Wilbanks, who gulped it down. When Wilbanks had recovered himself, Decker picked up the book and laid it back on the table. It was the new volume by H. G. Wells, *The War of the Worlds*.

"What makes you think you can protect her better than I can?" Wilbanks asked when he could speak again.

"For one thing, I'll be here to do it. For another, if no one knows where she is, no one can hurt her."

"You said she lives with your daughter."

"We've taken her to a safer place for the time being. Not to hide her from you, but to keep her away from the killer. You can't possibly fault us for that."

Wilbanks leaned his head back and closed his eyes. "No. No, I can't fault you for that."

"Give us a few days to see if Mr. Malloy can find out who killed Miss Murphy."

"Is there any hope of that?"

"I have learned to respect Mr. Malloy's abilities. If anyone can do it, he can."

"And if he doesn't?"

"You have every right to your child, Mr. Wilbanks, but allow me to suggest that you consider her future without you."

Anger flared in his eyes. "Do you think I haven't done that already?"

"I'm sure you have, but until yesterday, you didn't know about Catherine's current situation or the danger she might be in."

"And now I do. You aren't the only one with

influence in the city, Decker. I can protect Catherine, too."

"From whom?"

Wilbanks narrowed his eyes again. "What does that mean?"

"Exactly what I said. Do you know from whom you are protecting her?"

"No, and neither do you."

"That's true, but I'm in a position to protect her from everyone, at least for the time being. Are you prepared to consider everyone you know as a potential threat to her, even your other children?"

"What do you mean? My other children are no threat to her."

"Are you sure?"

"Of course I'm sure!"

"I think you're allowing your emotions to cloud your judgment, Wilbanks. I can't fault you for not wanting to suspect your own children of murder, but who would have more to gain if Catherine disappeared?"

When the time came, Malloy surrendered with grace and made no further protests to Sarah's plan to accompany him to see Wilbanks's attorney. They'd gone only a few steps down the sidewalk, however, when one of the girls from the Mission came running out of the alley beside the house to intercept them.

"Mr. Malloy, please wait!" She beckoned them to join her in the relative privacy of the shadowed space between buildings.

"What is it, Carrie?" Sarah asked.

A frail girl of about fourteen, Carrie glanced over her shoulder and wrung her hands before replying. "I didn't want to say nothing in front of Mrs. Keller. I didn't want her to think I lied to her before."

"I'm sure she wouldn't think that," Sarah said, trying to keep her voice calm, even though her heart was pounding.

"And I didn't, not really. All she asked us was did anybody come around when she wasn't here, asking about the ladies who volunteer here. I told her no, because that's not what happened at all."

"What did happen?" Malloy asked in the gentle voice he always used with Catherine.

"A woman came by when I was sweeping the front steps. Mrs. Keller was inside, so she *was* here, and she only asked us did somebody come by when she *wasn't* here, so I wasn't lying, was I?"

"No, of course not," Sarah said. "What did she want?"

"I didn't know at first, did I? So I asked did she want to see Mrs. Keller, but she said no. She was just wondering if we had any little children staying here. Said she was looking for a friend whose little girl had gone missing. I told her we'd only ever had one little girl here, but that was a long time ago. She asked me what happened to her, and I said she got taken in by a nice lady. I didn't tell her your name, though, Mrs. Brandt. I'm sure I didn't. I'm so very sorry!"

"That's all right, Carrie. You didn't know."

"When did this happen?" Malloy asked.

"I don't remember exactly. Four or five days ago, I think."

Malloy nodded his approval. "What did the woman look like?"

Carrie frowned. "I don't rightly know. She was wearing this big hat with a veil, so I didn't get much of a look at her."

"How old was she?" he prompted. "About Mrs. Brandt's age? Or older, like Mrs. Keller?"

"Like Mrs. Brandt, I'd guess, from her voice. She had a real nice voice."

"How was she dressed?" Sarah asked.

"Oh, real pretty. Her dress was kind of reddish, only not flashy. Stylish, it was."

"Did she say anything else?" Malloy asked.

"She thanked me for my help. She said she guessed her friend's little girl wasn't here, and she walked away. She seemed real disappointed, and I was sorry I wasn't able to help her. Please don't tell Mrs. Keller, will you?"

"We won't," Sarah said. "But thank you for telling us."

With a last, apologetic look, the girl scurried away.

"I don't think it was Anne Murphy," Sarah said. "I thought maybe she'd come back trying to get more information, but this was someone else."

"Young and stylish," Malloy said. "Could have been Emma Hardy."

"If Emma was looking for Catherine here, she must have seen Anne at some point and found out what Anne had done."

"I wonder if Emma has a temper," Malloy said.

Sarah thought about how she might react if someone she trusted had lost Catherine. Would she be angry enough to stab that person? "I know how I'd feel, but Emma had already left her child for nearly a year."

"That doesn't mean she wouldn't be mad about not being able to get her back. Even if she didn't care about Catherine, as long as she had her, she'd always be able to get money from Wilbanks."

"Would she have known Wilbanks was dying? That could have made her more desperate, too."

"Yes, she might think this was her last chance to get a settlement out of him or something. In fact, she wouldn't even need Catherine. She could just tell him he'd never see her again unless he gave them the money, and then she could leave town without producing the child. So maybe she wasn't as desperate as we think."

"If she was devious enough to think of that," Sarah said. "I don't think I would have, but then, I don't want to think Catherine's mother is anything but kind and loving and frantic to see her again."

"Just keep thinking that. Meanwhile," he said, taking her arm, "that attorney is waiting for us, and I'm dying to find out what he wants."

They took the elevated train up Third Avenue. The tracks lay three stories above street level, and riders amused themselves by looking into the windows of the tenement buildings only a few feet away as the train rolled past. This time of day, the El wasn't too crowded, so they easily found seats for the relatively brief ride that could have taken hours in the traffic-choked streets below.

When they emerged from the covered stairway at the Fifty-ninth Street Station, they might have been in a different city. Here no street vendors hawked their wares and no bedraggled children or mangy dogs raced down the sidewalks. Tree-lined streets ran between rows of well-kept houses. Decorative wrought-iron fences separated the tiny front lawns from the sidewalk. The people who lived here never had to worry about dodging the landlord or going to bed hungry.

Michael Hicks lived in a red brick town house with lace curtains. A maid admitted them and took them right upstairs to the formal parlor, where company would normally be entertained. A well-dressed man whose thinning hair and thickening waist marked his entry into middle age stood to welcome them, and to Sarah's surprise, a woman stood beside him.

Neither was smiling, since this wasn't a social call, and the woman looked as surprised to see Sarah as she was to see her. The woman's gaze swept her from head to foot, taking Sarah's measure as women did, judging and categorizing her in an instant. For a moment Sarah regretted not having dressed for the occasion. Then again, nothing in her current wardrobe would have indicated she was anything other than a midwife to the working class of the city. Besides, she'd long since stopped caring about such things as appearances. These people would soon have reason to judge her on who she was, not what she wore.

"Mr. Malloy," the man said. "I am Michael Hicks, and this is my wife, Lynne."

The two men shook hands, and Malloy nodded to Mrs. Hicks, then said, "And this is Mrs. Brandt," which was all they had decided to reveal at this point, although their host looked more than curious.

Hicks was too well mannered to leave guests standing while he interrogated them, so he invited them to be seated, and Mrs. Hicks offered them refreshment and rang for the maid to bring it. When the girl had gone to fetch it, the four of them sat for a long moment in silence. Only then did Sarah notice how tense the Hickses were. She and Malloy were anxious, of course, but she hadn't expected Hicks to be, and she hadn't expected Hicks's wife at all. Yet when she met Mrs. Hicks's eye, she saw her own anxiety mirrored there.

"Are you Mr. Wilbanks's daughter, Mrs. Hicks?" Malloy asked, breaking the awkward silence.

"Yes, I am." She was an attractive brunette who wore her age well, but Sarah was fairly certain she was not someone Carrie would have called young and stylish. "And you must be the woman who has the little girl."

"Your sister, yes," Sarah said, wanting to see her reaction. She winced slightly, and Sarah realized she couldn't blame her. How would she have felt to learn her father had a young child by a mistress?

"*Half* sister," Hicks said, "and I'll ask you not to distress my wife. She is already upset enough over this situation."

"We're not here to distress your wife," Malloy said, not bothering to hide his impatience. "We're here because you sent for me, and I'd like to know why."

"Very well. First, I must apologize for not saying more in my message, but I couldn't be sure who might see it. Mr. Wilbanks asked me to meet with you to see if we could come to some compromise about the child."

"Her name is Catherine," Sarah said.

Mrs. Hicks cried out, as if in pain, and turned on

her husband in a fury. "You should have told me!"

"I couldn't," he said in dismay. "I knew how hurt you'd be."

She turned back to Sarah. "He named her after my mother! He was carrying on with that actress all those years, and then he named her child after my mother *while she was still alive!*"

"I'm so sorry," Sarah said honestly.

"How could he have been so cruel?" she asked of no one in particular.

Sarah decided she would ask him herself if she ever got the opportunity.

"Lynne didn't know about any of this until yesterday," Hicks said.

"But you did," Malloy said.

"Yes, but I didn't find out until after Lynne's mother passed away a little over a year ago. My father-in-law confessed the whole sordid story to me then, but only because he wanted to do something for the child."

"Are you the one who advised him to marry Emma Hardy?" Malloy asked. Apparently, he had no qualms about distressing Lynne Hicks, no matter what her husband might desire.

"*Marry* her?" Mrs. Hicks echoed in horror.

"That was *his* idea," Hicks said quickly. "He wanted to know how to legitimize her birth and give her the same advantages you'd had in life. I had to tell him that marriage to the mother was the only way to do that."

For a moment, Mrs. Hicks looked like she might burst into tears, but a rap on the door signaled the return of the maid with a tea tray, and like the good hostess she had been trained to be, she reined in her emotions and went through the motions of seeing to the needs of her guests. By the time the maid was gone and they'd all been served with tea no one really wanted, the tension in the room had eased considerably.

"What kind of compromise does Mr. Wilbanks have in mind?" Malloy asked.

Hicks glanced at his wife, as if trying to gauge her tolerance for the subject. She apparently gave him some sort of silent consent, because he said, "First of all, he would like to see the child. To make sure she's all right, you understand."

"And if we bring her to him, how do we know he'll let her go again?" Sarah asked.

"He does have every legal right to keep her," Hicks reminded her.

"Which is why I asked. I know you have no reason to wish the child well, but I love her dearly, and I don't want to see any harm come to her."

"You can't think my father would harm her," Lynne Hicks said.

Sarah was glad to see her defending her father's integrity, no matter how angry she might be with him at the moment. "I don't think your father would harm her, but someone already murdered her nursemaid, and it might have been some-

123

body close to him who didn't want him to find the child."

"Oh, for heaven's sake, stop calling her 'the child,' " Mrs. Hicks said. "I'll have to get used to hearing her name eventually. Catherine. There, I've said it. Now you may say it, too."

"Thank you," Malloy said with just the slightest trace of sarcasm. "Do either of you have any idea who might have wanted to keep your father from finding Catherine?"

"No, we do not," Hicks said.

"Really?" Malloy said. "Because I'd expect Mr. Wilbanks's other children to be the ones most likely to want to get rid of an extra heir to his fortune."

Sarah winced at the baldness of this statement, but Malloy actually looked pleased when Hicks responded with outrage.

"How dare you make an accusation like that!"

Mrs. Hicks looked merely annoyed. "If you're trying to accuse me of murdering a woman I never met just so I'd inherit more of my father's money, you're wasting your time, Mr. Malloy. I'm not going to inherit anything from my father no matter how many illegitimate children might crawl out of the woodwork."

Malloy gave Sarah a questioning look. Luckily, she knew the explanation, or thought she did. "Your father already made a settlement on you."

"He called it a gift, when I married. He said

the idea of a dowry was too old-fashioned, but there was no reason to make me wait for my inheritance when we could make good use of it getting started in life," she said, glancing at her husband.

"And as you can see, we're quite comfortable now," he said. "We don't need or want any of David Wilbanks's money."

"What about your brother?" Malloy asked. "Did he get a settlement when he married, too?"

Sarah had expected another angry response, but instead the Hickses exchanged an uneasy glance.

"Ozzie receives an allowance," Hicks said.

"And is he going to inherit something?"

"He will inherit everything," Mrs. Hicks said.

"Unless your father decides to leave some of his fortune to Catherine," Malloy said.

"Ozzie would never hurt anyone," Lynne Hicks said.

"Ozzie would never have the *courage* to hurt anyone," Hicks added, earning a glare from his wife.

"Gilda would, though," Mrs. Hicks said.

"Who's Gilda?" Malloy asked.

"Ozzie's wife," Hicks said. "They haven't been married two years yet, but she's already impatient to get her hands on the old man's money."

"Didn't she have a dowry?" Malloy asked.

"She didn't need one," Mrs. Hicks said with a trace of bitterness. "She's a Van Horn."

"One of the Knickerbocker families," Sarah told Malloy, a distinction her own family bore. The families who had originally settled New York City in the seventeenth century enjoyed a unique social position in the city to the present day.

"They've lost most of their money," Hicks said, "but they're still the Van Horns. Mr. Wilbanks wanted some old society to go with his new money. He wanted Ozzie to be accepted in the best homes."

"And is he?"

"I suppose," Mrs. Hicks said.

"We don't see Ozzie and Gilda much," Hicks said.

"My brother is much younger than I, and we were never close," Mrs. Hicks added.

And perhaps Gilda Van Horn didn't consider theirs one of the best homes in the city, Sarah thought.

"Does Ozzie know about Emma Hardy and Catherine?" Malloy asked.

Sarah looked at him in surprise, because of course they already knew that Ozzie Wilbanks had gone to see Emma Hardy at least twice before she disappeared.

"I can't imagine Mr. Wilbanks has told him anything," Hicks was saying.

"Could he have found out some other way?" Malloy asked.

"This isn't getting us anywhere," Hicks said.

"Mr. Wilbanks wants to see the little girl." He glanced at his wife. "Catherine."

"We may be able to arrange that," Malloy said. He didn't look at Sarah so he didn't see the black look she shot him. "But he needs to understand we aren't going to make any permanent arrangements until we know who killed Miss Murphy and why."

"What kind of permanent arrangements does Father want to make?" Mrs. Hicks asked her husband. "He can't take care of a child. He's dying!"

"That is my concern as well," Sarah said.

"That's everyone's concern," Hicks said, not quite meeting his wife's gaze.

"Does he think I'll take her?" Mrs. Hicks asked, obviously appalled by the idea. "The child he conceived while my mother was dying?"

Her husband wisely did not reply to that.

"You don't need to concern yourself," Sarah said. "I love Catherine as if she were my own. I would have adopted her before now, but I'm a widow, and a single woman can't adopt. But before we knew who her parents were, I became her legal guardian. She is welcome to stay with me for the rest of her life."

"I'm sure she is," Hicks said, "now that you know who her father is."

"I'm not the least bit interested in his money," Sarah said.

"Aren't you?" Hicks said with a knowing smile.

Sarah glared at him, trying to think of the proper retort, but Malloy beat her to it.

"I should have introduced Mrs. Brandt better. We know who Catherine's father is, but you don't know who Mrs. Brandt's father is. He's Felix Decker. Even the Van Horns would be happy to get an invitation to his house."

Their surprise was almost comic, but Sarah couldn't enjoy it. "Mr. Hicks, you still haven't told us why you sent for Mr. Malloy today."

"Yes, I did," he said. "Mr. Wilbanks wants to see the child."

"And what's the rest of it?"

"The rest of what?"

"The threat," Malloy said before she could. "If we don't let him see Catherine, what will you do?"

But Hicks just shook his head. "It doesn't matter now. It's obvious to me that nothing I say would convince you to act against what you see as the child's best interests. I commend you both. Catherine is fortunate to have found such courageous protectors."

Sarah wasn't going to let a little flattery distract her. "And if we agree to allow him to see Catherine, will you give your word that we can have her back again?"

"I will inform Mr. Wilbanks that she is safest in your custody, at least for the time being. And, Mr. Malloy, when you identify the person who killed Miss Murphy, we can discuss Catherine's future."

6

By the time they left the Hickses' home, Frank felt like he could cheerfully strangle someone. Anyone. He was pretty sure he hated all rich people, except maybe Sarah's mother, and even she could be pretty annoying at times.

"What time does Brian get home from school?" Sarah asked as they walked aimlessly down the street in the general direction of the El.

Frank needed a minute to catch up with her thought process. His son had been the last thing on his mind. "I don't know exactly, but my mother usually has him home by four, I think."

"I'd like to go see him."

"Right now?"

"It will be after four by the time we get to your place."

Frank frowned, thinking about the reception they'd likely get. "Do you really want to see my mother?"

"I really want to see Brian."

When she turned to him, he was horrified to

see tears in her eyes. She never cried. "Maybe I should just take you back home so you can rest."

"No. I don't need to rest, and I don't want to go home. It will be hours until my parents arrive, and if we go now, Mrs. Ellsworth will be over to find out what's going on, and I just can't face her questions yet. I want to see Catherine, but I don't want to spoil her visit with my mother by showing up all upset and upsetting her. But if we go see Brian, I can put my arms around a child, and he'll be happy to see us, and maybe I can play with him and forget all of this for a while."

He couldn't argue with her reasoning, and the idea of seeing his son was certainly appealing. "All right. Let's go."

They took the Third Avenue El down to Ninth Street and walked over to the building where Frank lived with his mother and son.

Although he knew it didn't make any difference to Sarah, Frank couldn't help feeling ashamed of the neighborhood and the tenement building where he lived. The predominately Irish part of the Lower East Side was clogged with street vendors and housewives bargaining for their wares. This time of day, people were getting what they needed for their evening meals. Some were buying things to prepare, and those with a few cents extra were getting something already prepared.

Their progress was slow as Frank led Sarah

through the throngs. Finally, they reached his building. Inside, the open front door cast little light into the windowless hallway and up the stairway, but Frank's flat was only on the second floor—the most desirable location since it was above the noise of the street but with not too many steps to climb. Those on the fifth floor paid much less rent.

Someone was making cabbage. Someone was always making cabbage. The smell was probably a permanent part of the building.

When they reached his door, he took a deep breath to brace himself for his mother, and opened it. "Ma! It's me. I've brought Mrs. Brandt." There, she'd been warned.

Frank never knew what alerted his deaf son, but Brian always knew when his father was home and came running to greet him. This time he emerged from his bedroom, where he'd probably been playing. He couldn't hear Frank's warning, so the sight of Sarah was a very pleasant surprise. He threw his arms around her skirts and gazed up at her adoringly.

She was telling him how happy she was to see him, even though she knew he couldn't hear a word of it, as she lifted him into her arms.

"You're getting so big! I don't know how much longer I can carry you," she said.

Brian was signing to her, his little fingers flying with the words he'd learned at the expensive school Frank sent him to. She couldn't understand his signs any more than he could understand her words, but neither needed help understanding how happy they were to see each other.

"What's he saying?" she asked Frank.

"He's telling you what he did at school today," his mother said from the kitchen doorway. A fireplug of a woman who had never been pretty and whom life had treated harshly, she stood drying her hands on her apron. As usual, she was scowling, but he also noticed she looked a little scared, although what she had to be scared of, he had no idea.

"Hello, Mrs. Malloy. I'm sorry to barge in on you this way, but we were nearby, and I asked Malloy if we could see Brian for a few minutes. I hope you don't mind." Sarah gave his mother her best smile.

His mother didn't smile back. "I guess you'll be wanting supper."

"Thank you," Sarah said as if his mother had graciously invited her, "but we can't stay long. We have an appointment later."

"An appointment," she sniffed, looking at Frank as if to say, "Who do you think you are to have *appointments?*"

"If you've got some coffee, I'm sure Mrs. Brandt would like some," he said, pretending not to notice his mother's disapproval. "I know I would. And don't worry about supper for yourself.

132

I'll go out and get something for you and Brian before I leave."

"Coffee," she said in a tone that indicated she thought it an unreasonable request. "I'll make some."

Sarah carried Brian into his bedroom, where they would communicate in that mysterious way people had where words weren't necessary. Brian instinctively knew who loved him, and he gave his love unconditionally in return. Frank followed his mother into the kitchen to make peace.

"I know you just got home, and I didn't want to bother you," he said while she scooped coffee beans into the grinder with the jerky motions of the put-upon. "But Mrs. Brandt is having a tough time of it right now. Catherine's parents have turned up, and they want her back."

She'd started working the grinder, but she stopped and turned to him. "Catherine? The little girl?"

"Yes."

"And that's why you're here? Just to see the boy?"

"Yes, I told you—"

"I know what you told me. Who are they, these parents, and where have they been all this time?"

Frank gave her a brief version of the story while she finished making the coffee. She periodically registered her outrage with an astonished glance, but she made no comment until he'd finished.

"So she took Catherine to her parents' house until we can get this all sorted out," he said.

"Those people don't deserve the child."

Frank sighed. "The Deckers haven't done anything—"

"Not *them,*" she snapped. "The *girl's* parents. What kind of man carries on with an actress when his wife is dying, and what kind of woman gives her child to a stranger and leaves town for a year?"

At last, something Frank and his mother could agree on. "Which is why Mrs. Brandt doesn't want to turn the child over to them, not to mention the fact that she loves Catherine like she was her own. Besides, we don't know who killed the nursemaid or why, and until we do, Catherine might be in danger, too."

"Well, of course she is. You don't have to be a detective sergeant to figure that out!"

Frank couldn't argue with that. "So when Mrs. Brandt started crying in the middle of the street and asked if she could see Brian, I couldn't say no."

She made a derisive sound, but before he could figure out what she disapproved of this time, she said, "Go to your son. He sees little enough of you as it is. I'll let you know when the coffee's ready."

Frank found Sarah sitting on Brian's narrow bed, watching him play with his wooden train with tears in her eyes.

"He's going to wonder why you're crying," he said.

She blinked furiously as Brian jumped up to greet him and show him his train. When Frank looked back at her a few minutes later, she was smiling serenely, all trace of her misery banished.

A while later, his mother summoned them to the kitchen for the coffee, and Brian joined them. He got a cup like everyone else, but his contained milk with just a spoonful of coffee. Frank noticed with surprise that his mother had set a place for herself, too, and she joined them.

"Thank you so much, Mrs. Malloy," Sarah said, taking her seat at the table.

"Francis told me about your troubles. You mustn't let those people take the child from you."

Frank turned to Sarah, ready to rush to her defense, but she straightened up in her chair, a frown marring her lovely face. "But they're her natural parents. Don't you think they have a right to her?"

His mother made that derisive noise again. "People like that don't have a right to anything. That actress woman, she can't care anything for the girl. What kind of mother leaves her child like that, not even knowing where she is? A woman like that shouldn't be allowed to keep a cat!"

"You're absolutely right," Sarah said with a trace of her usual spirit. "But her father—"

"Making a baby don't mean a man is a father.

135

If he really cared about giving her a good life, he would've married her mother *before* he made her instead of trying to make up for it later."

Sarah turned to him, the color high in her cheeks. "She's right. I shouldn't feel sorry for them."

Frank didn't know what was stranger, his mother giving Sarah advice or Sarah taking it. "No, you shouldn't."

Sarah turned back to his mother. "When I found her, she'd been abandoned, and she'd been frightened so badly, she couldn't speak for months. Heaven only knows what she saw or heard."

Someone pounded a little too enthusiastically at the door, startling all of them except Brian, whose attention was on trying to figure out what Sarah was talking about. His grandmother started signing to him while Frank got up to answer the knock.

"Has it been hard to learn to sign?" he heard Sarah asking his mother as he left the room.

Frank opened the door to a beat cop who had a message to him from Headquarters. He'd expected to just leave it for Frank's eventual return and was surprised to find him at home.

Frank read the message as he walked back to the kitchen.

The two women looked at him expectantly. "Emma Hardy wants to see me."

• • •

Sarah wanted to run to the rooming house where Emma Hardy was staying, but Malloy wouldn't tell her where it was.

"Are you sure you want to meet this woman?" he asked her for at least the hundredth time in the last two blocks. Well, maybe he'd asked her more like three times, but it seemed like a hundred.

"Of course I want to meet her. She's Catherine's mother."

"And that's exactly why you shouldn't meet her. What if she cries and tells you how much she misses her daughter and how much she loves her? What will you do then? Give Catherine back to her and wish her good luck?"

Sarah tried to stop, but the surge of bodies around them kept moving forward, forcing her to go on or be knocked over. She grabbed Malloy's arm and pulled him into the alcove of a shop doorway, where they could concentrate on talking. "You're right to be concerned. An hour ago, I might have done just that, but your mother made me realize I can't."

"My mother is crazy."

"Everybody's mother is crazy, but what she said was perfectly correct."

"And it's just what everybody else has been telling you, too."

"Yes, but everybody else loves me and wants me to be happy, and they know I'd be shattered if I lost Catherine. I couldn't trust their judgment. But your mother . . ."

"My mother definitely does not love you."

"Of course she doesn't." Sarah knew Mrs. Malloy was terrified she was going to take Frank and Brian away from her and leave her with nothing, even though Malloy had never shown the slightest inclination to allow Sarah to do anything of the kind. "And she's not particularly interested in my happiness either, but if she sees that I can't allow Emma Hardy and David Wilbanks to take Catherine, then I know it's the right thing to do."

He still looked confused, but Sarah didn't have time to figure out why or even discuss it with him.

"We need to get to Emma Hardy. Let's go!"

He rolled his eyes. "I'm not the one who stopped."

He took her arm and propelled her back into the flood of pedestrians making their way home for supper. In the press, they had no more opportunity for discussion, and concentrated their energies on arriving at their destination safely.

Malloy stopped in front of one of the large old houses on a street just off Broadway. Its blistered paint and sagging porch marked it as a rooming house. "This is where Anne Murphy lived for most of the time after she left Catherine at the Mission," he said. "She only moved to the place where you visited her when Emma wrote that she was coming home. Emma wanted Anne to move to a different place so she wouldn't be easily found."

"And this is the place where Wilbanks thought Emma lived when she was in plays in the city."

"That's right."

"Didn't she bring her lover back with her this time?"

Malloy gave her a small grin. "Let's ask her."

Sarah marched up the steps with Malloy at her heels and knocked on the door with as much authority as she could manage. An attractive woman about her own age opened the door. She frowned at Sarah, then looked past her to Malloy.

"Miss Hardy?" he asked.

"Are you Malloy?" she replied.

He nodded.

"And who's this?" She jutted her chin at Sarah.

"Do you really want to discuss your private business in the doorway?" Sarah asked in the tone that usually made even women in labor obey her.

Emma Hardy blinked in surprise, then glanced over her shoulder. Sarah could see several women gathered in the hallway behind her and making no effort to pretend they weren't eavesdropping.

"Mind your own business," she told them, sending them flouncing off. "Come in," she told Sarah.

When she stepped inside, she noticed the brightly colored posters adorning the walls in the entrance hall. They gave the place a cheerier

139

air than most of the boardinghouses she'd seen.

Miss Hardy pointed to the parlor door, and Sarah went in. More posters hung here, but now Sarah could see they were faded and old. The worn furniture marked it as a common area, shared by all but enjoyed by none. Malloy followed her, and Emma Hardy closed the parlor door behind them.

"Now, who are you?" she asked Sarah.

Sarah smiled. "Mrs. Brandt."

Emma apparently saw no reason to acknowledge the introduction. She was a striking woman, and Sarah could see why she had caught Wilbanks's eye, even from the chorus. She'd pulled her dark hair up into a sloppy Gibson Girl knot, but it shone in the fading sunlight like a raven's wing. Her dark hair contrasted well with her milky skin, still smooth and clear. She wore a dress of deep burgundy, which might be the "red" dress Carrie had described. It hugged her womanly curves. Her large, dark eyes probably looked mysterious when she wanted them to. Right now they just looked angry.

"Let's sit down," Malloy said. "I think we have a lot to talk about."

Malloy and Sarah sat together on the sofa, and Emma took an overstuffed chair opposite them. Sarah noticed stuffing coming out of one of the arms.

"Where's Catherine?" Emma asked when they

were seated. "Mrs. Dugan said you know where she is."

Sarah glanced at Malloy, who said, "Mrs. Dugan is the landlady." To Miss Hardy, he said, "I do know where she is."

"Then give her to me."

"Why should I?"

"Because I'm her mother!"

Sarah felt the fury rise up in her like a tidal wave. "And what kind of mother goes off and leaves her child for a year without a thought?"

"I thought of her! I thought of her all the time I was gone!"

"And did you wonder where she was and what she was doing?"

"She was with Anne! I left her with Anne."

"Miss Hardy," Malloy said in that infuriating voice men use when they think women need to be calmed down. "We know you left her with Anne Murphy. Do you know that Miss Murphy was murdered?"

"Of course I know it! Mrs. Dugan told me first thing when I got here this afternoon. Anne was supposed to meet me with Catherine. So where is my child?"

"She's safe," Sarah said.

"I should hope so. I was furious when I found out Annie had left her at some settlement house, like she was an orphan or something. Just tell me where she is and I'll go get her."

141

"What will you do when you get her?" Malloy asked.

"What do you mean?"

"Just what I said. What are your plans for Catherine's future?"

"Her future is she'll live with me and grow up. What other plans do I need?"

"I'd be interested in how you plan to take care of her if you're an actress," Sarah said.

"That's none of your affair. I'm her mother, and she belongs with me."

"Does she?" Malloy asked. "And how does Mr. Vaughn feel about raising somebody else's child?"

Her shock was almost comical, but Sarah didn't feel much like laughing. "What does that mean?"

"Stop asking me what things mean, Miss Hardy, when you know perfectly well what they mean. I know about Parnell Vaughn and how you were living with him when David Wilbanks was paying Mrs. Dugan for you to live here."

"I never!"

"Mrs. Dugan told me everything, so don't bother to deny it. Now what are you and Vaughn planning to do with the child when you get her? Were you going to extort money from Wilbanks for her, by chance?"

"I . . . I don't know what *extort* means," she said, twisting her hands in her lap.

"Were you going to ask Wilbanks to give you

142

money in exchange for the child?" he said with elaborate patience.

"He wants her, I know. Why shouldn't I get something out of it? I gave up my career to have her. He owes me something, doesn't he?"

Any lingering sympathy she might have felt for Emma Hardy evaporated. "Whose idea was that?" Sarah asked.

Emma glared at Sarah. "It wasn't nobody's idea. It's just the right thing to do."

"We're not going to tell you where Catherine is," Malloy said.

The color bloomed in her cheeks. "You can't do that! She's my flesh and blood. You can't keep her away from me!" She turned her fury on Sarah, but before she could utter a word, her eyes widened in surprise. "*You!* Annie said some rich woman who volunteered at the Mission took Catherine. That was you, wasn't it?"

Sarah didn't answer, but it was no use. She felt the heat in her cheeks, and she knew Emma saw the truth on her face.

"Brandt, that's your name. That's what you said. You have Catherine, and I know your name. It shouldn't be too hard to find her now."

"I don't have her anymore," Sarah said. "I sent her someplace safe."

"That's easy to say, isn't it? You won't mind if I come to your house and look anyway, will you?"

"Miss Hardy," Malloy said, startling both of

them back to the present. "Did you forget that Anne Murphy was murdered?"

Her confidence vanished. Her gaze shifted from Malloy to Sarah and back to Malloy again, as if trying to judge which one was the more formidable opponent. "No, I didn't forget. How could I?"

"And don't you wonder who killed her?"

"What difference does it make who killed her? It's got nothing to do with me."

"Are you sure?"

The color had drained from her face, and she started twisting her hands again. "Why should it?"

Sarah wanted to slap her. "Because the reason Miss Murphy left Catherine at the Mission in the first place was because she was afraid someone would harm her."

"Who would want to hurt a child?" she asked.

"Maybe the same person you were afraid was going to hurt *you* when you left town a year ago," Malloy said.

She stared back at them for a long moment, as if trying to figure out what to say. For an actress, she wasn't very good at hiding her emotions, and Sarah could easily see how terrified she was, but not of them. "I don't know who you could mean. Nobody ever wished me any harm."

"Then why did you run away?" Sarah asked.

"I didn't run away. Whoever told you a thing like that? I just got a chance to be in a play and I took it. I was tired of living in that old house and I was tired of Wilbanks telling me what to do all the time, so I left. I wanted to have some fun." She tried to smile, but it did not quite reach her eyes.

"And you left your child with Miss Murphy."

"She loves little Catherine," Emma said, then frowned. "I mean she *loved* her. Half the time, I think Catherine thought Annie was her mother." She smiled as if that were a joke, but nobody smiled back.

"Let me get this straight," Malloy said. "Miss Murphy thinks you left town because you thought *you* were in danger. Then she hides Catherine at the Mission because she thinks the child might be in danger. For nearly a year, she lives in the same boardinghouse where you and she had lived, and nobody bothers her. But then she gets a couple letters from you telling her you're going to meet up with her and the child, and then suddenly, somebody kills her. Why do you think that happened, Miss Hardy?"

"How should I know? I hadn't seen her for nearly a year. Anything could've happened. Maybe she offended somebody. Maybe she got in trouble with somebody."

"A dresser?" Sarah said, not bothering to hide her skepticism. "What could she have done to make someone want to kill her?"

"I don't know! I told you, I hadn't seen her for almost a year."

"Until you got back to New York and went looking for her. What did you say when she told you she'd lost Catherine?"

"I didn't say anything because I never saw Annie. This morning I went to the boarding-house where she'd told me to meet her, but they said she wasn't there, so I come here to see if Mrs. Dugan knows where she is. She tells me Annie is dead and you've got Catherine. That's all I know!"

"I think you know at least one other thing," Malloy said.

"And what would that be?"

"Where Parnell Vaughn is."

"And what if I do?"

"Then you'd better tell me so I don't have to take you down to Police Headquarters and lock you up for the night."

"The devil, you say!"

"There's no need to swear, Miss Hardy. Just tell me where Vaughn is."

Now she really looked frightened. "What do you want with him? He doesn't have anything to do with any of this."

"I'd like to find that out for myself. Otherwise, I saw a beat cop on the corner. I'll just have him take you in and lock you up until I have time to get back there and ask you again. I'm pretty busy, so that won't be until tomorrow, maybe even the next day, so—"

"He's at the La Pierre Hotel. That's where we're staying." The look she gave Malloy could have drawn blood, but he merely smiled slightly.

"Thank you for your help, Miss Hardy."

"So what am I supposed to do about my daughter? When will I get her back?"

"I thought you didn't want her back," Malloy said.

"I never said that!"

"Oh, I guess you're right. You *didn't* say that. In fact, you're eager to get her back so you can sell her to her father."

She looked as if she wanted to scratch Malloy's eyes out, but Sarah had had enough of her theatrics. "Have you seen Mr. Wilbanks since you've gotten back to the city?"

"How could I? I only got back yesterday."

"Really? Where have you been for the past week?"

"The past week? What do you mean?"

"The week since your play closed in Philadelphia."

"How did you know that?"

Sarah gave up and turned to Malloy for assistance.

"We know your play closed over a week ago, Miss Hardy," he said. "I thought you were in a hurry to see your daughter, so why did it take you so long to come looking for her?"

"I . . . Parnell. That's it. He was sick. We had to

stay in Philadephia until he could travel. He was worn out from the tour. That's hard work, going from town to town for months on end, and Parnell doesn't have a strong constitution."

Sarah wondered if Malloy could check on how long they'd been in the city. Certainly, the La Pierre Hotel could tell him when Vaughn and Emma had checked in.

"I'm going to pay Mr. Vaughn a visit," Malloy said. "The two of you can try to hide or even leave town if you want to, but if you do, you'll never see your daughter again. Oh, and did we mention to you that Mr. Wilbanks is dying?"

Plainly, she'd had no idea. "Dying? What do you mean, dying? He was perfectly fine the last time I saw him."

"That was a year ago," Sarah said. "A lot can happen, and Mr. Wilbanks only has a few months left."

"So if you hope to get anything out of him, you'll need to be quick," Malloy added with another grin.

"I don't believe you!"

"Why would we lie to you?" Malloy asked. "It's easy enough to check. Just go see him. I'm sure his son would be glad for you to visit him."

Once again, the color drained from her face, and Sarah thought they had found the person who had frightened Emma Hardy off in the first place. "Maybe I will," she said.

Frank checked his watch as they left the boardinghouse. "We still have a couple hours before we have to meet your parents. I'd like to see Parnell Vaughn before Emma has a chance to tell him what to say to us."

"That's probably a good idea. Do you know where this hotel is?"

"Yes, and it's not a place I can take you. I also want to see this Vaughn fellow alone."

"In case you need to frighten him," she said.

He saw no judgment in her eyes, but he still hated that she knew he sometimes had to use violence in his job. "I'll walk you out to Broadway so you can get a cab home."

They both knew a woman alone would have a difficult time hailing a cab, so she didn't make any silly protests.

"Your mother was right," she said as they walked. "Emma Hardy doesn't deserve Catherine. She didn't even deny that she was going to sell her to Wilbanks."

"There's a lot worse things she could have done with her, you know."

They walked a ways while she thought this over. "Can you find out how long she's been in the city?"

"You mean if she's been here long enough to have killed Anne Murphy? I'll check with the desk clerk, but we already know she was."

"We do?"

"Didn't you notice? She said Anne told her some rich woman had taken Catherine from the Mission."

"That's right, she did! And Anne didn't know that until just a few days before she died."

"Not long enough to have written Emma a letter, so that means Emma got to the city and went to see Anne, probably to collect Catherine so she could make her bargain with Wilbanks. Then Anne told her what happened to Catherine."

Sarah nodded. "She wouldn't have been happy to hear that either. If she lost Catherine, she didn't have any hold over Wilbanks. That might've made her angry enough to stab Anne."

"It's possible. If she did stab her, she probably realized her best bet was to pretend she was just going to see Anne for the first time today and didn't know she was dead."

"Which is exactly what she did by coming here to ask about her. What are you going to ask Vaughn about?"

"I'll start with when they got to the city and if he was with Emma when she went to see Anne Murphy. After that, it will depend."

"On what?"

"He's supposed to be a drunk. It will depend on if he's been drinking and how much."

"Will it be better if he is drunk or if he isn't?"

"I won't know that until I see him."

They'd reached Broadway, and Frank stepped

into the street to hail a cab. As luck would have it, one stopped nearby to let off a passenger, and Malloy quickly secured it for Sarah, paying the driver after giving him her address and helping her inside.

"Try to eat something when you get home," he said.

"Try to eat something yourself. I don't even know if there's any food in my house, so don't wait until you get there."

"Mrs. Ellsworth will bring something over, I'm sure."

Sarah smiled. "She will if she sees you coming."

"If I'm late, start without me. We've got a lot to tell your parents, and you know most of it."

"I'll make my father wait until you're there to tell about his visit with Wilbanks."

He signaled the driver to go, and the aging vehicle with its sway-backed horse lurched into motion in an optimistic effort to join the steady flow of traffic.

Frank watched it for a few minutes, until she was well on her way. Then he turned south on Broadway and headed toward the lower part of the Lower East Side where the La Pierre Hotel housed those well-heeled enough to afford a real bed, however full of fleas or bedbugs, instead of the filthy wooden bunks and straw mattresses of a nickel-a-night flophouse.

The La Pierre was as bad as he remembered. At first he thought the front desk was deserted, until he noticed the soft snoring sounds. When he peered over, he saw the clerk curled up on the floor and fast asleep. With a grin, he started slapping the tap bell, sending up the kind of alarm that usually brought fire engines to the scene. The desk clerk awoke with a snort and jumped to his feet, looking around wildly to see what all the ruckus was about. When he saw Frank grinning at him, he grumbled, "What do you want?"

"I want to see your register, for starters." He pulled out his badge and let the clerk have a good look before pulling the large book over to him so he could skim the entries. He quickly found what he was looking for: Mr. and Mrs. Parnell Vaughn had checked in two days ago, the day before Anne Murphy was murdered. Even a fleabag place like this would expect a couple to pretend to be married. He checked the room number and headed for the stairs.

"What are you going to do?" the desk clerk called in alarm.

"I'm going to visit one of your guests."

"I don't want no trouble. We make our payments regular."

He meant bribes to the police department, and Frank was sure they did. A hotel like this would have a host of prostitutes servicing the clientele. Police interference would be very bad for business. "If there's trouble, I'll take it out of here," he called back as he climbed the stairs.

At the end of the grimy hall, Frank found the room he was looking for and pounded on the door. When nobody answered, he called, "Vaughn, are you in there?"

When that brought no response, he tried the knob and it turned. Well, if Vaughn wasn't here, he could at least have a look around. He pushed open the door, not sure what to expect.

What he didn't expect was to see Parnell Vaughn lying motionless on the bed.

Although the cab ride took longer than it would have just to walk the distance from Broadway to her house on Bank Street, Sarah was glad for the time alone. She realized she was bone tired from the strain of knowing that any minute someone might take Catherine away from her forever. How would she stand knowing the child she loved was being raised by someone else, someone who may not even care about her?

Someone who might never allow her to see Catherine again?

Emma Hardy's admission that she was willing to give Catherine to Wilbanks if he paid her well enough had chilled her heart. If Wilbanks was dead, what would Emma do with her? And suppose she did turn Catherine over to Wilbanks? What would happen to her when he died? Who would look after her? Lynne Hicks seemed like a nice enough woman, but she had no interest in raising her father's bastard child, especially when that child's name would be a daily reminder of how her father had betrayed her mother. Even though Sarah had never met him, Wilbanks's son seemed an even less likely candidate as a guardian for Catherine, especially if Wilbanks had provided for her in any way in his estate.

By the time the cab stopped in front of her town house, Sarah's head was pounding. Although Malloy had already paid him, she gave the driver a little extra and let herself into her house. The emptiness seemed to echo. How many years had she lived here alone and never thought twice about coming home to an empty house? The months since Catherine and Maeve had lived here with her had changed her forever.

She took off her hat and coat and had just started to wonder what she would do with herself until her parents arrived when someone knocked on her door. Did she dare answer it? What if it was someone wanting her to deliver a baby? She didn't have any clients who were due, but babies sometimes came early and many people never consulted her at all until the labor pains started.

"Mrs. Brandt? It's me!" a familiar voice called.

Sarah opened the door to Mrs. Ellsworth. She carried a plate that she'd covered with a napkin. "I didn't want to bother you, but I had some chicken left from supper, and I thought you might appreciate not having to cook for yourself this evening."

"That's very kind of you." Sarah felt a pang of

guilt for telling Malloy she didn't feel like talking to her neighbor. "You're probably wondering where the girls are."

"I have been worried, knowing that Catherine's parents were looking for her."

"I should have told you. Maeve and Catherine have gone to stay with my mother for a while."

"Oh, what a good idea. I saw your mother's carriage here earlier, and I was hoping that's where they'd gone." Not much happened on Bank Street that Mrs. Ellsworth didn't notice. "Why don't you come into the kitchen and let me wait on you. I'll heat this up and make you some coffee. There's probably some cake left from yesterday, too."

Sarah surrendered willingly, and she found that the coffee and the supper greatly relieved her headache. To her credit, Mrs. Ellsworth waited until she'd eaten before asking her what she'd learned about Catherine's parents since they'd last spoken. Even though that had been only yesterday, so much had happened. Sarah had to break the news that Anne Murphy had been murdered.

"Dear heaven, how horrible! That poor woman. Does Mr. Malloy think it has something to do with Catherine?"

"I wish we didn't think so, but what else could it be? At least we've identified Catherine's father, the mysterious Mr. Smith. My father went to see him today, and Malloy and I actually met with her mother just a little while ago." Sarah quickly filled Mrs. Ellsworth in on what she'd learned from Emma Hardy and Mr. and Mrs. Hicks.

"Malloy has gone to see this Parnell Vaughn. He said he wanted to question him before Emma had a chance to warn him."

"So many unsavory characters. I know it must break your heart that Catherine's mother is so heartless."

"To tell you the truth, it's almost a relief. As awful as it is to think Catherine's mother doesn't love her, if she were kind and loving and desperately wanted her child back, I'd have to give Catherine to her. How could I refuse?"

"You're so right. That is a relief. But if her father is dying, are you at least going to let him see her?"

"I don't think we can refuse that either, if we can figure out how to do it safely. I just wish we knew who killed Miss Murphy. Then we would know what to do."

"What do you think of that lawyer?"

"Mr. Hicks? He seems like a respectable man."

"Respectable? I never met a lawyer I'd call respectable."

Sarah didn't bother to hide her smile. "Well, at least he didn't look like a murderer to me."

"Who does? If people looked like murderers, Mr. Malloy's job would be a lot easier."

Sarah couldn't argue with that. "But I don't think he had a reason to kill Miss Murphy."

"Who did then?"

"I have to say Emma Hardy. Whoever killed Miss Murphy did it in a fit of temper. I imagine Emma was very angry when she found out Anne Murphy didn't know where Catherine was, and she might have lost control and stabbed her."

"What about her lover, this Parnell fellow?"

"I suppose he might have been angry, too. They probably both wanted the money Mr. Wilbanks would have given for her. I must admit, I wish it was Parnell Vaughn. I really hate the thought of Catherine's mother being a killer."

"So do I," Mrs. Ellsworth said. "But who else would have done it?"

"I don't know. I guess someone who didn't want her to tell Miss Hardy where Catherine was."

"And who would that be?"

"Well, Mr. Wilbanks's son, for one. Mr. Hicks told us he's the only heir, but if Mr. Wilbanks decided to leave some money to Catherine . . ."

"Oh, yes, money is the root of all evil, as we well know. Is Mr. Malloy going to speak with this son? Oh, my, I just realized he'd be Catherine's brother."

"Half brother," Sarah said, remembering how upset that knowledge had made Mrs. Hicks. Would her brother be equally appalled? "We haven't talked about his plans. We're going to meet with my parents here this evening to discuss what we've all learned, and I suppose we'll decide then."

Mrs. Ellsworth frowned. "Your parents are coming here this evening?"

"Yes, and so is Malloy."

"Well, then, I suppose I'd better be going."

"Mrs. Ellsworth, you don't have to leave."

"I don't want to intrude. You have a lot to talk about, and it's none of my business."

"Of course it's your business. You love Catherine as much as we do."

Mrs. Ellsworth smiled. "Of course I do, but I'm not family."

And before Sarah could think of any other arguments to make, Mrs. Ellsworth had gone back to her house next door.

Dressed in only his stained balbriggans, Parnell Vaughn looked as if he hadn't shaved in a few days. Or combed his mane of dark hair. His skin was an unnatural shade of gray.

Frank sighed. He was getting sick of finding dead bodies. Luckily, Vaughn didn't seem to be completely dead, just dead drunk. His chest rose and fell frequently enough to indicate there was hope Frank might be able to rouse him.

Frank strolled over to the washstand and found the pitcher half full. He carried it to the bed and dumped it over Vaughn's head.

Vaughn bolted up in the bed, sputtering and yelping and looking around wildly. "What the hell? Who are you?"

"Detective Sergeant Frank Malloy of the New York City Police."

He stared back blankly, as if Frank had spoken to him in a foreign language. "What are you doing here?"

"I want to talk to you."

"I haven't done anything wrong. Why would you want to talk to me?"

"Maybe somebody you know did something wrong."

He blinked his bloodshot eyes a few times. "Emma? Do you mean Emma?"

"Did Emma do something wrong?"

"God knows. Why am I all wet?" He looked up as if he expected to see where the water could have entered through the ceiling.

Frank returned the pitcher to the washstand, grabbed a grimy towel, and tossed it to him. While Vaughn rubbed it over his head, Frank glanced around the room. Except for the bed and the washstand, the furniture consisted of a battered wardrobe and a rickety chair. Two small trunks rested on the floor, propped open and overflowing with discarded garments, the luggage of two traveling actors.

Frank moved the chair over to the bed, turned it around, and straddled it. Vaughn gave up trying to dry himself and turned his bloodshot gaze back to Frank. "What do you want from me? Where's Emma?"

"I don't know where she is. How long have you been here?"

"Here? In this room?"

"In the city."

"A few days. I don't know." He cast about for something, feeling under the bedclothes. His expression lightened when he found it, but when he pulled the bottle out, it was empty. "You wouldn't have anything to drink, would you?"

"No. So what have you and Emma been doing since you got to the city?"

"I haven't been doing much of anything. I found a saloon and that's pretty much all I remember."

"What about Emma?"

"She never tells me what she's up to."

"You must have some idea. Why did she come back to the city?"

Vaughn feigned an interest in the bottle, holding it up to the feeble light coming from the window as if checking to see if it was really empty. Frank batted it out of his hands, sending it crashing to the floor.

"Hey!"

"I can do that to you, too, if you annoy me, so stop annoying me and answer my questions."

Vaughn rubbed a hand across his mouth and studied Frank warily with his large, dark eyes. In spite of the stubble and the dripping hair and the damage caused by his latest binge, Frank could see Parnell Vaughn was a handsome man. The liquor hadn't yet taken his looks, although that would come in time. Then he'd have to play old men on the stage, Frank supposed.

"What was your question?"

"What has Emma been doing?"

"She went to find her kid."

"Do you know where the kid is?"

He licked his lips, probably wishing he had a drink. "Annie has her, or at least she was supposed to have her."

"But she doesn't."

"No, Emma came back here screaming like a banshee because Annie put her someplace and now she's gone and she can't find her."

"I guess she was heartbroken to lose her little girl like that."

"Emma? Not likely. But she'd decided she better do something about her while she still could."

"What does that mean? While she still could?"

"I mean, well, do you know about the old man?"

"Wilbanks?"

"Yes, Wilbanks. Liked to call himself Smith when he'd come to diddle Emma in that house where he kept her. You know about that?"

"Yes."

"Cute little place, if you like the country."

"You were there?"

"Hell, yes. How else was I going to see Emma?"

"I thought you two lived together when she'd come to the city to be in a show."

"That was later. At first, before she had the kid and then for a long time after, he wouldn't let her go anywhere, so I'd go there to see her. It's not like he cared. He hardly ever visited, and even then, I think he would've cut her loose except for the kid."

"Sounds like you had a pretty nice deal. Wilbanks is keeping Emma and even letting her come to the city for weeks at a time. What made you leave town so sudden?"

Vaughn narrowed his eyes. "What do you care about all this? What do the *police* care about all this? It's not illegal for a man to keep a mistress."

"It's illegal to commit murder."

"Murder? Who got murdered? Oh, my God, not Emma!" His gray face went white.

Frank could have let him suffer for a while, but he took pity on him. "No, not Emma. Anne Murphy."

"Annie? No, that's not possible! Nobody'd kill Annie. She never hurt a fly."

"Maybe not, but somebody killed her just the same. Any idea who that could've been?"

"How should I know? I . . ." He blinked his large eyes several times. "Wait a minute, you think I did it?"

"I didn't say that."

163

"But you do. Or you think Emma did. That's why you're here, isn't it?"

"I'm here because I found letters from Emma Hardy in Anne Murphy's room."

Vaughn frowned as if trying to make sense of all this. "You didn't come here because of any letters. Emma wrote those when we were on tour. How'd you know to come *here,* to this hotel?"

"Emma told me where you were."

Frank watched the flush of anger rise up his face, turning it scarlet. "That bitch! I don't know what she told you, but I never even saw Annie. She went there by herself. She told me to stay here and rest. That's what she said, *rest,* but she meant I should stay here and drink. She even brought me a bottle so she'd know I wouldn't need to go out anywhere."

"When did she leave?"

"How should I know? I drink, then I sleep, then I drink some more. She comes and goes, and sometimes she wakes me up and sometimes she doesn't. But if she told you I hurt Annie, she's lying. I haven't been out of this room for days."

"Is that something Emma would do, kill Annie and try to blame you for it?"

Vaughn's eyes widened as he considered the question, and Frank could see the answer—the real answer—before he said, "No, of course not." But the fear in his eyes said that he could easily believe it of her.

Frank pretended to believe him, though. No sense upsetting him when he still had more questions. "What made the two of you come back to the city now?"

For a second Vaughn looked confused, but he recovered himself pretty quickly, considering his condition. "The tour was over. We had to come back to get another show, and Emma, she says we don't have to do this anymore anyway. She says we can get money from the old man if we give him the kid."

"But you had to be quick, because the old man was dying," Frank said.

"That's right."

So Emma had lied about that. She did know Wilbanks was sick. "How did she know he was dying?"

Vaughn had to think about that for a minute. "Some fellow told her, I think."

"What fellow? When?"

"I don't know who he was. It was in Chicago, I think. Or maybe later. Cleveland? I don't know."

"While you were still on tour?"

"Yeah, he came to her after the show and told her the old man was looking for the kid and he was real sick and wanted to see her before he died."

"Who was he?"

"How should I know? I never even saw him. But that's when she said we had to go back to the city. She said Wilbanks would give us some money for the kid. So she wrote to Annie and told her we were coming."

Frank knew the rest of the story. What he didn't know was who the man was who found Emma in Chicago or maybe Cleveland, although he had a pretty good idea.

Before he could decide if he had any more questions for Vaughn, the door flew open and Emma Hardy burst into the room.

"Get up and get dressed! We've got to—" She froze when she saw Frank straddling the chair in the middle of the room. "What are you doing here? What did you tell him?" she demanded of Vaughn.

Vaughn glanced at Frank and then back at Emma, as if trying to decide who was the bigger threat. "I didn't tell him anything. Where have you been?" Plainly, he had decided Emma was the bigger threat. Frank looked at her with new respect.

"It's none of your business where I've been," she said, eyeing Frank warily. "He's got Catherine and won't tell me where she is."

"He does? That's kidnapping!" Vaughn said.

Frank rose slowly to his feet. "No, it isn't. So, Miss Hardy, who was the man who told you Wilbanks was looking for you?"

She gave Vaughn a furious glance, then said, "I don't know. Some detective he hired to find me."

Frank nodded as if he understood, except he didn't quite understand it all, because Wilbanks had said his detective hadn't found Emma. "Why didn't he take you to Wilbanks, then?"

"Because . . ." Her gaze darted around the room, as if she hoped to find an answer there. "How should I know? You'll have to ask him," she said finally.

Frank thought she did know, and he was pretty sure he knew, too. "Because you didn't have Catherine. That's the reason, isn't it? Wilbanks wasn't interested in you, just the child. So you decided to go back to New York and make your own deal with Wilbanks."

She straightened her spine and gave him the kind of glare that actresses usually gave the villain of the piece. "The detective said he was dying and wanted to see her. How could I refuse that? So I wrote to Annie right away and told her we were coming back. I even warned her to move to a different place, where nobody could find her. I was afraid Catherine might come to harm."

"I don't think so. I think you were afraid the detective would find Catherine himself, and you'd miss your chance with Wilbanks." He waved away her sputtered protests. "What I don't under-stand is why you didn't come straight back to the city when you found out Wilbanks was looking for you."

"Don't you think I wanted to?" she asked, trying

to appear indignant, but she wasn't a good enough actress to fool Frank. "I would have done just that but I didn't have any money. They don't pay the actors until the end of the tour. That's the only way they can be sure we'll stay for the run of the play. So the only way we could get back here was to travel with the show."

Now Frank was pretty sure he had the answers to all his questions. "It's been a pleasure meeting you both," he said and started for the still-open door.

"Where are you going? When am I going to get my daughter back?" she asked.

"We'll talk about that after I find out who killed Anne Murphy," he said. "If you have any ideas about that, just leave me a message at Police Headquarters on Mulberry Street. Meanwhile, you should stay right here where I can find you. Wouldn't want you to miss out on your deal with Wilbanks."

He'd gone only a few steps down the hall when Emma started screaming, "What the devil is wrong with you, you drunken bum? I told you not to talk to anybody!"

She slammed the door, so Frank missed Vaughn's reply.

Sarah had just finished telling her parents about her and Malloy's visit to the Mission and their meetings with Michael and Lynne Hicks and Emma Hardy when Malloy arrived.

He gave her a small smile of greeting, but she knew from his eyes that he hadn't discovered anything that would solve Anne Murphy's murder. She led him into the kitchen, where her parents were seated at her kitchen table. They exchanged somber greetings, and Malloy took a seat.

He claimed he'd grabbed something to eat from a street vendor, but she noticed how quickly he devoured the cake she put in front of him, and she doubted it. Without asking, she gave him a second slice and filled all the coffee cups before joining everyone at the table.

"Mr. Malloy, why don't you tell us what you learned from this actor fellow," her father said. "And then I'll tell you what I learned from Wilbanks."

Malloy gave them an account of his visit with Vaughn and the actor's surprising revelations. Sarah listened in astonishment. "The detective, that must be the one Mr. Wilbanks hired."

"I don't think so," Malloy said. "Wilbanks said the detective he hired couldn't find Emma."

"But who else would have hired a detective?" her mother asked.

"Someone who wanted to find the child as badly as Wilbanks," her father said. "But perhaps not for the same reason."

Malloy nodded. "Emma says she didn't tell the

detective where Catherine was, but even if she let something slip, it wouldn't have been much help, because she had no idea Catherine wasn't with Anne Murphy."

"If this fellow found Emma, he might have found Anne Murphy, too," Sarah said. "Could he have killed her?"

"I doubt it. I don't have much respect for private investigators, but they don't usually go around killing innocent women. Besides, she was the only one who might help him locate Catherine."

"If that's what he wanted to do," her father said.

They all turned to him in surprise.

"Although none of us wants to think about it, whoever hired this other detective was probably trying to keep Catherine from being found at all, at least by Wilbanks," he said.

"You're right," Malloy said. "And killing Anne Murphy might prevent anybody else from finding her, too. So I guess we can't rule out the possibility of a hired killer."

"Or the person who hired the detective, who might have gone to see Anne himself after learning where she was," Sarah added.

"Or Emma Hardy," Malloy said. "She's got a temper. Vaughn himself said she might've attacked Anne Murphy when she found out Catherine was missing."

"This isn't getting us anywhere," her mother

said with a sigh. "Felix, what did you find out from Mr. Wilbanks?"

"Nothing as useful as Sarah and Mr. Malloy, but at least I convinced him not to insist on seeing Catherine just yet."

"How did you manage that?" Sarah asked.

"I suggested that one of his other children might want her out of the way."

"Now that I've met his older daughter, I can't believe she's responsible for Anne Murphy's death," Sarah said.

"Don't be so hasty," her father said. "Wilbanks admitted to me that Hicks had an investigator trying to locate her."

"Which is probably the same one Wilbanks thinks couldn't locate Emma," her mother said.

Malloy nodded. "But maybe the investigator did find her and reported that to Hicks, but Hicks didn't tell Wilbanks."

Sarah remembered Mrs. Ellsworth's comments about attorneys and almost smiled. She still couldn't think of Michael and Lynne Hicks as killers, but she remembered what Lynne had said about her brother. "Mr. Wilbanks also has a son. Did you see him when you were there, Father?"

"No, but I learned a lot about him today. He's got a reputation for gambling, and his father keeps him on a short leash."

"Mrs. Hicks said he married a Van Horn," Sarah said.

Her mother perked up at that. Marriages among the older families in the city were her special interest. "Really? Which one?"

"Gilda."

They watched as her mother searched her phenomenal memory. "Oh, yes, Gilda. A lovely girl, but a bit headstrong, if I recall correctly. Her family is one of the oldest in the city, of course, but well . . ." She gestured helplessly.

"They don't have a penny to their names," her father said, completing her thought for her. "Mrs. Decker thinks it's bad manners to talk about money," he added to Malloy.

"And what my father means," Sarah said with a smile, "is that the Van Horns have allowed their fortunes to dwindle to the point that they must maintain their homes with just three servants."

"They've tried putting their sons to work," her father said, "with mixed results, and they marry their daughters off to newly minted millionaires who don't expect a dowry." He turned to his wife. "Whose daughter is this Gilda?"

"Ralph, I believe. I remember hearing something about her when she married, but I can't quite recall exactly what."

"A scandal?" Sarah asked, wondering if it could have anything to do with their situation.

"No, I'm sure I'd remember a scandal. I'm thinking it was just a rumor or a story someone told me. I'd forgotten whom she married. His name would have meant nothing to me then, I'm sure, but I do recall she wasn't entirely happy about the match, even though it was highly advantageous for her financially." She gave Malloy a little shrug, as if to apologize for mentioning money.

"Do they live with Wilbanks?" Malloy asked.

"I believe so," her father said.

"Mrs. Hicks told us that Ozzie Wilbanks is his father's only heir, so he has the most to lose if Wilbanks decides to claim Catherine," Malloy said. "I need to pay him a visit."

"And perhaps Sarah and I should visit Gilda," her mother said, earning a scowl from both men.

"Elizabeth, just because I permitted you to assist Mr. Malloy with an investigation once before does not mean I will ever allow it again."

Her mother stared back at him in wide-eyed amazement. "Are you saying you felt it was permissible for me to assist Mr. Malloy in investigating the murder of a virtual stranger but not in a matter that involves our only grandchild?"

Sarah didn't know what astonished her more, her mother's open defiance of her father or the fact that she had referred to Catherine as her grandchild. She realized her mouth was hanging open and closed it with a snap. She braced herself for her father's response, knowing it would not be loud but would be no less withering for all of that.

The color that rose in her father's face wasn't anger, however, and his expression could only be called chagrin. "Forgive me, Elizabeth. You're right, of course. Sarah, I know I can depend on you to keep your mother from any situation where her safety might be in jeopardy."

"I will do my best, Father," she said, managing not to sound as shocked as she felt.

"So we only need Mr. Malloy's approval of your scheme then," her father said.

To his credit, Malloy replied without any trace of surprise. "Wilbanks already knows Mrs. Brandt has Catherine and that she's your daughter, but the son may not. He didn't even realize his older children knew about Catherine until the past few days. Mrs. Hicks knows about Mrs. Brandt now, but if the son doesn't, the son's wife also may not. What were you going to talk to her about, Mrs. Decker?"

Plainly, her mother hadn't thought that far ahead, but she would die before admitting it in front of her husband. After only a moment's hesitation, she said, "I thought we might pretend we feel compelled to allow Mr. Wilbanks to take custody of Catherine. She is, after all, his daughter, and he has a legal right to her. We can pretend we're distressed about this, of course, since Sarah is so fond of the child, and I was hoping to allay her concerns by obtaining Gilda's assurance that she will love Catherine as her own when Mr. Wilbanks is gone."

Her father was too surprised at the brilliance of this plan to speak, but Malloy said, "Do you really think you can convince her you'd be that obliging?"

"Oh, heavens, yes, Mr. Malloy. Women of my social class are experts at pretending to be totally witless when the occasion demands it."

This time both men were too surprised to speak.

Sarah bit back a smile. "I think this is an excellent plan, Mother. I'll even manage to shed a few tears if necessary."

Malloy had to clear his throat. "Well, at the very least you'll find out how much this Gilda knows about Wilbanks and his mistress, and how she and her husband feel about it."

"And how she feels about her husband and her father-in-law, and how eager she is for her husband to inherit the family fortune," her mother said. "I think I'll even try to find out what that gossip was about her when she married Ozzie Wilbanks, unless I happen to remember between now and then."

"Yes, well," her father said with uncharacteristic uncertainty. "Uh, Mr. Malloy, is there any way I can assist you?"

"As a matter of fact, I was just thinking that maybe you should go along with me when I visit Ozzie Wilbanks. There's no reason he'd agree to meet with a police detective, and I can't force him to, but he might see you out of curiosity, and if I happened to be with you . . ."

"Excellent plan. I'll be happy to use whatever influence I have."

The four of them spent a few minutes deciding where and what time to meet the next day.

"Our carriage is waiting," her father said. "May we drop you somewhere, Mr. Malloy?"

"Thank you, no. It would be out of your way, and I don't have far to go."

Sarah couldn't help thinking of the sensation her parents' carriage would cause if it pulled up in front of Malloy's tenement.

Her parents put on their coats and started to go, but for a moment, Sarah realized her father was hesitant to leave her there alone with Malloy. Then he appeared to shake it off and the two of them left.

Sarah turned to Malloy, wanting to reach out for the comfort of his arms and knowing she didn't dare. Pretending they were just friends was difficult enough already. Instead she smiled. "Did my mother surprise you?"

"Your mother always surprises me. Just when I think I know what to expect from her, she does something completely amazing. I actually feel sorry for your father."

"I know. I expected him to be angry at her and instead he apologized."

"He thinks of Catherine as his grandchild, too."

Tears sprang to her eyes. "Oh, Malloy, what will I do if they take her away?"

"Nobody is going to take her away, even if I have to pack the two of you up and put you on a train to California."

This surprised her so much, she forgot she wanted to burst into tears. "California?"

"I'm sure your father will have a closer hideout, but if it comes to that, then yes, California. You're not going to give Catherine to those people, I promise you that."

"Thank you, Malloy. I don't know how I'd bear this without you."

He looked surprised for a moment, and then he said, "You're your mother's daughter. You'd bear it somehow."

With that he left, leaving her staring after him as he disappeared into the night. Yes, he was right. She'd bear it somehow, even without him, but she was so very grateful that she didn't have to.

Frank had lain awake for a long time last night, going over everything he'd learned yesterday. To his chagrin, he remembered that he'd never gotten an answer from Vaughn to one of the most important questions he'd asked, the one about why he and Emma had suddenly decided to flee the city. The only clue he had was Wilbanks's claim that he had proposed marriage to Emma and that she had refused. Marriage to Wilbanks would have given Emma everything she could have ever wanted in life, so Frank found it impossible to believe she would have turned it down. Even if she truly cared for Vaughn, which she must if she was willing to tolerate his drinking and stay with him all these years, she could have kept him as her lover. No, Emma had another reason for leaving town, and Frank was pretty sure it involved Ozzie Wilbanks.

By the time he arrived at the Decker home late the next morning, he'd worked out a plan for getting Ozzie to tell him everything. To his credit, Decker was waiting for him, as eager as Frank to confront the person who might give them the information they needed to find Anne Murphy's killer.

Decker's carriage took them the few blocks to Wilbanks's house. Frank didn't complain or point out they could have walked the distance faster. If he'd learned nothing from Sarah Brandt, he'd learned the importance rich people put on appearances. Besides, it gave them a chance to make their plans for how their interview with Ozzie would go.

"What will we do if Ozzie refuses to see us?" Frank asked as they pulled up at their destination.

"He won't refuse."

Frank was still marveling at his confidence when the driver opened the door and Decker stepped out onto the sidewalk. Frank followed, standing aside as Decker knocked on the door and informed the maid who answered that he needed to see Oswald Wilbanks on an urgent matter of business. Once again they were escorted into the receiving room.

"What business do you have with Ozzie?" Frank asked when they were alone.

"None, but I'm sure he'll be curious enough to see me. Men like him are always looking for the main chance, and the prospect of being sought out by Felix Decker will be too tempting."

He was right. The maid returned almost instantly to show them up to the parlor where they had each met with the elder Wilbanks. Today, the fire in this room had not been lit. The man who greeted them appeared to be in his late twenties, although his pale, brown hair had already begun to thin and too many late nights had left his skin sallow and his waistline thick.

"Mr. Decker, it really is you," he said, extending his hand. "I confess, I was afraid one of my friends was playing a joke on me. It's a pleasure, sir."

"The pleasure is mine," Decker said. "I've been hearing things about you, young man, and I wanted to see for myself if they are true."

While Ozzie basked in the perceived compliment, Frank bit back a smile. Decker had indeed heard things about Ozzie, but none of them were good. As they had agreed, Frank continued to allow Decker to lead the conversation. Frank would step in only if necessary.

When the two men had finished taking each other's measure, Decker said, "May I present my associate, Detective Sergeant Frank Malloy of the New York City Police."

Ozzie's surprise was almost comic. His jaw dropped and he did not offer his hand. "The police?"

"Yes," Decker said with the same hearty tone, as if he were completely oblivious of Ozzie's reaction. "We're here to discuss your family's situation concerning a young child whom I believe is your father's daughter by his mistress, a Miss Emma Hardy."

"I . . . I don't know what you're talking about," Ozzie tried.

"Nonsense. We're all men of the world, Mr. Wilbanks. There's no need to pretend ignorance. We know you're acquainted with Miss Hardy and understand her situation."

"Well, yes, I suppose I do." He was still eyeing Frank with deep suspicion.

"Perhaps we should sit down," Decker said.

This snapped Ozzie back to remembering his responsibilities as host. "Of course, please sit down. May I offer you something? A drink perhaps?"

"It's a bit early for me," Decker said. "Mr. Malloy?"

Frank shook his head, but Ozzie had already gone to the sideboard, where a collection of crystal decanters sat. "I hope you won't mind if I do, then. This is something of a shock, you understand."

Ozzie poured himself a liberal measure of amber liquor and took a big gulp of it before even moving away from the sideboard. Decker had chosen a grouping of chairs by the front windows, and Ozzie joined them there. Apparently fortified by the drink, he managed an unconvincing smile. "I'm sorry, Mr. Decker, but I'm afraid I don't understand your interest—or the interest of the police—in what is only a family matter."

"Well, you see, it's a family matter for me, too.

181

The child, Catherine, has been living with my daughter for the better part of a year."

"Your daughter?"

"Yes, my daughter does volunteer work at a settlement house that cares for young girls. The child was abandoned there, I understand, but perhaps you already know all this."

"As a matter of fact, I do. My father told me all about the girl yesterday. Until then, I had no idea."

"Don't be coy," Decker said. "We know you knew about her long ago, Mr. Wilbanks. We also know you visited Emma Hardy on at least two occasions while she was still under your father's protection."

Ozzie frowned. "So what if I did?"

"May I ask what you and Miss Hardy discussed?"

Ozzie needed a minute, during which his gaze darted between Frank and Decker and back again, as if trying to decide which of them was in charge. Even though Frank hadn't yet uttered a word, Ozzie replied to him.

"As you can probably understand, I was quite upset to learn my father kept a mistress. I went out to see if I could convince her to . . . to release him."

"And you were successful," Decker said.

Ozzie seemed surprised at this. "Oh, no, not at all. I didn't know about the child, you see, not until I went out there the first time. I thought her hold on him was purely sexual, but when I saw the child, I knew it was more than that. Father might allow a mistress to leave him, but he would never shirk his responsibilities to a child."

"And what would he think his responsibilities were to this child?" Frank asked, since Ozzie was still addressing him.

Ozzie took another gulp of his drink to cover his unease, then tried to sound casual as he said, "To support her, of course."

"And that's all?" Frank asked.

"What do you mean?"

"I mean, did your father intend to do more than just support the child?"

Ozzie gave them another unconvincing smile. "What else could he have done?"

Decker returned the smile. "He could have married Miss Hardy after your mother died."

Color blossomed in Ozzie's cheeks. "That's absurd!"

"Is it?" Frank asked. "Your father told me that's exactly what he intended to do."

"That's the first I've heard of it."

"And what would you have done if you'd heard of it last year?" Decker asked, surprising Frank.

"I don't know what you mean."

"Yes, you do," Frank said. "You knew your father intended to marry Emma Hardy, and you went out there to threaten her, to tell her what would happen to her if she did agree to marry your father."

To Frank's surprise, Ozzie's shoulders sagged with relief. "Is that what she told you? That lying little bitch, of course she did! Well, that's not what happened at all."

"What did happen then?" Frank asked.

Ozzie sank back in the chair, obviously comfortable now with their conversation and no longer feeling threatened. "I guess maybe I did think I'd threaten her that first time I went to see her. I didn't know about the child yet, as I said. All I knew was my father was keeping a woman, and I wanted to see her for myself. My mother was still alive then, although she died soon after, but I didn't know how little time she had left. I wanted to defend our family's honor, I think, and see if I couldn't convince her to release my father from her clutches."

"So you did threaten her that first time?" Frank asked.

"No. Well, maybe. She might think so. I was angry, of course. Then I saw the child, and I was even angrier. How dare he do that to my mother? I don't even remember what I said to her, but I do remember she laughed at me. She said if I so much as laid a hand on her, my father would cut me off without a cent." Plainly, the memory still rankled, and a flush rose up his neck.

"Did you believe her?" Frank asked.

"My father is a very . . . Well, under the circumstances, I hate to say he's a 'moral' man,

184

but he has his own standards, and he obeys them. Harming a female, even a lying, scheming little piece of trash like Emma Harding, would violate his standards."

"So you were afraid your father would dis-inherit you, his only son, for interfering with his mistress?" Decker asked skeptically.

"He's threatened to before, for far less serious offenses," he said, not bothering to hide his bitterness.

"All right," Frank said, "so you were afraid to threaten her the first time. Why did you go back to see her again?"

This time Ozzie drained his glass, then cast a longing look at the decanter across the room before replying. "I had to protect my father."

"From what?"

"From *her*," he snapped. "My mother died, and Michael told me Father was going to marry that whore."

"Michael Hicks?" Frank asked.

"Yes, of course. Who else? He tells Michael everything."

"Is Michael the one who told you about Miss Hardy in the first place?" Frank asked.

"Uh, no, he wasn't."

"Who was?"

"My, uh, my wife."

"Your wife? How did she find out?"

"I'm not sure."

Decker made an impatient sound. "Come now, Wilbanks. You can't expect us to believe you didn't ask your wife how she came by such scandalous information. Is it common gossip?"

"Not common, no. I mean, my father was very discreet. He had no wish to embarrass my mother or us."

"Then how did she learn of it?"

"She . . . Well, she suspected something. Father would leave town quite regularly with no explanation, so she had him followed."

"She hired a private investigator?" Decker asked, exchanging a knowing glance with Frank.

"Heavens, no, nothing so elaborate. She asked her cousin to see what he could find out, and he was the one who discovered my father's little hideaway."

"Which cousin is this?" Decker asked, probably thinking his wife would want to know exactly how he fit into the family tree.

"Terrance. Terrance Udall. You can ask him yourself. We did nothing wrong. He was with me the second time I went to see the whore."

But Frank remembered what Anne Murphy had told Sarah about that visit. Emma had been badly frightened. "Exactly what did you say to Miss Hardy that time?"

"Me? Not much. Terrance did most of the talking. He's a bit hotheaded, I'm afraid. He may have even raised his voice to her, but she gave it

186

right back to him. She's a harridan, that one. I don't know what my father sees in her."

"Did Terrance threaten her?" Decker asked.

"Not really."

Frank had had enough of Ozzie Wilbanks. He gave him a look that made him squirm in his chair. "Then what did he *really* say to her?"

"I, well, she might have considered it a threat, although that's not how we meant it."

"You'd best not try Mr. Malloy's patience, Mr. Wilbanks," Decker said mildly. "What did he say to her?"

Ozzie cleared his throat. "Well, he said something to the effect . . . I mean, I don't remember the exact words but something like, if she married my father, she would regret it for the rest of her life."

"And did he indicate the rest of her life might not be very long?" Frank asked.

"I think he may have," Ozzie said unsteadily, then tried to take another drink from his empty glass. "You understand that I didn't approve of his actions, but there's no controlling Terrance when he sets his mind to something. We just meant to save my father from himself. Nobody marries his mistress. He'd be a laughingstock."

"But rich men have been known to marry chorus girls," Decker said.

"Nobody in the Van Horn family has," Ozzie said.

And that was when Frank really understood the problem. "Your wife didn't want a chorus girl in the family."

"And especially not her bastard child," Ozzie said. "You should understand, Mr. Decker. My wife comes from an old, respected family. She simply couldn't bear the thought."

Frank wondered how she bore the thought of marrying into the Wilbanks family, but maybe their money had helped ease the pain. "So Cousin Terrance . . . he's not a Van Horn?"

"On his mother's side."

Frank nodded as if that explained everything. "So Cousin Terrance threatened Emma and she left town."

"Oh, no, not at all."

"But you said he threatened her," Decker said.

"He did, or at least he tried, but Emma just laughed at him the same way she'd laughed at me. Then she called us names and told us to get out of her house or she'd tell my father we tried to rape her and then we'd find out what he was capable of, so we left."

"But she did leave town shortly after that," Decker said.

"I don't know what she did after that. All I know is my father stopped going to see her, and then he got ill, and that's the last I heard of Emma Hardy and her brat until Michael told me the other day that she was back in the city."

"And when did he tell you that?" Frank asked, as if the answer didn't matter.

"I don't know. A few days ago, I guess. Now I'm going to have to ask you to leave. I have an appointment, and I'm afraid I'm already late."

When they were back in the carriage, Decker said, "How much of that do you believe?"

"Most of it. Ozzie Wilbanks is a terrible liar, so it's easy to tell what's true and what's not."

"But?"

Frank smiled in approval at Decker's perception. "But he told me some things he didn't realize."

"For instance?"

"For instance, Michael Hicks was apparently keeping much closer tabs on Emma Hardy than David Wilbanks knew."

"So you think it really was Wilbanks's investigator who found Emma when she was on tour?"

"Yes, and for some reason Hicks didn't tell Wilbanks."

Decker frowned. "And Hicks apparently knew Emma was back in the city, but he didn't tell Wilbanks that either. I wonder why."

"Why don't we ask him?"

Sarah went early to her mother's house so she could visit with Catherine and have the noon meal with her before she and her mother left for their "morning" visit with Gilda Wilbanks. Sarah was both pleased and dismayed to hear what a wonderful time Catherine was having in the Decker household, where every servant doted on her and her every wish was instantly granted. Leaving her was difficult but at least she knew Catherine was safe and in good hands, even if she was being hopelessly spoiled.

Since her father hadn't returned the carriage yet and the day was fine, Sarah and her mother decided to walk the few blocks to the Wilbanks home. Sarah's mother presented her card to the maid and asked to see Mrs. Wilbanks on an important family matter. They weren't sure Gilda knew who they were, but the maid came back and escorted them upstairs to the rear parlor.

This room was the less formal parlor the family would use every day, although the furnishings were still expensive and elegant. A lovely young woman in a becoming bottle-green gown came forward to meet them. She wore her golden hair in a Gibson Girl knot. Artfully arranged stray curls bobbed against her cheeks and her long, graceful neck. Her smile was practiced and slightly guarded.

"Mrs. Decker, how kind of you to come."

"Yes, *kind,*" a male voice mocked.

Sarah and her mother looked over in surprise to see a young man standing in the corner. His golden good looks mirrored Gilda's, and his smile was even less sincere.

"May I present my cousin, Terrance Udall. He has been offering me his support during this difficult time. I'm sure you understand."

Sarah didn't understand at all, but she decided not to mention that as her mother was introducing her to Gilda and Terrance.

"Yes, Mrs. Brandt," Gilda said. "You're the one who has the little girl, if I'm not mistaken." So she knew exactly who they were.

Sarah was glad she had taken pains with her appearance today. Her clothes weren't the latest fashion, but at least she didn't look like the poor relation that she was. "Her name is Catherine."

Gilda raised her perfectly arched eyebrows but only said, "Please sit down. I've ordered some tea to be brought up."

Sarah and her mother chose the sofa while Gilda and Terrance chose chairs opposite them. When they were settled, Gilda said, "May I ask what brings you here today?"

"Of course you may," Mrs. Decker said. "I gather that you know all about Catherine."

"Yes, and you can imagine what a shock it was to us."

"You had no idea?" Sarah asked.

"Not in the slightest. Mr. Wilbanks is not the sort of man one would suspect of keeping a mistress."

"What about you, Mr. Udall?" Sarah said. "Did you suspect?"

Udall, who had been observing the proceedings with a smirk, sobered instantly. "I have learned never to be surprised by anything, Mrs. Decker."

Which, of course, didn't answer her question. "As I'm sure you know, Mr. Wilbanks would like for me to return his daughter to him."

Gilda and Terrance exchanged a glance. "Are you aware that Mr. Wilbanks is gravely ill?"

"Yes, we are," Sarah said, "which is why we are here."

"My daughter has grown very fond of Catherine," her mother said. "We believed her to be an orphan when Sarah took her in."

"A natural assumption," Gilda said. "I understand she was abandoned at some charitable institution."

"But of course she isn't an orphan," Udall said. "And she belongs with her family."

Sarah and her mother looked at him in surprise. Her mother was the first to recover. "We only want what's best for the child, and certainly, she should be with her father."

Sarah didn't have to feign her pain at this statement. "He does have a legal right to her, and I couldn't in good conscience keep her from him, no matter how much it hurts me to give her up."

Her mother nodded. "But as you pointed out, Mr. Wilbanks may not be with us much longer, and Catherine is very young. We wanted to meet you and determine that you are willing to take over the responsibility of raising her."

"And if she's not," Udall said, his smirk firmly back in place, "you would be happy to take her yourself, I'm sure."

Sarah wasn't exactly sure how to answer him, but she said, "Of course I would."

Udall's smirk widened. "And I suppose Mr. Wilbanks has told you that he intends to provide for her quite generously in his estate, which will greatly ease the burden of raising a child not your own."

"Mr. Wilbanks has told us no such thing," her mother said in her most withering voice. "And in any case, we are perfectly capable of providing for the child ourselves."

"Please excuse Terrance. He tends to be overly dramatic as well as overly protective of me."

"Do you need protection, Mrs. Wilbanks?" Sarah asked.

"No, I do not," she said with a smile.

Sarah smiled back. "Then let's be honest, shall we? I'm sure you have no interest in raising the child of your father-in-law's mistress and neither does Mrs. Hicks, to whom I've already spoken about this matter."

"You have? When was that?"

"Yesterday."

"You're wasting no time, are you?" Udall said.

"I was summoned by Mr. Hicks," Sarah said,

stretching the truth a bit. "But I'm sure you can understand my eagerness to get this matter resolved, especially since one person has already been murdered."

Gilda and Udall exchanged another glance, their shock obvious. "Surely, you don't think the nursemaid's death has anything to do with us," she said.

"I have no way of knowing if it has anything to do with you or not, but it certainly has everything to do with Catherine."

"I don't see how," Gilda said.

Sarah seriously doubted this, but she was willing to play along. "Miss Murphy was the only person who knew what had become of the child. With her dead, she might never be found."

"And yet she has been found," Udall said.

"Only because the killer didn't know Miss Murphy had already contacted the people at the Mission where she left Catherine. If she hadn't done so, no one would ever have known what became of her."

"My goodness," Gilda said in mock astonishment. "What convoluted reasoning. In your version of events, the killer must be a member of a highly respected family of impeccable reputation who murdered a total stranger in order to keep a dying man from seeing his child. Why should anyone believe such a thing when people of the lowest order are also involved and are far more likely to have killed this woman?"

"I don't see why," Sarah said, mocking Gilda's own words.

"Do people like that really need a good reason? From what I know about the child's mother, she's capable of anything. She must have been furious to learn this nursemaid had lost her child. Who could blame her for lashing out at her?"

This was not going at all the way they had expected, but Sarah was learning a lot about Gilda Wilbanks that she never would have suspected. Before she could decide what to say next, the maid arrived with the tea. By the time they had all been served and the maid had withdrawn, Sarah had formulated her next step.

"Solving Miss Murphy's murder is a matter for the police, of course."

"The *police*," Udall echoed with his annoying smirk.

He was right to be contemptuous, of course. Usually, the police would take little interest in the death of someone like Anne Murphy. Her mother stiffened beside her, taking instant offense on Malloy's behalf, however. "You might be surprised—"

"He's right, Mother," Sarah interrupted, not wanting to give too much away. "We may never find out who killed Miss Murphy, so our concern must be for Catherine and keeping her safe."

"So safe that no one ever sets eyes on her?"

Gilda said. "How do we know you even have the child, or that she's even the right child? The city is full of abandoned children. I should like some proof before we go any further with this."

As much as Sarah disliked Gilda Wilbanks, she had to admit her request was only reasonable. Still, if someone in this house had already killed to keep Catherine from being found . . . "Her mother can identify her."

Gilda smiled knowingly. "I'm sure she can, and she would have every reason to identify *any* female child as her daughter since her only hope of profiting from this is to produce one. I'm actually surprised she hasn't already thought of this and enlisted some poor urchin to the cause."

"Whose word would you accept, then?" Sarah's mother asked.

"I believe Father Wilbanks is the only one with no ulterior motive who could identify her."

Such a clever solution, Sarah realized. And she had been so cleverly outmaneuvered. The only way to prove Catherine was Wilbanks's child was to allow him to see her, and since he was so ill, the only way to do that was to deliver her to the home of those with the best reason to want her dead.

"That didn't go at all the way we planned," her mother said as they walked away from the Wilbanks home.

"No, it didn't, and the worst part is that she is absolutely right. I've just been thinking in terms of allowing Wilbanks to see Catherine as a kindness to him, but without his word, we really have no way to prove she's his daughter."

"Which is only important if you're interested in her inheriting anything from him."

Her mother was right, of course. "Catherine doesn't need anything from her father or anyone else, but I can't help hating the thought of someone as unpleasant as Gilda Wilbanks inheriting everything."

"Unfortunately, family wealth isn't usually distributed according to who deserves it most. Your father said everyone expects Ozzie Wilbanks to squander the family fortune in just a few years, in any case."

"How lovely that would be for Gilda." Sarah sighed. "Of course there's another reason to allow Mr. Wilbanks to see Catherine—because he wants to see his child before he dies."

"Yes, and whether we need him to identify Catherine or not, we must bring them together soon."

"I just wish we could figure out how to do that without Gilda and her husband finding out."

"Oh, I think we must make sure they *do* find out, so they know without a doubt who Catherine is."

Sarah sighed again. "No matter what else happens, I know one thing: Gilda Wilbanks will not get custody of Catherine. Malloy offered to put me on a train to California with Catherine if necessary."

"Let's hope it doesn't become necessary. Perhaps your father and Malloy fared better than we did today."

They could hardly have done worse, Sarah thought.

Frank and Mr. Decker decided that they were more likely to find Michael Hicks in his office in the middle of the day, so they located the address and went there after lunching in a small, elegant restaurant Frank would never have considered entering, where they knew Decker by name and they didn't even ask him to pay. There were places in the city where cops weren't asked to pay, but that was a form of bribery to ensure protection from harassment. This, Frank understood, was different. Decker would probably receive a bill in the mail, and the restaurant owners weren't the least bit worried that it wouldn't be paid.

Hicks was in his office, and he wasn't too busy to see them. Frank figured people were seldom too busy to see Felix Decker. Hicks didn't seem surprised by their visit, or maybe he just hid it well. The men shook hands, and Frank and Decker took the offered seats in front of Hicks's expansive desk. The room was meant to impress, with its dark paneling and rich appointments. The heavy draperies blocked any hint of sunlight that might bring cheer to the place. The effect could be either comforting or intimidating, depending on whether Hicks was on your side or not. Frank had the uncomfortable feeling Hicks hadn't chosen his side in this yet.

"What can I do for you gentlemen?" he asked.

Frank let Decker start, as they had agreed. "You can explain to us why you never told Mr. Wilbanks that your investigator had found Emma Hardy weeks ago and you've known exactly where she's been ever since."

Hicks never even blinked. "I can see why you might find that puzzling, but I assure you, my motives were for the best."

"And what were those motives?" Frank asked.

Hicks calmly folded his hands on his desk, as if they were discussing the weather. "Mr. Wilbanks is very ill, as you've seen. His only concern is seeing his daughter . . . Catherine . . . before he dies. In the report I received, my investigator had located Emma Hardy but the child was not with her and had not been with her for months. I'm sure you can understand how upsetting that information would be to Mr. Wilbanks."

As much as Frank hated to admit it, he was right, but he wasn't going to let him off too easily. "So you lied to Mr. Wilbanks?"

"I did not lie. I merely did not tell him. For all I

knew, the child was dead or Emma had abandoned her somewhere and we would never find her. I decided to leave Mr. Wilbanks in ignorance with a bit of hope, at least until we knew for certain what had become of her."

"What else did your investigator find out that you didn't tell Wilbanks . . . and us?" Frank asked.

Hicks's clear gaze never faltered. "I had instructed him to do whatever was necessary to locate the child. We didn't foresee that Emma wouldn't have her, of course, but when he discovered that, he decided to try to motivate Emma to go to her."

"So he told her that Wilbanks was dying," Decker said.

"Yes. He told her Mr. Wilbanks still wanted to provide for Catherine and was thinking of leaving her some money in his will, but he wanted to make sure she was all right first. He also indicated Wilbanks would make it worth Emma's while if she brought the child to see him."

"Your investigator sounds very resourceful," Decker said.

Hicks shrugged. "He simply understands that most people will do whatever is in their financial best interest."

"Yes, and Miss Hardy would have found it difficult to resist the opportunity to take Mr. Wilbanks for a fortune," Decker said.

Frank saw a flaw in their reasoning, but now

was not the time to point it out. "So what did your investigator do after he tempted Emma with this promise of riches?"

"He followed the troupe for a few days, expecting Emma to go straight to New York or wherever she had left Catherine. He was surprised when she didn't, and for a while we both feared the child must be either dead or irretrievably lost, but he eventually learned that she didn't have the means to return until she got paid at the end of the tour. He saw her mailing a letter, though, and managed to get a look at the address. We decided this person must have Catherine, so I instructed him to return here and locate her."

"Anne Murphy," Frank said.

Hicks nodded.

"And did he locate her?" Decker asked.

"Yes, but he quickly determined she didn't have the child either."

"And before she could get her, someone killed her," Frank said.

Hicks tried to maintain his composure, but he couldn't stop the flush that crawled up his neck. "You can't believe I had anything to do with that."

This time Frank shrugged. "It was an easy way to make sure no one found Catherine."

"But I wanted to find her and bring her to David."

"We know that's what Mr. Wilbanks wanted,

but was it really what *you* wanted?" Frank asked.

"Yes, it was, and I had no reason to wish the child harm, as you well know. Or Miss Murphy either, for that matter. You're wasting your time here, Mr. Malloy. If you want to find out who killed that woman, you should be talking to Emma Hardy, and in case you don't know, she's staying at the La Pierre Hotel with an actor named Parnell Vaughn."

9

Hicks escorted them out to the lobby, where several young men sat at high desks, scratching away at important papers with their pens. One young man stood at the front counter, however, idly chatting with the man seated there.

"Don't you have something to do, Udall?" Hicks asked. Frank got the impression he asked that question a lot of this particular young man.

"Yes, sir, of course I do, but I hoped to speak to Mr. Decker." He smiled, and Frank knew he'd gotten away with a lot of mischief with that smile.

"Are you acquainted with Mr. Decker?" Hicks asked, apparently immune to Udall's charm.

"No, sir, but I made the acquaintance of his lovely wife just this afternoon."

This got Decker's attention, as Udall had meant it to. "And where did you meet my wife, young man?"

"At my cousin's home."

"You're Cousin Terrance," Frank said, remembering Ozzie's description of the man who had tried to terrorize Emma Hardy. "A Van Horn on your mother's side."

Udall's smile flickered for a moment as he tried to figure out who Frank might be and how he knew so much about him. "You have the advantage of me, sir. Have we met?"

Hicks, who seemed to enjoy Udall's momentary discomfort, quickly introduced the men, taking great delight in informing Udall that Frank was with the police. "Mr. Udall is one of my clerks, or at least he is when he bothers to come to the office."

Frank remembered what Decker had said about the Van Horns putting their sons to work with mixed results. Judging from his expression, Decker remembered it, too.

"I had to go to Gilda this afternoon when I heard what's happened," Udall said. "She's extremely upset, you know. Is that why you're here, Mr. Decker? About the child?"

"I'm sure that's none of your business," Hicks said.

Udall furrowed his noble brow. "The welfare of an innocent child should be everyone's business, don't you agree, Mr. Decker?"

"Yes, it should," Frank replied for him, "especially for those who know her. You met her, didn't you, when you and Ozzie Wilbanks went to see Emma Hardy."

Udall's confidence evaporated into dismay. "I'm

afraid I don't know what you're talking about."

"Oh, yes," Decker said. "Ozzie told us just this morning how the two of you went out to try to frighten Emma Hardy into leaving Wilbanks and taking her little heiress with her."

Plainly, this was news to Hicks. "Is this true, Udall? Did you go with Ozzie to see this woman?"

"Ozzie wanted to go. He wanted to see his father's . . . uh . . ." He glanced around, belatedly realizing how many other clerks could overhear their conversation.

"Paramour," Malloy said helpfully.

"Yes, well, he wanted to go see her, and I was afraid of what he might do. He has quite a temper, you see, so I went along to make sure he didn't get himself into any trouble. But I only had a glimpse of the child. Ozzie had no time for her, although now that I think of it, she's his sister, isn't she? He really should have taken more interest."

Frank had to admire this young man. He was the best liar he'd encountered so far in this case. He supposed being the son of a socially prominent family with no money meant Udall had to get by on his charm and good looks, and lying was always a useful skill for someone like that, too. Frank wondered why he hadn't captured himself a rich wife yet. He'd have to ask Mrs. Decker about that. If she didn't know, she'd find out. "That's funny. When we spoke with Ozzie Wilbanks this morning, he said you were the one who lost his temper with Miss Hardy."

"Me? That's ridiculous. Why should I care enough to lose my temper with her?"

"Maybe you were outraged about the innocent child," Frank said. "Was that why you threatened her?"

Udall narrowed his pale blue eyes. "I never threatened that woman, and even if I did, let me remind you that no harm has come to Miss Hardy, nor is it likely to. And if Ozzie and I scared her off so she didn't marry Wilbanks last year, then we performed the man a service and should be rewarded accordingly."

"I'll suggest it to him the next time I see him," Frank said.

Hicks had been enjoying this exchange, but now he said, "Udall, you'd best get back to work now."

"Yes, sir. Mr. Decker, sir, it's been a pleasure. Mr. Malloy . . . good day." Apparently, it hadn't been a pleasure to meet Frank.

Frank was smiling when he and Decker stepped out into the street.

"I don't think that man was entirely truthful with us," Decker said.

"Which one?"

"Well, now that you mention it, we do know for a fact that Hicks lied to us."

"He didn't lie. He just didn't tell us the truth,"

206

Frank said, still smiling. "And as for this Udall fellow, he's a piece of work."

"He certainly is. I'm so glad Elizabeth met him. She'll be able to tell us all about him."

Frank was sure she would. "Let's go find her then."

Sarah and her mother had just come down from the nursery when Malloy and her father arrived and joined them in the family parlor.

"You look like you had an interesting day," her mother observed.

"We certainly did," her father replied. He seemed very pleased with himself, or at least pleased about something. He and Malloy actually exchanged a conspiratorial glance. Sarah found herself blinking in surprise.

"We met Terrance Udall," Malloy said.

"So did we," her mother said, delighted.

Malloy grinned. "We know. We were hoping you could tell us why he hasn't married some featherbrained heiress."

"Malloy, would you like some coffee?" her father said, pulling the cord to summon the maid.

"Yes, thank you."

Her mother patted the seat beside her on the sofa, and Malloy took it, watching her expectantly. "Where did you encounter Mr. Udall?" she asked.

"He works for Michael Hicks," her father said, taking a chair on his wife's other side.

"I thought you were going to see Ozzie Wilbanks," Sarah said.

"We did," her father said. "Mr. Malloy, would you tell the ladies what we learned today?"

Malloy was only too happy to do so, Sarah noted, and her father allowed it. He described their visit with Ozzie Wilbanks, giving their impressions of him. Her father interrupted only occasionally and added his opinions when Malloy asked.

"He seems an odd match for Gilda," her mother observed. "She's quite clever and even a little ruthless, or I miss my guess."

"According to Ozzie, Gilda is the one who figured out Wilbanks had a mistress," Malloy said.

"How did she do that?" Sarah asked.

Malloy frowned. "He said she got suspicious when Wilbanks kept leaving town, but now that I know Udall works for Hicks, I'm wondering if he didn't get wind of it there and tell Gilda about it."

"That's certainly possible," her father said. "Attorneys hear all sorts of secrets that they can't tell another living soul but that anyone in their office might find out by just paying attention."

"I'm guessing Udall paid a lot of attention to Wilbanks and his business because of his connection to Gilda," Malloy said. "At any rate, according to Ozzie, Udall was the one who supposedly found out where Emma lived."

"Wait a minute," her mother said while Sarah was still absorbing what Malloy had said. "Gilda told us she had no idea that Wilbanks had a mistress until a few days ago."

"Gilda must be a good liar, too," Malloy said to her father, who nodded sagely.

Sarah was starting to think this whole encounter was a dream. Since when did Malloy and her father share confidences? Since when did her father defer to Malloy? Since when did her father defer to anyone at all?

"We believed her," her mother said, oblivious of Sarah's confusion, "so she's at least a passable liar. What else did Ozzie tell you?"

"He admitted he'd gone to see Emma—"

"Only after Malloy let him know we already knew he did," her father said.

"But he claimed she wasn't frightened by his threats. She had the upper hand with Wilbanks and she knew it. Udall was the man he took with him the second time he visited Emma."

"Was he the one who frightened her so?" Sarah asked.

"That's what Ozzie claimed, but Udall said it was Ozzie," Malloy said. "Ozzie wouldn't frighten a fly, though, so it must have been Udall."

"But regardless of who made them, Ozzie

claimed she laughed off these threats as well," her father said.

"Then we went to see Hicks, to find out why he didn't tell Wilbanks his investigator had found Emma in Chicago and had been following her ever since."

"I've been wondering that, too," her mother said.

"Hicks claims that when the investigator found out Emma didn't have Catherine, he didn't want to worry Wilbanks, so he decided not to tell him anything until they knew what had happened to Catherine and where she was."

"That's understandable," her mother said.

"Or self-serving," Sarah said. "I haven't made up my mind about Mr. Hicks yet."

"Neither have I," Malloy said. "But we couldn't get much more out of him, and just as we were leaving, Mr. Udall introduces himself to Mr. Decker by claiming to have recently met his lovely wife."

Sarah sniffed indignantly. "Didn't he mention he'd met his lovely *daughter,* too?"

"As a matter of fact, he did not," Malloy said, "which is only one more reason to distrust him."

"I should think so," her mother said. "And what did Mr. Udall have to say for himself?"

"Not much worth repeating," her father said with a small grin. "Except to claim an unselfish interest in Catherine's well-being."

Which, of course, thoroughly frightened Sarah. "Oh, dear, and that leads directly into our conversation with Gilda Wilbanks and Mr. Udall. Gilda insisted that we produce Catherine to prove not only that she is truly Mr. Wilbanks's child but also that she exists at all."

"She's not a very trusting person," her mother said, "but then liars typically aren't."

"I thought you were going to upset her by offering to give her Catherine to raise," her father said.

"We very quickly abandoned that plan," Sarah said with a sigh. "Gilda is not easily intimidated, and she seems to have had a plan of her own, which was to assume we were only interested in using Catherine to extort money from Mr. Wilbanks."

"That's ridiculous," her father said.

"Of course it is, but you can't really blame her for assuming that. In any case, we left with both sides feeling stymied."

"The only thing Sarah and I are now sure of is that we must allow Mr. Wilbanks to see Catherine as soon as possible. He's really the only unbiased person who can verify her identity as one of his heirs, and Sarah and I have agreed we need to divert as much of Mr. Wilbanks's fortune away from Gilda Wilbanks as possible."

Her husband gaped at her. "Isn't that a little cold-blooded, Elizabeth?"

"You didn't meet Gilda Wilbanks."

"And speaking of money," Malloy said, "something Hicks said made me realize we still don't know something very important: why Emma ran away in the first place."

Her mother frowned at him. "What does that have to do with money?"

"Oh, sorry. Hicks said something that got me thinking. He said people usually do what's in their financial best interest."

"Do you disagree?" her father asked.

"No, that's usually true, but in this case, Emma didn't."

"Yes, she did," her mother said. "She came back to the city specifically to get money from Wilbanks."

"But why did she run away in the first place? Wilbanks had just proposed to her, or at least that's what he said, and we have no reason to doubt it. What could have been better for her than marrying Wilbanks? She would have had his name, his protection, and his money, too, and instead she ran away."

Sarah couldn't believe they still hadn't found the answer to this. "You're right. Anne Murphy said Emma ran away because she thought she was in danger, and she scared Anne enough to hide Catherine at the Mission."

"But according to Ozzie Wilbanks, she had just laughed off his threats," her father said. "So it seems unlikely she was frightened of him, at least."

"Didn't you ask her about that when you saw her?" her mother asked.

"I never got the chance. I did ask Vaughn, but I realized later that he'd never answered me."

"So now you need to visit Emma Hardy again," her mother said. "I don't suppose you'd like some assistance."

"Mother," Sarah said, shaking her head.

"There are only two women involved in this situation, and since we've already visited Gilda, I'm afraid Mr. Malloy will leave us with nothing to do," her mother said.

"I'm sure you'll manage to keep busy," her husband said with a knowing smile. "Mr. Malloy, I'd be happy to accompany you to see this woman."

"I don't think that will be necessary. Besides, I don't want to take you to that neighborhood. You'd probably get your pocket picked."

"Won't you get your pocket picked as well?"

Malloy just grinned. "They'll know I'm a cop."

When he returned to the La Pierre Hotel the next morning, Frank had no trouble with the desk clerk, who greeted him this time with an ingratiating smile and asked how he could help. He found Vaughn alone in his room, and amazingly, he was up and dressed. He'd even shaved, although he had a nasty bruise under his left eye. A half-full bottle of whiskey sat on the bedside table.

"What happened to your eye?" Frank asked.

Vaughn instinctively reached up and touched it. "Walked into a door."

Drunks, Frank thought. "Where's Emma?"

"Emma doesn't tell me what she's up to," Vaughn said, smiling the same way the desk clerk had.

"I think she probably does, so if you want to avoid a trip down to Police Headquarters, you'll answer my questions. Now where is she?"

His ingratiating smile vanished. "She went to see Wilbanks."

"Wilbanks? What for?"

He shrugged. "She wants her kid back."

"Wilbanks doesn't have her."

He shrugged again.

"Does she think he still has feelings for her?" Frank asked, trying to make sense of this.

"Emma can be very appealing when she wants to be."

"Ah, so she's going to try to revive his affection for her. Doesn't that bother you, Vaughn?"

"Why should it?"

"Don't you have feelings for her yourself?"

"Her arrangement with Wilbanks doesn't have anything to do with me."

"Oh, yeah, I remember now. You used to visit Emma at that house Wilbanks paid for, and that didn't bother you either. What kind of a man are you, Vaughn?"

"A practical one."

Frank shouldn't have been surprised. He'd seen men turn their wives and daughters out to sell themselves in the street. Compared to that, Emma's arrangement with Wilbanks was almost decent. "There's something I don't understand, Vaughn, and maybe you can help me."

"I will do my utmost, Mr. Malloy, if it means you will go away and leave me alone."

"You and Emma had a good life when Wilbanks was keeping her, so why did she suddenly run away?"

He licked his lips, probably thinking he'd like a drink. "She didn't run away."

"She left her home, her protector, and her child, and the two of you left town without a word. That sounds like running away to me."

"She was just tired of it, tired of Wilbanks and the kid. She wanted to be on her own again."

"Then why not just tell Wilbanks he could have Catherine and come back to her life in the theater?"

"I . . ." His gaze darted around the room, then settled on the whiskey bottle. "She was afraid."

"Afraid of what?"

"Of Wilbanks's son. He'd come to see her. He

said he'd hurt her if she didn't give up on Wilbanks."

"She wasn't afraid of Ozzie Wilbanks."

Vaughn's eyes widened. "Yes, she was! Well, maybe not him, but his friend."

"Ozzie and his friend told me she just laughed off their threats."

"Of course she did, to their faces. She's an actress, and she didn't want them to know they'd frightened her. But she said she had to get away before they did something, and that's why we left town."

Vaughn was lying, but Frank wasn't going to get the truth out of him without a lot of work, and he didn't have time for that today. Maybe, if he was lucky, he'd be able to catch up with Emma, though, and maybe she'd tell him just because he asked. He left a grateful Vaughn, who was already taking a swig of whiskey before Frank had even left the room.

He rode the El uptown, and made his way to Wilbanks's house. He'd probably missed Emma, but maybe he could get Wilbanks to tell him what she'd wanted. The maid took a bit longer than usual to answer the door, and when she did, her cheeks were flushed and her eyes wide with alarm, but not, Frank realized, because a policeman was at the door. Instead, she kept glancing back over her shoulder.

Before he could ask for Mr. Wilbanks, the faint

echo of voices raised in anger came drifting down to them from the floor above, and the girl gave a gasp of dismay. Maybe he wasn't too late for Emma after all.

"I'm with the police," he said before pushing past her and bounding up the stairs, two at a time. She didn't even try to stop him.

Frank easily found the source of the shouting. It was the parlor where he'd met Wilbanks the first time, and someone had carelessly left the door ajar.

"You can't throw me out, and when I'm your stepmother, neither of you will be welcome here!" Emma Hardy said in a voice that probably carried to the last row in the theater as Frank stepped into the room.

Wilbanks sat in his usual chair, a lap robe over his knees. His face was scarlet, a bloodstained handkerchief pressed to his lips, and his eyes frantic. Emma stood beside him, her hand resting possessively on his shoulder, and her expression as haughty as he'd ever seen a woman's face. Maybe he'd underestimated her acting ability. She glared at Ozzie and a woman who could only be his wife, Gilda, who stood before her and Wilbanks, their expressions outraged.

Wilbanks noticed him first, and the look in his eyes turned from frantic to pleading. Frank was pretty sure what he wanted, too. He cleared his throat, and the others turned to him in surprise.

Ozzie recovered first. "Mr. Malloy, what are you doing here?"

"I came to speak with Mr. Wilbanks. So nice to see you again, Miss Hardy." To his surprise, she smiled.

"You could not have arrived at a better time," she said. "I've just been telling Ozzie and his wife the good news. I've decided to accept David's proposal of marriage."

Frank wondered what Wilbanks thought about that, but from the way he was gasping, he obviously could not speak at the moment. Besides, Frank enjoyed Ozzie's and Gilda's reactions too much to care if Emma's claim was true or not.

"Mrs. Wilbanks?" Frank said, nodding. "I don't think we've met."

Even furious, Gilda was lovely, but she didn't waste any of her charm on Frank. "No, we have not."

"My dear," her husband said quickly, "this is Detective Sergeant Malloy with the New York City Police."

"Good. Arrest this woman." She waved her hand at Emma Hardy, who huffed in protest.

"I haven't done anything wrong!"

"She's trespassing," Gilda said.

Frank looked at Wilbanks, who shook his head slightly. "I don't think I can arrest Mr. Wilbanks's fiancée for trespassing without his permission, but Miss Hardy, maybe you're ready to leave. I'd be happy to escort you back to your hotel."

Emma obviously knew when to make her exit. She leaned down to Wilbanks and said, "I think you should rest now, my darling, but don't worry, I'll be back tomorrow, and we can make our plans." She kissed him lightly on the cheek, which drew a gasp from Gilda Wilbanks. Pretending not to notice, Emma strolled past Gilda and Ozzie toward the door, looking around as she went, as if taking stock. "What a dreary room," she said. "I'll have to completely redo it."

Gilda gave her a look that should have knocked her dead, but of course, Emma paid her no attention. Frank nodded his farewell to the Wilbanks family and followed her out. As he closed the door behind him, he heard Ozzie say, "Father, I'm going to send for your doctor."

The maid met them at the top of the stairs and escorted them out, returning Emma's slightly shabby cape to her before opening the front door for them. Emma, Frank noticed, wore a singularly ugly hat and the reddish dress she'd worn the last time he saw her. It probably was the best dress she owned.

"What was that all about?" he asked as they walked down the front steps.

"You're like a bad penny, aren't you? What are you doing here anyway?"

"I came looking for you. Vaughn told me

you'd be here," he added at her questioning look.

"I'll have to thank him for that," she said acidly.

"You should be glad I showed up when I did. Another minute, and Gilda Wilbanks would've clawed your eyes out."

"I'm not afraid of her or that milksop Ozzie."

"What about that milksop Terrance Udall?"

They were halfway down the block now, and she stopped and turned to him. "Is that dear Gilda's cousin? He's harmless, too. Rich people are so used to having other people wait on them that they can't accomplish anything themselves." So much for Vaughn's claim that she was terrified of them.

"Are you really going to marry Wilbanks this time?"

"Didn't I just say I was?" She started walking again.

"Yes, you did, which makes me wonder why you didn't do it a year ago when he asked you the first time."

She looked at him sharply, and seeing he was serious, she smiled. "I didn't want to."

"Why didn't you want to?"

"Mr. Malloy, you're starting to annoy me."

Frank grabbed her arm and jerked her to a stop. "And you're starting to annoy me, Miss Hardy."

She pulled her arm from his grasp and glared at him. "What do you want from me?"

"I want to know what made you leave your

daughter and run away a year ago, and I want to know who killed Anne Murphy and why."

"I already told you, I just got tired of Wilbanks and I wanted to get away."

"So you left your child behind?"

"You can't take a child on tour, Mr. Malloy. I thought I left her in good hands. I had no idea Annie would lose her."

Frank could have argued that point with her, but why bother? "Are you really going to marry Wilbanks this time?"

"Why shouldn't I?"

"Because I don't think he still wants to marry you."

She smiled again, as if this amused her. "He didn't want to marry me back then either. All he cared about was Catherine. I did him a favor by leaving town, and he did me a favor today by letting me scare his precious son out of what little wits he has. I was just getting some of my own back after they came barging in telling me to get out of their house. It's not their house yet, you know."

"Then you aren't really going to marry him?"

"You just said you don't think he wants to marry me, and you're probably right. In any case, I don't want to marry him either."

"Why not? Isn't marrying a rich man the dream of every chorus girl?"

"Not *every* chorus girl."

221

"All right, so you still won't tell me why you wouldn't marry Wilbanks. Who killed Anne Murphy?"

"How should I know?"

"Don't you have any idea?"

"Not a one."

"That's funny," Frank said, "because I can think of at least three people who didn't want you to find Catherine and might've killed Anne so you never would."

"Who? Ozzie and his lovely bride?" she scoffed.

"And her cousin."

"Yes, you're right. I'm sure one of them did it. Why don't you go arrest them?"

"Or maybe you hadn't thought of them because you know who really killed her."

"How could I know that?"

Frank met her gaze squarely, refusing even to blink, and watched her eyes narrow as the truth dawned on her.

"You can go straight to the devil, Malloy." With that she turned on her heel and walked swiftly away.

He let her go, sure she'd give him nothing more. What she *had* given him was simply confusing. She'd missed an opportunity to accuse the Wilbanks family of killing Anne Murphy, and he had no idea why. Was it because she already knew who did? But if she did, why hadn't she told him? Or if the killer was someone she wanted to protect—like herself—why hadn't she tried to put the blame on someone else? Nothing Emma Hardy did made sense to him. He wondered if it would make sense to Sarah and her mother. He'd be sure and ask them at the first opportunity. In the meantime, he'd realized he needed to see Michael Hicks's investigator, who may know something Frank didn't.

"Just think, Sarah," her mother said as her carriage carried them through the city streets so slowly, she could have passed it walking without even exerting herself. "If you didn't have to earn your living, you could go on visits like this with me every day."

Sarah didn't want her mother to know her true feelings about such a prospect. She dearly loved her mother, but the thought of returning to the life her mother led—an endless round of meaningless social engagements with people who talked only about themselves or gossiped about other people—made her want to throw herself into the East River. "You're very kind to take me along today."

"I realized I needed to do something of which your father would approve, and what better errand than finding out as much as we can about Gilda Wilbanks?"

"I must admit, I'm very curious about her. I just

wish you could remember the rumor you heard about her."

"I know, but believe me, if there's anything at all to it, Olivia will know."

Olivia Van Horn greeted them warmly, probably because she hadn't seen Sarah in years and desperately wanted to know what she had been doing with herself all that time. Her home was located in the section of Fifth Avenue known as Marble Row. After her husband's death, she had taken a small flat in a luxurious building where she could enjoy the comforts of wealth without the expense of an army of servants. She was one of the Van Horns who didn't have a penny to her name, at least by Sarah's mother's standards.

Her parlor contained what was left of the family's heirlooms—sideboards and tables from another age holding priceless porcelains—and plush furniture long past its prime. Olivia herself was like an heirloom. Still beautiful although her blond hair had gently turned to silver, she looked as fragile as one of her porcelains and almost as old.

When they were seated and served with tea and cakes, Olivia Van Horn said, "Sarah, you must tell me about yourself. Your mother hardly ever mentions you except to say that you are doing well. I must know everything. Is it true you're a midwife?"

As much as she would have preferred to talk

about Gilda Van Horn, Sarah realized that society gossip was tit for tat. She couldn't expect to learn anything without sharing something herself. Too bad she didn't know any juicy stories about anyone else in society that she could share instead. As briefly as she could, she brought Mrs. Van Horn up to date on her life story, managing not to mention a word about having ever assisted a police detective in solving murders.

As soon as Sarah had finished and before Olivia could think of another question to ask, her mother said, "We met a young relation of yours the other day."

"You did? Who was that?"

"Gilda Wilbanks."

"Oh, Gilda isn't *my* relation. She was Gilbert's, of course. Ralph Van Horn's daughter. The Van Horns are prolific. I can hardly keep up with all of them. How did you happen to meet her?"

"Felix had some business with her father-in-law," her mother said. "I thought it would be good for Sarah to make a friend her own age."

"Oh, I thought perhaps Sarah had occasion to see her professionally, as a midwife, I mean. She's been married to that Wilbanks boy for years now, and nothing in the way of offspring to show for it."

"I think it's only been a little over a year," Sarah said, stretching the truth a bit. "Much too soon to give up hope."

"How did she seem to you?" Olivia asked.

"What do you mean?" her mother asked.

"Oh, I don't know. She wasn't too happy about the match, you know."

"Really?"

Sarah had to bite back a smile at her mother's innocent stare.

"Oh, yes. Well, it's not like she tried to run away or anything. That would have been foolish. The Wilbanks boy is going to inherit a fortune, and Gilda's side of the family has to think about those things."

Sarah knew that Olivia's side of the family had to think about those things, too, but she merely nodded encouragingly.

"Gilda has a lovely home," her mother said. "Well, it's her father-in-law's house, of course, but I understand he's very ill."

"That's what I've heard. How tragic."

"Yes, it is. But I think Gilda will do well when the time comes. She seems very settled."

"I'm glad to hear it. Such a fuss at the time. You remember, don't you?" Olivia's faded blue eyes gleamed with her eagerness to tell.

"No, I don't. Not as bad as the Vanderbilt girl, I hope."

Sarah nearly choked. Consuelo Vanderbilt had been forced to marry an English duke she hardly knew and shipped off to a castle in England.

"Oh, no, nothing like that. The Wilbanks boy is

an American, after all. No, she just had some silly notion about marrying for love."

"That's not so silly," Sarah said.

"Isn't it?" Olivia said, giving Sarah a critical stare. "And what happens when you're left penniless? There's nothing romantic about that."

Sarah could have taken offense, but she had the strangest feeling Olivia was talking about herself.

"No, there isn't," her mother agreed, with an apologetic glance at Sarah. "But Gilda doesn't have to worry about that now. Unless she's pining away for her lost love."

"Oh, I doubt it very much," Olivia said. "She's much too practical. Besides, her family would never have allowed her to marry him even if he was rich as Croesus."

"And why not?" her mother asked.

"Because they were cousins, of course."

10

Sarah's mouth dropped open but only for a moment before she managed to say, "You don't mean Terrance Udall by any chance, do you?"

"As a matter of fact, I do. However did you know?"

Sarah glanced at her mother, wondering how much they dared tell Olivia, knowing it would be all over the city within days.

"When we called on Gilda, Mr. Udall happened to be visiting her, too. He's a . . . a charming young man."

"Oh, my," Olivia said in obvious distress. "Did you . . . Oh, my."

"What is it, Olivia?" her mother asked. "What's wrong?"

"Oh, nothing, I'm sure. It's just . . . How unwise of her to be seeing Terrance. I wonder that her husband allows it."

"Perhaps he doesn't know," her mother suggested. "Mr. Udall is her cousin, after all. It must seem very innocent to him for a member of her family to call."

"That must be the case. But she's a fool. Anyone might tell him, and to tempt fate like that . . . Well, she's insane to risk her marriage for a wastrel like Terrance Udall, that's all I can say. And it's always the female who pays the price in situations like that. If Mr. Wilbanks were to divorce her, do you think Terrance would want her? And even if he did, they'd be poor as church mice. Love flies out the window when the wolf is at the door."

Sarah's father had said something very similar years ago when her sister Maggie had married a poor man. She'd always wondered if it were true.

Sarah's mother said something meant to comfort, but Olivia was having none of it. "I wonder if her mother knows. Someone needs to talk sense to the girl before it's too late."

"I'm so sorry we upset you. I would never have mentioned Gilda if I'd realized . . ."

"You couldn't have known, but I'm glad you did."

After another few minutes of meaningless conversation, Sarah and her mother took their leave. When they were safely in the carriage, her mother turned to her. "Gilda wanted to marry Terrance Udall. I know I never heard that, or I would have remembered."

"And now we know why Terrance is taking such an interest in Ozzie's inheritance . . . because it's Gilda's inheritance, too."

229

"How very unselfish of him," her mother said, "to want the woman he couldn't have to be rich and happy with another man."

"I'm sure Malloy would say it's *too* unselfish."

"And I'd have to agree with him. What do you suppose they're up to?"

Sarah sighed. "I don't even want to guess, because none of the possibilities are very nice."

"Well, perhaps we're wrong. Perhaps we've completely misjudged Gilda Wilbanks. Perhaps she is just fond of her cousin, and she's trying to help him meet a nice young lady from a wealthy family."

"I just wish I thought you were right, Mother."

Frank was a little concerned about Terrance Udall seeing him back at Michael Hicks's office and wondering what he was up to, but Udall was nowhere in sight when he arrived and told the clerk he wanted to know what agency Hicks used to do his investigations. The clerk had to check with Hicks, of course, but to Frank's surprise, with no argument at all, the man returned and handed him a piece of paper with the name and address of the Kirby Detective Agency on it.

Frank had never heard of it, but that wasn't surprising. When the Pinkerton Detective Agency gained success after the War, dozens of private inquiry agencies had sprung up all over the country. Kirby probably only worked for Michael Hicks and maybe a few other attorneys. Since few people trusted the police, and for good reason, wealthy people who needed investigations usually relied on private agents.

He found the address on Sixth Avenue in a discreet office building. A female secretary sat at the desk in Kirby's front office, and she frowned up at Frank. "May I help you?"

She didn't sound like she thought that was possible, but Frank tried his most charming smile. "I think so. Attorney Michael Hicks sent me to speak with Mr. Kirby."

She still didn't look happy, but apparently, he'd said the right thing. She went into the inner office, and returned in a few moments. "Mr. Kirby will see you."

She showed him in and said, "I didn't get your name."

"Detective Sergeant Frank Malloy of the New York City Police."

She rolled her eyes. There wasn't much love lost between private detectives and the police. The police considered payments to private investigators money lost that could've gone to them as bribes. Private investigators were usually former cops who left because the force was too corrupt or too incompetent. Frank knew how they felt. The secretary closed the door, leaving him alone with Kirby.

The office was simply furnished and Mr. Kirby looked like a simple man of middle age, clean shaven and neatly dressed with dark hair graying a bit at the temples.

"Mr. Malloy, I'm Clarence Kirby," he said, rising from where he sat behind his desk. His handshake was firm, his palm dry. "I understand Mr. Hicks sent you. What can I do for you?"

"I had some questions about a case you worked on for Hicks, Emma Hardy."

Kirby frowned. "Have a seat, Mr. Malloy. May I ask what your interest is in that case?"

Frank took the offered chair. "It's personal. You see, I know the family who has Emma Hardy's daughter, and they aren't willing to give the child up unless they're sure it's the right thing."

"I see," Kirby said.

"I don't think you see at all, so I'll explain it to you. I know you were hired to find Emma after she disappeared. By the way, do you have any idea why she ran away in the first place?"

"You haven't told me anything yet that makes me want to share information with you, Mr. Malloy, so if you don't mind, I'll not answer that question just yet."

"Fair enough. I understand you found her on tour with some play. You approached her and tried to find out where the child was, but you didn't have much luck. You found out she wrote to Anne Murphy, so you came back to the city and found her, but she didn't have the child either, and so you killed her."

Kirby reared back in his chair, his eyes wide. "I beg your pardon!"

"You heard me. You killed Anne Murphy."

"I did no such thing. I'm a private investigator, not an assassin!"

"But you know who did."

"Of course I don't know. In fact, I only know she was murdered because Mr. Hicks told me. I'd stopped watching her as soon as I learned she had no idea where the child was."

Frank studied him for a long moment, waiting to see if his outrage cracked to reveal a hint of guilt. It did not. "I beg your pardon, Mr. Kirby, but I had to be sure."

"Sure of what? That I didn't kill that poor woman? I would have told you that if you'd just asked."

"And it would've been easy to lie if I just asked. You should know that."

Kirby's anger faded into a reluctant grin. "I used to know it. It's been a long time since I questioned a suspect, though."

"I guess you don't have much call for that in this business."

"No, I'm happy to say. Mostly, it's just following some swell to a cheap hotel to find out he's cheating on his wife so she can get a divorce and marry her own lover."

Frank glanced around at the modest office. "Is your operation as small as it looks?"

"Oh, yes, just me and Abby. She types my reports and sends the bills. I used to have other agents, but the clients always wanted me, so it didn't make sense to keep them on. If I need help, I bring in another agency."

"What do you think of Emma Hardy?"

Kirby leaned back in his chair, and Frank knew he'd finally told Kirby enough to make him willing to share information. "She's a hellion. Knows what she wants and goes after it. Near as I can tell, she worked Wilbanks perfectly. She's not much of an actress on the stage, but she must be pretty good between the sheets, if you know what I mean."

"Some men see what they want to see in a woman."

"There's that, of course, but from what I've heard, Emma never let him see what she was really like either."

"She must've done a good job, if he was willing to marry her."

"That was mostly for the child, I think, although he couldn't have known what he'd really be getting with her, or he never would've considered it. So you know where the child is? What happened to her?"

Frank told him.

Kirby shook his head. "Too bad Anne Murphy

never knew. She was terrified when she couldn't find her."

"Terrified of what? Do you know?"

"Well, I gather she cared for the little girl, and she became terrified when she couldn't find her, but I think it was more than that. I never talked to her myself, you understand. I didn't want to reveal my identity. But I talked to people who knew her. She thought somebody wanted to hurt the child. I guess that's what Emma told her. So she was afraid they'd found the child and something had happened to her."

"If she found out some man was asking her friends about her, she might've thought *you* were the one after the child. That would've scared her, too."

"Maybe, but she was also scared of what Emma would do if she got back and found out Anne didn't have her kid."

"Should she have been?"

Kirby gave him a pitying stare. "Have you met Emma Hardy? Of course she was right to be scared. Emma might not have cared about the girl, but she cared about the money she could bring in. If she got back here and found out Anne Murphy had lost track of her, well, let's just say I wouldn't want to be in Anne's shoes."

"Do you think Emma would have killed her?"

"Not if she was thinking straight. Anne might still be some help in finding the kid, but in a fit of temper, sure. She smacks Vaughn around some, I hear."

"What?"

"Didn't you know?"

"No, I never heard of such a thing, a woman hitting a man. Why doesn't he just hit her back?"

"You'd expect him to, wouldn't you? But he doesn't. I've seen it once or twice before. I know, usually it's the man beating up his woman to keep her in line, but every now and then you see it the other way around."

Frank remembered Vaughn's black eye. He said he'd walked into a door. How many women had offered that excuse for bruises their husbands had given them? "So she's been known to be violent."

Kirby nodded. "I understand Miss Murphy was stabbed."

"With a kitchen knife by someone visiting her in her room."

"Another woman then."

Frank frowned. "What makes you say that?"

"She lived in a boardinghouse. She wouldn't have brought a man up to her room."

Of course. Why hadn't any of them realized that before? "She wouldn't have thought twice about inviting her old friend Emma to her room, though."

Kirby nodded. "Anne probably even suggested it, so they could talk privately, knowing Emma would make a fuss when she found out about the child."

Could it really be that simple? Of course it could. Frank felt like an idiot. "So it was probably Emma that Anne Murphy was afraid of because she knew how angry Emma would be about Catherine."

"She wouldn't have expected Emma to murder her, though," Kirby said. "Emma would need her help to find the child."

"Once she calmed down, Emma probably realized that herself, but it was too late." Frank shook his head. "I didn't want it to be her."

"Why not?"

"Because she's Catherine's mother."

"I see. You're fond of the child."

Frank didn't want to discuss this with Kirby. He rose. "Thank you for your help."

"I hope we meet again under happier circumstances."

Frank paused at the door. "Are you still on this case?"

"No, Mr. Hicks said he had all the information he needed."

Frank wondered if that was true.

Once outside the building, he stepped back against the wall to allow the other pedestrians on the sidewalk to move past him while he considered what to do next. It was almost suppertime, and he hadn't seen Brian in too long. He saw no reason to ruin Sarah's evening with news that would keep until tomorrow, and Emma

Hardy seemed unlikely to murder anyone else, at least not in the near future. Yes, tomorrow was soon enough to arrest Catherine's mother.

Sarah's mother arrived at her door remarkably early the next morning.

"Oh, Sarah, when are you going to get a telephone?" she asked before she'd even taken off her coat.

"When I can afford one."

"What did Mr. Malloy say when you told him about Gilda and her cousin?"

"I haven't spoken with him."

"Really? I thought for sure he'd at least report to you what he'd learned yesterday from Emma."

Sarah took her mother's coat and hat and hung them up in the hall, then led her back to the kitchen, where the coffee left from her breakfast was still on the warmer. "What's Father doing today?"

"He went to his office, but he told me to contact him immediately if we learned anything new."

"At this point, I don't know what we could learn that's new unless someone decides to confess to killing Anne Murphy."

Her mother sat down at the kitchen table while Sarah poured coffee for them both. "You sound discouraged."

"I am." Sarah sat down across from her mother. "I don't even know what the right thing to do is anymore. We've been hiding Catherine to keep her safe, but we've also kept her from her own parents. We may not think much of either of them, but they're still her parents, and they have a right to see her."

"I know. If Mr. Wilbanks were in better health, I would invite him to visit Catherine at our home. At least we could be sure no harm would come to her there."

"I'm sure he wouldn't be able to travel, though," Sarah said, "so we would have to bring her to him."

"Gilda, it seems, will accept nothing less than his personal identification of her, too."

"Which means she'll want to be present, and I'm sure Ozzie will, too. Mr. and Mrs. Hicks should probably be there as well."

Her mother smiled wanly. "At least there's safety in numbers. With so many witnesses, no one would dare lift a finger to her."

"That's probably true, but what if Wilbanks won't let us take her back again?"

"How could he stop us?"

"By force, if necessary. He can afford to hire help for that, and we already know he has Mr. Hicks to work on the legalities. He *is* her father."

Her mother had no answer for that. They sipped their coffee in silence for a while.

"And what about Emma?" her mother asked finally.

"What about her?"

"She's Catherine's mother."

"I know she is, but I can't get over the fact that she abandoned her."

"I'm sure she would argue otherwise. And she is her mother. She must love her in her own way."

"Her own way is very unusual. I never thought I'd hear you defending her, Mother."

"I'm not defending her. I'm merely trying to be reasonable. Perhaps if we were kind to Miss Hardy, we could . . ."

"Could what?" Sarah asked when she hesitated.

"We could win her cooperation. If she was willing to give Catherine to Wilbanks for a financial consideration, perhaps she would do the same for us."

"Mother, I don't have anything to give her."

Her mother laid a hand on her arm. "I know that, dear, but your father and I do."

"Oh, Mother, I couldn't possibly—"

"You couldn't possibly *refuse,* particularly if we didn't ask your permission."

Sarah felt the sting of tears. "I've always resented it when you and Father did things you thought were best for me without consulting me."

"Would you resent it if we did this for you?"

"I . . . I think it would be very difficult to be anything but grateful. Even still, I can't ask you to allow yourselves to be blackmailed, which is what this would be."

"You wouldn't be asking us to do anything, and

what good is having money if you can't help the people you love? If we've learned nothing else in this life, we've learned that."

Sarah knew they'd learned it by losing their older daughter, a hard lesson indeed. "Thank you, Mother."

Frank stopped by Police Headquarters that morning to get a patrolman to go with him to the La Pierre Hotel. Even though people there would know he was a cop, if Emma decided to put up a fight, some of the other residents of the hotel might decide to come to her rescue. Only a fool would cause trouble in that neighborhood without someone to back him up. Frank spent an hour locating the patrolman he wanted. Gino Donatelli, one of the few Italians on the force, was also one of the few patrolmen he would trust in any situation.

"This woman is little Catherine's mother?" the young man asked him as they made their way downtown. This time of the morning, the pedestrian traffic was relatively light, so they didn't have to push their way through crowds, at least.

"Yes, and I think she might be a murderer, too."

Gino crossed himself. "Poor Mrs. Brandt." Gino adored Sarah Brandt. "This will be very hard for her."

It'll be very hard for me, too, Frank thought, but he said, "There's a man with her, but I don't think he'll be any trouble. He's a drinker, and if we're lucky, he'll still be passed out from last night."

"This drunk, is he Catherine's father?"

"No. Her father is some rich man who lives uptown."

Gino had to hear the whole story, which helped pass the time as they walked the long blocks to their destination.

As usual, the hotel was quiet at this time of day. Most of the residents were sleeping off their rowdy night. The desk clerk frowned when he saw Gino in uniform.

"I don't want no trouble," he said, glancing around to see if anybody had noticed a uniformed policeman in the lobby.

"Neither do I," Frank said. "If you hear any, send for the cops."

The desk clerk didn't think this was a bit funny. Cops were bad for business. He fumed as Frank and Gino climbed the stairs.

Frank paused outside Emma's door. "Your job is to keep anybody else from coming in if she starts screaming or something."

"What if he puts up a fight?"

"Then I'll call you. Otherwise just stay out here and don't let anybody else in."

Gino pulled his nightstick from the loop on his belt and held it ready.

Frank tried a regular knock first. No sense in alarming them or waking up the neighbors. He thought he heard some noise from inside, but nobody came, so he knocked again, a little more insistently.

"Go away," Vaughn called, surprising a grin from Gino.

"It's Malloy. I've got some news for you."

He waited again, but still nobody came. With an exasperated sigh, he tried the door and it opened. "These people never lock their room," he muttered and pushed it open.

The window shade blocked what little light might find its way to the window and cast everything in shadow. Frank blinked a few times until he made out Vaughn's form on the bed. He sprawled on it diagonally, and plainly, he was the only occupant of it. Frank couldn't believe Emma would be out and about so early, but he was pretty sure if she were here, she'd be complaining by now.

Frank took a step into the room. Now he could see Vaughn still wore his suit pants but only a dingy balbriggan undershirt on top, with the first three buttons undone. "Vaughn, where's Emma?"

Vaughn opened his eyes for a second, then slammed them shut again, groaning softly. "She's here somewhere."

Frank doubted that, but he looked around anyway and that's when he saw her. Or at least he saw her feet and the bottom of her skirt. She lay on the floor on the other side of the bed, in the narrow space between the bed and the wall. He sighed in disgust. He hadn't realized she drank, too. What a pair they were. Well, at least if she was passed out drunk, he wouldn't have much trouble taking her in.

He walked around the foot of the bed, wondering how he'd get her out of there. Lucky he'd brought Gino. It might take both of them to carry her down the stairs. He gave her foot a gentle nudge with his toe. "Emma, wake up."

She didn't move.

He nudged a little harder, but still got no response. With a disgusted sigh, he went to the window and gave the shade a jerk that sent it flying up and slapping around the rod several times before it finally settled. The noise brought another groan from Vaughn, and he threw his arm over his eyes to protect them from the feeble sunlight.

Frank went back and glared down at Emma, and to his surprise, she glared back at him. At least that's what he thought for a full two seconds before he realized she was really staring at nothing because she was dead.

"Strangled," the medical examiner said. Doc Haynes had finally arrived after several hours to get the body. Deaths in the Lower East Side weren't a big priority with the coroner's office. "I'll be able to tell you more after I do the autopsy."

"And it's Friday, so that means you won't have

anything until at least Monday. Am I right?" Frank asked.

"You're right. I don't know what you expect me to find, though. The lover strangled her, didn't he? He was the only other person in the room."

True. Frank had no trouble at all figuring out how it happened either. Emma had started smacking on Vaughn or whatever she did, and he just couldn't take it anymore. Before he knew it, his hands were around her throat, and then she was dead. Unable to face what he'd done, he'd drunk himself into a stupor. He'd done a good job of it, too, because he still hadn't woken up, even when Frank and Gino had carried him to another room after finding the body.

"All you have to do is check his hands," Haynes added.

"His hands?"

"Yeah, she's got blood and probably some skin under her fingernails. She would've scratched her killer up pretty good."

"Thanks. I'll remember that."

Frank had summoned another beat cop to guard Vaughn and set Gino to questioning the other hotel residents to see if they'd heard anything. Not surprisingly, nobody had. People in this part of the city were always deaf, dumb, and blind when a crime was committed. Frank went through all of Vaughn's and Emma's stuff. He found a box of papers and letters at the bottom of one of their trunks that he'd go through later, but not much else.

Haynes and his orderlies had just carried Emma Hardy's body away when the beat cop guarding Vaughn shouted that he was waking up. Frank went down the hall to the room where they'd put him earlier.

Vaughn moaned and then he somehow managed to roll over just in time to puke over the side of the bed. Frank swore and the cop swore. Well, at least it had happened here and not while Frank was questioning him.

"Get a wagon to take him to Headquarters," Frank told the beat cop. "I'll meet you there."

Before too long, a Black Maria arrived and a couple of burly cops hefted Vaughn to his feet and half dragged, half carried him down the stairs and out to the street. Gino frowned after them. "What?" Frank asked.

"He should've woken up by now."

"What do you mean?"

"I mean if he was drunk, if he *got* drunk after he killed her—"

"He probably just got *drunker* after he killed her," Frank said.

"Yeah, well, drunker then, but even still, he should've come out of it by now. He's more than drunk. He still don't even know what's going on."

"He probably killed her," Frank said. "They were alone in the room."

"They were alone in the room when we found

them, and she was dead and he was dead to the world. We don't know what happened before that."

Frank wanted Vaughn to be the killer. He wanted this to be neat and easy, but Gino was right. "I trained you too well."

"I know. It gets me in trouble all the time."

"Let's go to Headquarters and see if he remembers anything. Maybe he'll make it easy for us."

But Gino shook his head. "That fellow don't remember his own name."

By the time Frank and Gino got back to Headquarters, Vaughn was in one of the interrogation rooms. Somebody had poured water over his head and given him some coffee, but he was still groggy. When Frank and Gino came in, he didn't even lift his head off the table.

"Vaughn, wake up," Frank said, slapping the scarred wooden table that was the main piece of furniture in the room. Two battered chairs made up the rest, and Vaughn sat in one of them. Frank sat down across the table from him. Gino stood by the door.

Vaughn dragged himself upright and stared at Frank through rheumy eyes. One of them still sported a greenish bruise. His skin was the color of putty, his hair hung in greasy strings, and he needed a shave. "Malloy?"

"Good, you're not as stupid as you look," Frank said. "Tell me what happened last night."

"Last night?"

"Don't annoy me, Vaughn. I'm already in a bad mood. Last night. What did you do?"

"I . . . I don't remember."

This was not surprising. "What *do* you remember?"

He scrubbed his hands over his face. "Emma was mad."

"About what?"

"I . . . Wilbanks. His son, I think."

That made sense. She'd been pretty angry the last time Frank had seen her. "Did she tell you she was going to marry Wilbanks?"

"No."

"Well, she was," Frank lied. "I think she told you, and you got mad and strangled her."

"She isn't going to marry Wilbanks."

"What makes you so sure?"

"She can't. She's not going to marry him."

"Why can't she?"

Vaughn blinked a few times. He seemed to be coming out of his fog. "I'm not going to tell you. Emma would be mad if I did."

"Vaughn, Emma won't be mad at anything anymore. She's dead."

"No, she's not."

This was going to be a very long day. "Vaughn, Emma is dead. You strangled her."

Frank waited, giving him a chance to come to terms with it, since he obviously had no memory of killing her.

"No," he said again and looked at Gino. "She can't be."

"She is," Gino said solemnly.

"No, no, she can't be! We're going away together. She's going to get the money from Wilbanks, and then we won't have to worry about anything ever again. That's what she said."

"When did she say that?" Frank asked.

"All the time. She said it all the time. Before she went to see him, she said it."

"Before she went to see him yesterday, you mean?"

"Was that yesterday?"

"Yes, she went to see Wilbanks yesterday, and she told his family she was going to marry him."

"That can't be right." He rubbed his eyes like a sleepy child. "Maybe she said it, but she'd never do it. She was going to get the money and we were leaving town. And then she was mad."

"What was she mad about?"

"Wilbanks. She was mad at the son. He threw her out or something."

"How did she expect to get money from Wilbanks if she didn't have the child?"

Vaughn's eyes started drooping again. Frank gave him a light slap to get his attention. "What's wrong with you? What did you take?"

"Nothing. I . . . It was the whiskey. There was something in the whiskey."

"What whiskey?"

"The bottle he brought."

Frank felt a chill slither down his spine. "The bottle who brought?"

Vaughn was scratching his head. "I need a drink."

"Answer my questions, and you can have one," Frank lied. "Who brought you a bottle?"

"I don't know. Some fellow. He wanted to talk to Emma."

Frank glanced at Gino, who gave him an "I told you so" look. "Who was he? What was his name?"

"I don't know. I don't remember. Nice fellow. He gave me a drink."

"Then what happened?"

"I don't know. I felt funny. *I don't remember*. I need a drink."

"Vaughn, listen to me. Emma is dead. Somebody strangled her. Do you remember what happened?"

Vaughn stared at him for a long moment. "Emma is dead?"

"That's right. Somebody strangled her. Was it you?"

Vaughn's bloodshot eyes filled with tears. "Emma's dead? She can't be dead."

"She's dead, Vaughn. Somebody strangled her, and you were the only one in the room with her."

"No, no, I'd never hurt Emma. I loved her. She said we'd always be together, and she'd take care of me."

"Then why did you strangle her?"

"I didn't! I'd never hurt her." His voice broke. "Emma, Emma!" He dropped his head onto his arms and began to sob.

Frank swore.

"I told you we didn't know what happened in that room," Gino said.

"He could be lying," Frank said, even though he didn't believe it himself.

"He could be," Gino agreed without much conviction.

Then Frank remembered what Haynes had said about Emma scratching her killer. He pulled Vaughn's hands out from under his head. Not a single scratch.

Frank sighed. "Lock him up and go back to the hotel. Take somebody with you, and see if you can find somebody who saw this visitor. The desk clerk had to see him, at least. Tell him you're going to pack up all of his customers and bring them back to question them if he doesn't tell you the truth. That'll put the fear of God into him."

"It won't do any good. Nobody will admit to seeing anything."

"I know, but we have to try."

"What will you do?"

Frank pushed himself to his feet. "I've got to go tell the rest of Catherine's family that her mother is dead."

11

Sarah sighed with relief when she heard someone ringing her doorbell. After her mother left, she'd started cleaning her house in hopes that the activity would distract her. Instead, it had only given her more time to think about her situation. She hoped it was a delivery. She needed the distraction.

Then she saw Malloy on her doorstep, and she realized she hadn't wanted it to be a delivery at all.

"Malloy," she said, smiling in spite of everything. He didn't smile back as he came in. In fact, he didn't even meet her eye. "What is it? What's happened?"

He waited until she'd closed the door behind him. "Emma's dead."

She needed a full minute to take it in. "Dead? How could she be dead?"

"Somebody strangled her."

"Dear heaven! Who?"

"I don't know." He handed her a battered wooden box so he could slip out of his coat and hang it up.

"What's this?"

"I found it in Emma's room. It's full of letters and papers. I thought there might be something important in it, so I brought it along to go through later."

By silent agreement, they made their way to the kitchen, and Sarah set the box on her desk in the front room as they passed through. The breakfast coffee was gone, but she started a new pot, then sat down opposite him at the table.

"What happened?" she asked.

He told her how he and Gino had found Emma.

"Wait, Vaughn was alone in the room with her body? But you just said you don't know who killed her."

"He was passed out. Not just drunk, but like somebody'd slipped him a Mickey Finn. We took him down to Headquarters, and he kept falling asleep while I was questioning him."

"Who would have given him a Mickey Finn?"

Malloy smiled suddenly and shook his head.

"What's so funny?" she demanded.

"You. I'll bet your mother doesn't know what a Mickey Finn is."

"Everybody knows that."

"Ask her."

"I will. So who could have *slipped him a Mickey Finn?*" she asked with a grin of her own.

"He claims some fellow came to see Emma last night. The fellow gave him a bottle, or maybe just a drink from a bottle, and he says it made him feel funny and he doesn't remember anything else, and now Emma is dead."

"That's pretty far-fetched."

"Yeah, even a drunk like Vaughn could make up a better story than that. All those plays he's been in, he probably knows a lot of stories he could've told us."

"Are you saying you think it's true because it's so unbelievable?"

"Well, I guess it's possible that he strangled her when he was drunk and doesn't remember it now. That happens with drunks. But if he just didn't remember, he'd probably say so. I think his story is true because if he'd decided to lie about it, he would've made up a better story."

"But who would have wanted to kill Emma?"

"Ozzie Wilbanks, for starters. I almost forgot, you don't know what happened yesterday. Emma went to see Wilbanks."

"Oh, my. That must have delighted him."

"It didn't make Ozzie or Gilda very happy either. I don't know what happened between her and Wilbanks, but when I got there, Emma was telling Ozzie and Gilda that she had decided to marry Wilbanks after all."

"What did Wilbanks say about that?"

"Nothing. He'd had one of his coughing fits, and he couldn't speak."

"How did you happen to walk in at just the right moment?"

"I went to see her at the hotel, and Vaughn told me where she was. I figured she would've already left, but I got lucky."

"Do you think Wilbanks would really marry her?"

"No, and neither did she. I think she just said it to annoy Ozzie and his bride."

Sarah considered this for a moment. "Do you think someone did believe she'd marry him and killed her to stop it?"

"By 'someone,' do you mean Ozzie?"

"I guess I do."

"I don't know, but why else would somebody bother to kill her? She didn't have Catherine, and even if she did . . ." He straightened in his chair, obviously realizing the awful truth at the same moment she did.

"Even if she did, *she* wasn't the threat," Sarah said, her blood turning cold. "*Catherine* is the threat."

"We're not going to let anything happen to her, Sarah."

The coffee had started to sputter, and she jumped up to rescue it, grateful for the distraction. This was just too horrible.

"Both of the women who were closest to Catherine are dead," she said, pulling cups and saucers out of the cupboard.

"I thought I'd figured out who killed Anne Murphy."

"Who?"

"Something Kirby told me got me thinking—"

"Who's Kirby?"

"Oh, he's the investigator Hicks hired to find Catherine. I went to see him to find out if he knew anything we didn't."

"Did he?"

"He said Emma, uh, hits Vaughn."

"What? That's crazy. Women don't hit men." She set the cups on the table.

"He said they sometimes do, and the men won't hit them back for some reason."

Sarah shook her head. "Maybe because they've been trained that it's not right to hit a woman."

"Maybe. Knowing Vaughn and Emma, I'm not real surprised, actually. He got a black eye a couple days ago. He said he walked into a door."

Sarah poured the coffee. "That's unbelievable."

"That he walked into a door?"

"No . . . Well, yes, I guess. I meant it's unbelievable that a woman would hit a man and blacken his eye."

"Kirby's point was that Emma was known to be violent when she's angry. Then he said something I should've realized right away: Anne Murphy and the killer were alone in her room at the boardinghouse."

"Why is that . . . Oh! I see. Men aren't allowed upstairs, at least in decent boardinghouses." She sat back down.

"But she would've invited Emma upstairs, the same as she did you and Maeve."

"And you think that's what happened, that Emma went up to Anne's room, and Anne told her Catherine was missing, and Emma got mad and stabbed her?" Sarah thought this over. "Did she bring the knife with her?"

"I think Anne already had the knife in her room. She was scared, remember? Emma had told her she was leaving the city because someone wanted to kill her, and for all Anne knew, they wanted to kill her and Catherine, too."

"So the knife was handy for the killer, who maybe hadn't planned to do Anne any violence at all until Anne provoked her by telling her that her daughter had vanished."

Malloy nodded. "That's what I was thinking, and I went to the hotel to take Emma in and see if I couldn't get her to confess."

"And instead you found her dead." Sarah sighed. "I hoped she wasn't the killer."

"Who else would Anne have invited up to her room, though? It had to be a female."

Sarah saw a flaw in that logic. "But the landlady wasn't there the morning Anne was killed, and neither was anyone else. Who would know if she invited a man upstairs?"

"Remember how scared she was. I doubt she would've let a strange man into the house at all. Kirby had been asking people about her, and I'm sure someone told her. She probably thought he was one of the men Emma was afraid of, so she would've been extra careful."

"Maybe he didn't ask. Maybe he didn't even knock. Maybe he waited until Anne was alone and snuck in."

"I guess that's possible, but how did he know which room was hers?"

"Stop ruining my theory with logic," she said.

"Sorry. So we know Emma could've killed Anne, and maybe she did and maybe she didn't, but Emma certainly didn't kill herself, so there's at least one killer on the loose and maybe two."

"There's always the possibility that Vaughn killed her and he just dreamed up the fellow with the Mickey Finn."

Malloy sighed and drank the last of his coffee.

"Would you like some more?" she asked.

"Yes, but I need to go see Wilbanks."

"Why?"

"To tell him about Emma. She was his fiancée, after all, at least the last I heard. I'm sure he'll want to know."

"And you want to see how Ozzie reacts, too, don't you?"

"Ozzie and Hicks."

Sarah raised her eyebrows. "You think Mr. Hicks could have been the man who drugged Vaughn and strangled Emma?"

"I know, that's hard to picture, but maybe he

hired somebody. I just want to see how surprised he is."

"I guess I should go tell my mother. She'll never forgive me if I don't."

"I'll wait for you. We can go uptown together."

Sarah needed only a few minutes to change her clothes and smooth her hair. They took the El uptown, and then parted company. Sarah almost wished she could have gone with Malloy. She'd never met any of the Wilbanks family except Gilda, and she wasn't really related to Catherine. On the other hand, she already felt sorry for Wilbanks and guilty for keeping his child from him. Seeing the dying man might soften her heart even more, and she couldn't risk Catherine's safety over sentiment.

Frank greeted Wilbanks's maid with a friendly smile when she opened the door.

"Oh, Mr. Malloy, I was that glad to see you yesterday," she whispered as she let him in. "That woman was so awful. Poor Mr. Wilbanks." She'd certainly changed her mind about him since his first visit.

"How is he today?"

"Not well. The doctor told him he had to stay in bed. He was coughing something awful. Exhausted himself, poor man."

"Do you think I could see him for a few

minutes? I have some important information for him that might make him feel better."

"Oh, I don't know about that. I couldn't say, myself. I'd have to ask Mr. Oswald."

Frank wanted to talk to Ozzie anyway. "All right. I'll wait while you ask him."

The maid frowned. "But Mr. Ozzie is out."

"When do you expect him back?"

"I . . . Not for a while."

Frank smiled again. "Then he won't know, will he? Go ask Mr. Wilbanks if he feels well enough to see me." When she hesitated, he added, "If anybody gets upset, I'll tell them I forced you to let me in."

Still not quite certain but apparently grateful enough for his help yesterday to take a chance, she went upstairs and returned in a few minutes. "He's anxious to see you, Mr. Malloy. He said he has something to tell you, too."

She led him up several sets of stairs to Wilbanks's bedroom. She tapped on the door and a middle-aged man opened it instantly. He looked Malloy over with disapproval. "Ordinarily, I wouldn't let you in at all, but Mr. Wilbanks wants to see you. He's very weak, though, so you can't upset him."

"This is Henry, Mr. Wilbanks's valet," the girl said.

Frank recognized Henry's concern as genuine affection for Wilbanks. He figured Henry already knew all the family secrets anyway. "You can stay, and if you think it's too much for him, just let me know."

Henry didn't like it, but he said, "Come in."

Frank stepped into the room. The heavy drapes were drawn, making a dark room even darker. The mahogany furniture gleamed dully in the gaslight, and a fire made the room uncomfortably warm. Wilbanks lay in the enormous four-poster bed, nearly swallowed in the bedclothes, but he beckoned Frank urgently with one slender hand.

Henry brought a chair to the bedside, and Frank sat. "I'm sorry to bother you, sir, but I have some news."

His eyes brightened. "Catherine?"

"No, Emma."

He frowned. "I'm not going to marry her." Every word was an effort, his voice little more than a gasp, and Frank wondered what it cost him to speak at all.

"I know. She said that herself after we left yesterday. She was just trying to make your son mad, I think."

He nodded, relieved.

"But it doesn't matter anyway. Emma is dead. Someone murdered her last night."

Frank wasn't sure what reaction he had expected, but Wilbanks's expression went from surprised to shocked to horrified in a few moments. "How?"

"She was strangled in her hotel room. She wasn't alone there. She had a lover, a man named Parnell Vaughn."

His eyes widened in surprise. "He did it?"

"We think so," Frank lied. No use upsetting Wilbanks with any wild theories.

"Thank God," Wilbanks whispered.

Frank studied his face, trying to read the expressions roiling there. "Did you think somebody else might've done it?"

Wilbanks met his gaze for a long moment, then turned his head away. "Tired."

"I think you'd better go now," Henry said.

Frank thought so, too. He wasn't going to get anything else out of Wilbanks, but when Henry would have ushered him out, Frank grabbed his arm and pulled him into the hallway. "Who did Wilbanks think might've killed Emma Hardy?"

"Really, I don't know—"

"Yes, you do, and if you don't want me to go back in there and get it out of Wilbanks, you'll tell me."

"You wouldn't dare!"

Frank gave him a look that said he would dare that and a whole lot more.

"I can't speak for Mr. Wilbanks, of course . . ."

"Henry," Frank said in warning.

"But I believe he may have been concerned because he had not told Mr. Oswald that he had no intention of marrying that woman."

"You mean he let Ozzie believe she was telling the truth?"

"Well, he was very ill yesterday, you see, and he couldn't speak for a long time. The doctor came, and he told Mr. Wilbanks not to talk at all. He would write things down for me when he got like that. He told me . . . well, he wrote it . . . that he wasn't really going to marry her. He wanted me to know that. I told him I would tell Mr. Oswald to ease his mind as well, but he said not to. He said . . . He said to let him stew a while." The last pained Henry almost as much as it would have pained Wilbanks to say.

"And Wilbanks thought maybe Ozzie had gone to visit Miss Hardy and made sure the wedding didn't happen."

"As I said, I can't speak for Mr. Wilbanks."

He didn't have to, of course. "Did Ozzie go out last night?"

"Mr. Oswald goes out every evening."

"Thank you for your cooperation, Henry."

So Wilbanks thought his son might've killed Emma, believing he was saving his father from making a disastrous marriage, Frank thought as he made his way back down the stairs. The marriage would've been more disastrous for Ozzie than for Wilbanks, of course, at least in Ozzie's mind. No matter how terrible a wife Emma might have been, Wilbanks would be dead in a few months, but Ozzie would have to live many years knowing his stepmother and half sister had gotten a portion of what should have been his.

Was that enough to send him down to the Lower East Side late at night to hunt down and kill Emma Hardy? And was Ozzie capable of making such a successful plan? Whoever had killed Emma must have known she wasn't alone at the hotel and had brought the drugged whiskey along to knock Vaughn out before taking care of Emma. Udall could have told him that. Or had he intended the whiskey for Emma and been surprised to find her lover there, too? Had he just been lucky to have the drugged whiskey to take care of Vaughn so he could kill Emma without interference?

He'd be sure to ask the killer all those questions when he identified him, he thought with a sigh.

Michael Hicks had left the office for the day by the time Frank got there. Although the fellow at the front desk claimed he did not know where Mr. Hicks had gone, Frank took a chance and went to Hicks's house, where Hicks and his wife received him in the parlor.

Lynne Hicks didn't look at all happy to see him, and Michael looked positively apoplectic.

"What are you doing here, Malloy?"

"I came to tell you that Emma Hardy is dead."

As Frank had expected, this took some of the

starch out of them. Mrs. Hicks made a startled sound and looked at her husband, who, in turn, gaped at Frank. "Dead? How could she be dead?"

"Someone killed her, Mr. Hicks. I apologize for being so blunt, Mrs. Hicks."

Lynne Hicks waved away his concern. "Who did it?"

"I'm not sure," Frank said, watching Hicks's face carefully. He saw no reaction.

"Where did it happen?" he asked.

"In the hotel room where she's been staying."

"Where she's been staying with that Vaughn character?" Hicks asked.

"Who's Vaughn?" his wife asked.

"Her lover," Hicks said.

"I thought Father was her lover."

Hicks sighed. "She has another lover. An actor. He was on tour with her, apparently."

"Oh, my."

"Did you know Emma Hardy went to see your father yesterday, Mrs. Hicks?"

"Yes." Her expression told him just how much she hated Emma Hardy.

"May I ask how you know that?"

"Really, Malloy," Hicks said. "What does that matter?"

Frank didn't bother to answer him. He just kept staring at Lynne Hicks, who finally said, "My brother told me. Because Father was so ill. He telephoned. He thought I should come, in case . . ."

She dropped her gaze, apparently fighting tears.

"In case Mr. Wilbanks died," Hicks finished for her, not bothering to hide his disgust. "But of course, David wasn't dying at all. I think it was just wishful thinking on Ozzie's part."

"You must've been pretty surprised when you found out your father had decided to marry Miss Hardy," Frank said.

Mrs. Hicks's cheeks were flaming when she looked up again. "It was a . . . shock."

"I guess it was a shock to your brother, too."

"It was a shock to *everyone,* Mr. Malloy," Hicks said, still angry. "Of course, we only had Ozzie's word for it. Mr. Wilbanks was much too ill to confirm or deny it."

"Why would Ozzie lie about it?" Frank asked.

"He wouldn't," Hicks said, "but . . ."

"But we would have liked to have Father confirm it," Lynne Hicks said.

"So you didn't believe it?" Frank asked.

The couple exchanged a glance. "Let's just say, we hoped it wasn't true," he said.

"It wasn't," Frank said.

This time they both gaped at him. "How do you know?" she asked.

"Your father told his valet last night, but he asked him not to tell Ozzie just yet."

"That would be like him," Lynne Hicks said. "But why would he tell Ozzie a lie like that in the first place?"

"He didn't. Emma told it, and your father had started coughing and couldn't deny it or maybe he just decided not to. Whatever happened, somebody went to Emma's hotel and killed her later that night."

They needed a moment for his meaning to sink in. Lynne Hicks got it first. "Are you accusing my brother of murdering that woman so she couldn't marry Father?"

"Would you be surprised if I did?"

"That's outrageous, Malloy," Hicks said. "How dare you say such a thing to my wife?"

"Two women are dead, Mr. Hicks. I want to find out who killed them."

"You should pin a medal on whoever killed Emma Hardy," Hicks said, earning a disapproving glare from his wife.

"Really, Michael, that's heartless of you. If you aren't careful, Mr. Malloy will be accusing *you* of killing that woman."

"Not if he has any sense. And he won't be accusing your brother either."

"But who else would want to prevent a marriage between her and your father?" Frank asked.

"You're assuming that's the reason she was killed, and you have no way of knowing that at all," Hicks said. "Besides, you said yourself that actor was with her. Surely, he's the one who killed her. Some kind of lover's quarrel, perhaps. If he thought she was going to marry

David, he might have killed her in a jealous rage."

Frank decided not to mention his theory that Vaughn had been drugged by a mysterious visitor. "It could've happened that way."

"Then you should be arresting Vaughn, not bothering us."

"I did arrest him, but I can't think of any reason he might've killed Anne Murphy."

"Why do you need one?"

"Because it's hard to believe Anne Murphy and Emma Hardy, two women involved so closely with your father and his child, were killed by different people for different reasons. I want to find out who killed them both and why, so I'll know if little Catherine is safe or in danger."

"No matter what else you may believe, Mr. Malloy, you may be certain we wish the child no harm," Lynne Hicks said. "And please believe me when I say that I'm very glad she has someone who cares about her."

"Then maybe you can also understand how important it is to find out why these women were killed. If it was to prevent Mr. Wilbanks from dividing up his fortune, then Catherine is in more danger than ever."

"Mr. Malloy, my brother may be many things, but I must agree with my husband. Ozzie doesn't have the courage to kill anyone."

"Nobody wants to think somebody they love is a killer, Mrs. Hicks."

• • •

"Good heavens!" Sarah's mother said for about the tenth time in as many minutes as Sarah finished telling her about Emma Hardy's murder. They sat in the family parlor at the Deckers' home. "I just can't believe it. But you know what this means, don't you?"

"What it means? I have no idea."

"It means that when Mr. Wilbanks passes away, Catherine will be an orphan. There won't be anyone to object to your keeping her."

"I hope you don't expect me to be happy that poor woman is dead."

"I didn't say you had to be *happy* about anything at all. Certainly, Miss Hardy's death is tragic. She's Catherine's mother, after all. She may have been a poor mother, but children do love their parents, no matter how bad a job the parents might do."

"I wonder what she remembers about Emma, or if she remembers her at all."

"She's very young, of course. She probably remembers very little."

The door burst open and Catherine came running in. "Mama!"

Sarah caught her in her arms and pulled her into her lap for a hug and a kiss. Sarah inhaled her sweet scent and never wanted to let her go.

"Is it time to go home?" Catherine asked.

"Do you want to go home?"

Catherine frowned and Maeve said from the doorway, "She misses you, but otherwise, I think she'd be happy to stay here forever."

"We had ice cream," Catherine said, as if that explained it.

The adults laughed, and Catherine smiled uncertainly, not quite sure why they'd laughed but glad they had.

"I miss you, too, sweetheart, but I'm not going to make you go home just yet. You can stay for a few more days."

"And you'll come to visit me?"

"Of course I will, as often as I can."

Catherine sighed contentedly and snuggled more comfortably into Sarah's lap.

"Are you enjoying your stay, too, Maeve?" Sarah asked.

Maeve came over and sat down on the sofa beside Sarah. "Of course I am. We had ice cream."

This time even Catherine laughed.

Sarah coaxed the child to tell her what else she had been doing besides eating ice cream. By the time she had finished, Catherine's supper was ready, so Sarah ate with her and Maeve in the nursery, and they played with Sarah's old toys and some new ones her mother had bought to amuse Catherine during this visit, until it was time for bed. How strange to tuck Catherine into the bed where Sarah had slept so many years ago.

As she smoothed the child's fine hair away

from her eyes, she thought about the loss Catherine had just sustained, even though she had no idea the mother she hadn't seen in so long was dead. On impulse, she repeated the question she'd asked before. "Darling, do you remember anything about where you used to live before you came to the Mission?"

Her little face grew solemn. "No."

"It's all right if you don't," Sarah said hastily.

"I don't want to go back."

So she did remember something, but not something good. "You won't ever have to go back, darling."

"Promise?"

"I promise." There was, after all, no one left to go back to.

Catherine sat up and threw her arms around Sarah's neck. "Will you stay with me until I fall asleep?"

Sarah blinked to hold back her tears. "Of course."

Catherine fell asleep in minutes, and Sarah found her mother in the parlor. Her father had returned home while she was upstairs with Catherine, and she greeted him. "Did Mother tell you about Miss Hardy?"

"Yes, it's a nasty business. I think you should stay here until this matter is settled."

"I'm not in any danger, Father."

"How can you be sure? Catherine's mother and

her nursemaid are dead. You're her mother now."

"Yes, but I have no intention of marrying Mr. Wilbanks or trying to get money from him."

"Whoever killed those other women may not know that."

"Who do *you* think killed them?" Sarah asked to distract him from trying to tell her what to do.

He frowned and glanced at his wife. "I wish I thought it was that Vaughn fellow. Your mother said Mr. Malloy found him in the room with Miss Hardy's body."

"Yes, but Malloy thinks he was drugged," Sarah said.

"I'm afraid I respect Mr. Malloy's opinion too much to disagree, then. That only leaves the members of Wilbanks's family, though."

For a moment, Sarah was too surprised to speak. She'd never expected to hear her father say he respected Frank Malloy.

Before she could recover, her mother said, "I'm afraid you're right, Felix. If Catherine and Sarah are in any danger, it must be from Mr. Wilbanks's family. I've been thinking about that for the past hour, and I've decided the best thing to do is to take Catherine to visit Mr. Wilbanks."

"You think we should take them right into the lion's den?" her father asked incredulously.

"Yes. Don't you see? It's the only way, since we don't know who killed those two women and may never find out. To be completely safe, since we don't know who is responsible, we should make sure that both of his other children and their spouses are there so they will see and hear Sarah tell him that she will take care of Catherine when he is gone and she does not expect or even want him to leave the child anything at all."

"I thought you'd decided you wanted to keep some of Wilbanks's money away from Gilda."

"What a terrible joke," her mother said. "But of course Sarah doesn't want or need anything from him."

"He might leave Catherine money anyway, though," Sarah said.

"Then say you'll refuse it." Her mother turned to her father. "That's possible, isn't it?"

"To refuse an inheritance? Yes, it is. And I'm sure Wilbanks will see the wisdom of it, if the bequest would put the child in danger."

"So, we must notify Mr. Wilbanks at once that we want to arrange for Catherine to visit," her mother said. "Remember, this was actually Gilda's idea, although for exactly the opposite reason. She hinted that Catherine might be an imposter in some elaborate scheme to get some of the Wilbanks fortune. She wanted us to produce the child to prove her identity while Mr. Wilbanks is still alive, since he is the only one who could identify her. I would very much like to turn the tables on her."

Sarah was actually smiling by the time her

mother had finished her explanation. "Mother, that's brilliant!"

"My dear, you are a constant source of amazement to me," her father said. "I had no idea you had such a devious mind."

"Is that a compliment?" she asked.

Her father needed a moment to decide. "Yes, I believe it is."

"Then thank you." She turned to Sarah. "We need to contact Mr. Malloy, of course. He should accompany you."

"I should go, too," her father said.

"I would like to be there, as well," her mother said, "but think about it. There'll be Mr. Wilbanks, his children and their spouses, Sarah, Catherine, and Mr. Malloy. I think that's more than enough."

"But what if one of them truly is the killer?" her father said. "Sarah and Catherine will need protection."

"Can you and I protect them better than Mr. Malloy? Besides, if the killer is indeed present in that group, he won't dare act with so many witnesses. They'll be safer there than anywhere."

"Mother is right, Father. I know you want to protect us, but as soon as this meeting is over, we'll both be perfectly safe forever."

Her father frowned, but he said, "I'll see what Mr. Malloy suggests. How can we get in touch with him?"

In the end, Sarah wrote a note to Malloy

explaining their plan, while her father penned one to Wilbanks, requesting a meeting with him and his family the following afternoon at which they would present Catherine. They dispatched a servant to deliver the letters, then sent Sarah home in their carriage.

As the carriage rolled through the dark city streets, quiet now at this late hour, Sarah felt the tension easing from her body for the first time in many days. By tomorrow at this time, it would all be over and Catherine would be safe.

12

Sarah slept well that night and rose early, since she'd asked Malloy to come over this morning to discuss their plans. To pass the time, she decided to finish the cleaning Malloy had interrupted yesterday, and when she entered her office, she noticed the box he had brought with him from Emma Hardy's room still sitting on her desk. They'd both forgotten all about it.

She picked it up and carried it into the kitchen, thinking she'd go through it in case it contained something Malloy should know about. Then someone tapped on her back door.

"I'm sorry to bother you so early," Mrs. Ellsworth said, handing her a plate of cookies. "But I saw you leaving with Mr. Malloy yesterday, and I thought he might have given you some news."

"Not good news, I'm afraid. Coffee?"

"Oh, yes, thank you, but I can't stay long. Nelson and I are taking his young lady friend to a museum for the day."

"How exciting," Sarah said. Mrs. Ellsworth's son had been unlucky in love before, and everyone was glad to see him keeping company with a nice young woman. "This sounds serious."

"Well, her family is hoping and so am I, but they won't hear of the two of them going off without a chaperone, so I have to go with them. I'm afraid I'll find it too difficult to walk any distance, however, so they should have plenty of time alone," she added with a twinkle.

She took a seat at the table and gave the box a curious glance. "I hope the girls are all right."

"The girls are fine, I'm happy to say, but Catherine's mother is . . . Well, someone murdered her."

"Good heavens! How horrible! Do you have any idea who did it?"

"Not yet." Sarah told her what little she knew as she served her some coffee.

"Well, I don't suppose she'll have many people mourning her," Mrs. Ellsworth said.

"I know. That's so sad. I keep reminding myself she was Catherine's mother, though, and I try to think well of her for that."

"And Mr. Malloy is certain this actor fellow didn't kill her?"

"He's fairly sure. Vaughn drinks rather heavily, I understand, so it's possible he did it and just doesn't remember, but Malloy thinks he wouldn't have made up such a ridiculous story about the mysterious stranger with the drugged whiskey if it wasn't true."

"I can't even imagine how horrible this must be for you, Mrs. Brandt."

"The worst part was not knowing what to do, but my parents and I have come up with a plan we think will work." She explained it to Mrs. Ellsworth as they finished their coffee. "I'm waiting for Mr. Malloy so I can see if he agrees or has any other suggestions to make."

"It certainly sounds like an excellent idea, and if it works, well . . ." She glanced meaningfully at the box still sitting on the table. "Did I interrupt you in something important?"

"Oh, I almost forgot. Malloy found this box of papers in Emma Hardy's trunk. He was going to go through them later, but he left them here, so I thought I'd see if there was anything important in there."

"May I help?"

Sarah knew Mrs. Ellsworth must be dying of curiosity, although she doubted there would be little of interest. "I can't imagine Emma would mind if it helps catch her killer."

She lifted the lid and saw a collection of what appeared to be letters and bills and a few important-looking papers. She dumped them on the table. Mrs. Ellsworth pulled out two letters, and Sarah began sorting the other papers.

"This Emma didn't seem to have many friends,"

Mrs. Ellsworth said, holding up the letters. "Looks like both of these are from Anne Murphy."

"They're probably the replies from letters Emma sent. How did Miss Murphy know where to send them, though?"

"They're addressed to General Delivery in Pittsburgh and"—she checked the second one—"Philadelphia."

"I guess those were places they performed on their way back to the city. I know Philadelphia was their last stop. It would be easy enough to go to the post office and pick up her mail, I suppose. See if Miss Murphy told her anything interesting."

"I feel guilty, reading someone else's mail," she said, but Sarah noticed she didn't hesitate, pulling the first letter out of the flimsy envelope.

The rest of the papers were past due bills and contracts for Emma and Vaughn with the touring company. Sarah had given up finding anything important when she unfolded an official-looking paper and stared at it for a long moment, trying to make sense of it.

"This is interesting," Mrs. Ellsworth said, glancing up from her letter. "Miss Murphy tells her that she took Catherine to the Mission and she'll go get her when Emma arrives in the city." When Sarah didn't respond, Mrs. Ellsworth said, "What is it?"

"It's . . . it appears to be a certificate of marriage."

"Oh, my, did Mr. Wilbanks already marry her? But I thought that's why she ran away, because she didn't *want* to marry him."

"No, she didn't marry Mr. Wilbanks, and now I know why she ran away when he asked her. She was already married!"

"To whom? That Vaughn fellow?"

"Yes! They'd been married for . . . for over nine years!"

"Long before she met Mr. Wilbanks, I'm guessing."

"Yes! But if she was married to Vaughn, why did she take up with Wilbanks in the first place?"

Mrs. Ellsworth grinned. "Oh, Mrs. Brandt, I'm sure you can figure that out without too much effort."

"I suppose you're right. Even married women can be tempted by a rich man, and Emma seemed to be more susceptible than most. What I can't understand is why Vaughn put up with it. Did I tell you that he used to visit Emma at the house Mr. Wilbanks had provided for her?"

"Oh, my! I don't imagine Mr. Wilbanks had any idea."

Sarah shook her head. "What kind of a man not only allows his wife to be another man's mistress but actually visits her in the house the other man pays for? I guess that means he must have met Catherine, too. I wonder who she thought he was. And how on earth could a man stand being confronted with his wife's child by someone else?"

"I just hope he didn't take it out on Catherine . . . Oh!"

"What?" Sarah asked.

"I just remembered that time Catherine got so upset when she saw whiskey in your house."

"That's right! I'd completely forgotten. Malloy had made me drink some . . ."

"For medicinal purposes, of course."

"Of course," Sarah said with a little smile at the memory. "And then Catherine was so frightened of it. I wonder if Vaughn's drinking had anything to do with her reaction."

"Perhaps he gets violent when he drinks."

"No," Sarah said, remembering. "No, that's not it at all. Emma is the violent one."

"What do you mean?"

"Malloy told me she hits Vaughn."

"That's ridiculous. How could a woman hit a man? She'd be too frightened he would hit her back."

"Malloy tells me some wives beat their husbands the way some men beat their wives."

"I never heard of such a thing."

"Of course not. What man would admit to it? But if that's true, perhaps Catherine saw Vaughn drinking and Emma hitting him. I hate to think that, though."

"But it would certainly explain why she hates the sight of hard liquor."

"Yes, it would. Oh, Mrs. Ellsworth, what she must have seen and heard in that house. I just pray she doesn't remember it."

"Children are very resilient, you know. And she's done so well, living here with you and Maeve."

"If only I can keep her here with me."

"There's no reason why she shouldn't stay with you, especially now, with Miss Hardy dead."

Sarah smiled ruefully. "When you say it like that, it sounds like *I* had a good reason for killing that poor woman."

"She wasn't a 'poor woman,' so don't start feeling sorry for her. She abandoned her husband to become a rich man's mistress and bore him a child and then kept her husband on the side while her lover supported them both. Then she abandoned her lover and her child without a word. What kind of a woman does those things?"

"She bore him a child," Sarah whispered, having hardly heard the rest.

"What?"

"*She bore him a child.* But she was already married to Vaughn when she took up with Wilbanks. She said Wilbanks was Catherine's father, but how would she know? How *could* she know for certain?"

"Oh, my goodness, you're right. Maybe Mr. Wilbanks isn't Catherine's father at all!"

• • •

Sarah's note had said she'd be at home this morning. Frank hadn't wanted to come too early, and apparently, he'd timed his visit just right because Mrs. Ellsworth and her son were just leaving their house as he reached Sarah's front stoop. From the way they were dressed, they were going someplace special. At least Mrs. Ellsworth wouldn't be dropping in right in the middle of their conversation.

He exchanged greetings with them.

"Oh, Mr. Malloy, Mrs. Brandt has some interesting news for you," she said. "Something we discovered in that box of papers from Miss Hardy's room."

"I guess I have to get up pretty early to be ahead of you, Mrs. Ellsworth," he said in admiration.

"Oh, I was just worried about Catherine and ran over for a minute this morning to see how she was doing."

Frank pretended to believe this and bade them good morning. Sarah opened the door before he even knocked.

"Malloy," she said with the smile he loved. It made him forget he should be annoyed with her for making plans without him. "I was watching for you. Did Mrs. Ellsworth tell you what we discovered?"

"Oh, no, she just told me enough so I knew she'd helped." He slipped off his coat. "I didn't remember that box until I got home last night, and then I got your message, and I didn't think about anything else but that."

"I'm sorry we didn't consult you before we made the arrangements with Wilbanks."

She didn't look particularly sorry, and that should have annoyed him, too. If her plan hadn't been so good, it would have. "We'll talk about that in a minute. What did you and Mrs. Ellsworth find?"

She took his coat and hung it up. "You won't believe this. Remember you were wondering why Emma ran away when Wilbanks proposed to her?"

"You found out why?"

"Yes. She was already married to Vaughn."

He stopped in his tracks. "Of course! That makes perfect sense. When did they get married?"

"Almost nine years ago."

Dumbstruck, he followed her into the kitchen, where he found the marriage certificate lying on the table, waiting for him. He let her serve him some coffee while he considered this new information and all the ramifications. "What kind of a man lets his wife become another man's mistress?" he finally asked.

"What kind of a woman leaves her child for a year without giving her a thought?" she replied. "They were certainly a pair. And do you know what this means?"

He had no idea. "What do *you* think it means?"

"It means Catherine might not be Wilbanks's daughter at all."

"That would certainly make everything a lot simpler, wouldn't it?"

"At the very least, it raises doubt, which is one more reason for Wilbanks not to leave anything in his will to Catherine."

Frank sighed. "Maybe you should tell me how you came up with this plan to visit Wilbanks this afternoon."

"Of course. I hope you're not too upset that I came up with it without you. Well, *I* didn't come up with it. Mother did."

"Your *mother* did?"

"Yes. You should have seen Father's face."

"I can imagine."

"I don't think you can, but at any rate, Mother thought of it, and it makes perfect sense. If the killer is a member of Wilbanks's family who is concerned because he intends to leave part of his fortune to Catherine, then the best way to ensure her safety is to make sure Wilbanks decides not to."

"And your father agreed to this?"

"He said he would do whatever you advised. So what do you advise?"

Frank took a deep breath. "I've been thinking about this, and as much as I hate to admit it, it's a good idea."

Her eyes lit up the way they always did when she was going to do something reckless. "You really think so?"

"It's still dangerous," he said. "One of those people may have already killed two women."

"I know, and he wouldn't hesitate to kill again. But even if you knew for certain that one of them killed Anne and Emma, you'd never be able to arrest them."

She was right, of course. Rich people didn't go to prison. Rich people didn't even go to trial. Too many highly placed officials were willing to look the other way for the right price. "Which is the only reason I'm going to let you do this. If we can't stop the killer, we can at least take away any reason he might have to harm Catherine. Your mother was absolutely right about that."

She laid a hand on his arm, and he felt the warmth of it to his bones. "Thank you, Malloy."

"Don't thank me. I haven't done anything yet. Now how did you think this would work?"

She straightened in her chair and withdrew her hand. He missed it already. "We thought you and I should go with Catherine. We'll meet at my parents' house and take her over in their carriage. We thought that would be the safest way."

"Don't your parents want to go along, too?"

"Of course they do, but my mother pointed out how many people would be there—Mr. Wilbanks, Ozzie, Gilda, and Lynne and Michael Hicks.

286

Then you and I and Catherine. She's going to be overwhelmed as it is without adding two more to the crowd."

"And your father agreed to this?"

She shrugged. "He said he would do what you thought best."

"He did?"

"Yes."

That was interesting, but he'd try to figure it out later. "Then I think it's best that he not go along. He may think he'd be a help in an emergency, but I doubt it. We also need to tell Catherine not to eat or drink anything while we're there."

"Oh, Malloy!" The blood drained from her face. "Do you really think . . ."

"And we shouldn't either," he added. "One of those people could be a killer, someone who didn't think anything of murdering *two* women. He drugged Parnell Vaughn and strangled Emma Hardy. Do you know how long it takes to strangle someone? A long time, and you have to look right into their face while you're doing it."

For a second he thought he'd gone too far, but she stiffened her shoulders. "You're right, of course. We can't take any chances, and we won't be safe until we leave that house."

They spent a few minutes discussing when they would meet. Then Frank said, "I'd better get going then. I want to speak with Parnell Vaughn before we go to see Wilbanks."

"Should I go with you?"

"To Police Headquarters?" he asked with a grin.

She smiled back. "I guess not. Still, I'm very anxious to hear what he has to say."

"Don't get your hopes up, Sarah. He's lied about a lot of other things. He'll probably lie about this, too."

"Yes, and it's hard to tell what he might think was in his best interest to say. What does he have to gain or lose either way?"

"I don't know. Maybe he thinks Wilbanks will give him something for keeping his mouth shut. It's hard to tell what a drunk will do. I've got to ask him, though, because if he admits it, that will mean Catherine is out of danger completely."

Vaughn didn't look much better than the last time he'd seen him. The cells at Headquarters were filthy and dangerous, and Vaughn seemed much the worse for wear when the officer brought him to the interrogation room. His face was gray, and he had the shakes pretty badly, as Frank had expected.

When they were alone, Frank pulled a small bottle of whiskey out of his pocket and set it on the table. Vaughn reached for it like a drowning man, but Frank snatched it away.

"Not so fast. I need to ask you a few questions first."

"I already told you everything I know. I didn't kill Emma. I swear it." His eyes were leaking tears, but Frank couldn't tell if they were for Emma or because Frank wouldn't give him the bottle.

"Why didn't you tell me she was your wife?"

He wiped his mouth with the back of his hand. "What makes you say that?"

"I saw the marriage license. The two of you were together a long time."

Vaughn was staring at the bottle. "You said you had some questions."

"Were you married to Emma Hardy?"

He dashed at his watery eyes. "You know I was."

"Why did you keep it a secret?"

"We didn't."

Frank pretended he was getting up to leave.

"Wait! I . . . Emma used her maiden name because nobody wants to hire a married woman in the theater. People thought we were just lovers, so we let them think it."

"And did they think you were lovers when she took up with Wilbanks?"

"What does that mean?"

"It means why would a man let his wife become some other man's mistress?"

"I didn't know!"

"How could you not know?"

"We . . . we weren't living together then. We had a fight, and she left me."

"What did you fight about?"

"She . . . she thought I had another woman."

"Did you?"

"No! I never! Emma was jealous, though. She . . . Couldn't I have just a little sip? I can hardly think."

"In a minute. Why was Emma jealous?"

"I don't know. I never gave her any reason, but she always was. That time she got real mad and broke a bottle over my head. I had to go to the hospital, and she never came to see me or anything. When I got out, she'd moved into that boardinghouse she liked."

"Nell Dugan's?"

"Yeah, that's the one. She said she was going to divorce me. I knew she didn't have the money for that, so I figured I'd just wait her out. She'd left me before, but she always took me back."

"Only this time she got a better offer."

"She never had a man like that interested in her before. I mean you've always got the stage door Johnnies who hang around. The girls are pretty and some of them aren't any better than they have to be. Any fellow in an expensive suit with money to buy them dinner can have whatever he wants. Emma never had time for that kind, though, at least not until Wilbanks came along."

"And Wilbanks wasn't an ordinary Johnnie."

"No, he was rich, and he told Emma he could give her whatever she wanted."

"What did she want?"

"She wanted to be the star. She thought he'd finance a show for her. She wasn't going to spread her legs for a dinner, but for that . . . Well, she'd do anything for that."

"And why didn't he finance the show for her?"

"Because of the kid. She never expected that. We'd been married for three years by then, and nothing ever happened in all that time. She thought she couldn't have kids, and then a couple months with him—an old man like that!—and she's puking every morning."

"You saw this?"

"Well, not exactly. She was still living at the boardinghouse, but we'd see each other at the theater, and she told me things. I wanted her back, and I told her I did, but she says she's got to get rid of the kid first and then get Wilbanks to back the show for her. There'd be a part for me, she said. We'd be together again."

"But it didn't work out that way," Frank said, holding the bottle up for him to see.

Vaughn's eyes widened and he licked his lips. "He didn't want her to get rid of the kid. She never expected that either. Neither of us did. She tried everything, but he wouldn't budge. The best she could do was get him to promise he'd get her a show after the baby came."

"So he put her up in her own house. That must've been horrible for her."

"It was!" he said, obviously not noticing Frank's sarcastic tone. "She was miles away from the city with nothing to do. I'd go visit her when I could, but she hated it."

"You didn't hate it all that much, though, did you? She'd let you stay there for free and she'd give you money, too."

"Just a few dollars, from the household money, when I was between shows. It's not like he gave her anything for herself."

"And what did you think of the baby?"

"I didn't think anything of her. Anne took care of her. I hardly ever saw her. Please, just one sip."

Disgusted, Frank handed him the bottle and waited while he pulled the cork with trembling fingers and took a healthy swig. Vaughn set the bottle down carefully, bracing it with both hands while he waited for the liquor's warmth to seep into him. When he picked up the bottle again, Frank snatched it away.

"Hey!" He was halfway across the table when Frank backhanded him down into his chair again.

He cursed in frustration, rubbing his face and glaring balefully at his tormentor. "What was that for?"

"To remind you who's in charge. You can have the rest of it when you tell me everything I want to know."

"I've already told you everything!"

"What do you remember about last night?"

Judging from the tears that flooded his eyes, he remembered that Emma was dead. "I loved her so much."

"Then help me figure out who killed her. What do you remember about the man who came to your room last night?"

He squeezed his eyes shut and clamped both hands on his head, as if trying to keep it from flying off. He sat like that for a few moments. "I've been trying to remember, but everything's so fuzzy, like it was a dream."

"What did he look like?"

"A swell."

"How do you know that?"

"Nice suit. Well spoken. Good manners."

"His name?"

"I don't know. I don't think I heard it, or if I did, I've forgotten. He said he was there to talk to her about Wilbanks. He had a deal for her, he said. She was smiling."

"Did she know him?"

"I . . . Maybe. I don't know. Emma, she might've been smiling because of the deal. Money always made her happy."

"How did she hope to make a deal when she didn't have the child?"

"He didn't talk about the child. He said . . . I remember now. He said he'd give her money just to go away."

"Did she believe him?"

"I don't know. I just remember she was smiling. And he said we should celebrate, and he pulled out the bottle."

"And you were willing to celebrate anything with a drink, weren't you?"

Vaughn's eyes narrowed with hatred. "I took what he offered, yes."

"Did Emma?"

"She didn't like to drink. She took a sip or two, I think."

Maybe enough to make her easier to kill, Frank thought. "Then what happened?"

"She . . ." He frowned, squinting with the effort. "I remember, she wasn't smiling anymore. I tried to ask her what was wrong, but I couldn't make my mouth move. Then I fell asleep, and the next thing I remember is being here with you slapping me around."

Frank sighed and handed him the bottle. He took another swig, then glared at Frank again. "Now what?"

"Now you're free to go."

"What?"

"You heard me. They're holding your belongings at your hotel. You can go back there if you want. I don't care."

"You're not going to arrest me?"

"I did arrest you. Now I'm letting you go."

"What about Emma? What about the man who killed her?"

"If you remember his name, let me know. Otherwise, we'll probably never find him."

"Damn."

"Yeah, well, better finish the bottle before you leave. Otherwise, somebody will take it away from you."

As Frank left the dingy little room, he heard Vaughn say, "Emma," on a choking sob. He supposed he should be glad someone was mourning Catherine's mother.

Sarah had gone to her parents' house hours before the time she'd agreed to meet Malloy there. She wanted to spend time with Catherine and to prepare her for what was coming. She didn't want her to be frightened, but she wanted her to be prepared. Of course, when she told Catherine that Mr. Malloy would be going with them, nothing else mattered.

Her father didn't usually go to his office on Saturday anyway, so he'd been driving her mother to distraction all morning. Sarah had to inform him that Malloy felt he should not accompany them.

He took the news with good grace. "In his place, I'm sure I would feel I could adequately protect you and Catherine, but I can't help thinking having another man along whom he can trust would be an advantage."

"Father, you've already been a tremendous help to us in this whole matter. I'll always be grateful, but to be completely honest, your strength is more in using your influence and less in using your . . ."

"Strength?" he said helpfully when she couldn't think of anything diplomatic to say.

"Exactly."

"And you would be just one more person whose safety Mr. Malloy must consider," her mother said. "And one more loved one for me to worry about."

"Thank you, my dear, for putting me firmly in my place."

Her mother simply smiled serenely, confident her work was done.

At last Malloy arrived, and Sarah went to meet him the instant he entered the parlor.

"Vaughn?" she whispered.

"They were separated. He said there's no possibility."

"What's that?" her mother asked.

"Nothing important," Sarah said, fighting the wave of disappointment. "Mr. Malloy was just telling me Parnell Vaughn still doesn't remember who killed Emma."

Her parents greeted Malloy, who joined her on the sofa.

"Has Sarah explained to you why we'd like for you both to remain here?" he asked.

"Yes, she has," her father said. "But if you've changed your mind, I'm perfectly willing to assist you."

"Thank you, Mr. Decker, but I don't think that will be necessary. Your coachman will be with us, and I really don't expect any trouble while we're with Wilbanks. Even the most brazen killer wouldn't dare attack someone under his roof. And of course, after we've told the family why we came, there won't be any reason to harm Catherine anymore."

"When you explain it like that, I feel so much better," her mother said.

"I wish I did," her father said. "I won't feel better until you're all back here, safe and sound."

They sent for Catherine, and Maeve brought her in. She was a vision in a dress Sarah had never seen before, a delightful creation with enough ribbons, bows, and ruffles to delight any little girl's heart. Her brown hair had been brushed smooth and tied back with a pink ribbon. When she saw Malloy, she gave a squeal of delight and ran to him.

He caught her up into his lap and allowed her to hug and kiss him. "I'm so happy to see you!" she cried.

"I'm happy to see you, too. You look very pretty."

She smiled, lowering her head modestly but still watching Malloy out of the corner of her eye. "My dress is new."

"Mrs. Decker has been spoiling her," Maeve reported without a trace of disapproval.

"I like being spoiled," Catherine informed them, and in spite of the tension, they all laughed.

"Mama said we're going to visit some people," she told him.

"Yes, we are. What else did she tell you?"

"She said I'm not allowed to eat or drink anything while we're there, no matter who gives it to me, and if I do that, I can have ice cream later."

"Ice cream?" he said with just the proper amount of reverence. "I'd like to have some myself."

"Maybe if you don't eat or drink anything there, you can have some, too." She glanced around, as if waiting for someone to confirm or deny this theory. When no one spoke, she said, "But if not, I'll share mine with you." She smiled sweetly, and he tried to smile back, but couldn't quite do it. "Are you crying?" she asked.

"Of course not. I've just got something in my eye." He finally managed a smile.

"Come along, Catherine," Maeve said quickly. "Let's get your coat so you'll be ready to go."

Catherine scrambled down, and when she was gone, all four of the adults remaining had to wipe their eyes.

"I'll protect them with my life, Mr. Decker," Malloy said.

"Let's hope it doesn't come to that."

13

Although Sarah and Malloy tried to be cheerful, Catherine must have sensed their tension. She was silent during the carriage ride, snuggling tightly up to Sarah and holding her hand. At least a dozen times during the short ride Sarah wanted to jump out and carry Catherine back to the safety of her parents' house.

When they pulled up in front of the Wilbankses' house, Malloy stepped out first and scanned the street. Traffic was light in this neighborhood, and few people were on the street here on a chilly Saturday afternoon. The only vehicle in sight was a hansom cab near the corner. The driver was examining his horse's front leg, a common sight. City traffic took a toll on the animals.

Seeing no sign of danger, Malloy helped Sarah and Catherine alight.

The maid answered their knock instantly and took their coats. She stared so intently at Catherine that Sarah was sure she must know everything. Then she took them up to the parlor, and while she was announcing them, Malloy bent down and picked Catherine up. Sarah glanced at him in surprise, but his grim expression told her it was his way of protecting her from whatever was to come.

The tension hung like a fog in the room, engulfing them as they entered. An older man, thin to gauntness, sat by the fire with a blanket over his legs. He must be Mr. Wilbanks, and his hopeful expression almost broke Sarah's heart. If she had doubted at all, she now knew for sure he loved Catherine. She nodded at Michael and Lynne Hicks, who stood on either side of Mr. Wilbanks's chair. Michael looked solemn, and Lynne looked nervous. Gilda Wilbanks stood off to one side, her face a mask of hauteur. The man beside her must be her husband, Oswald. He seemed merely bewildered.

"She looks just like Alice," Lynne Hicks said in wonder. "That's our daughter," she added to Sarah.

"No, she doesn't," Gilda said.

Lynne glared back at her defiantly. "You didn't know Alice at this age."

"Catherine," Malloy said in that gentle voice he always used for her, "we're going to play a game. You like games, don't you?"

Catherine seemed uncertain, but she nodded.

"There's a lot of people in this room. I want you to tell me which ones you already know.

You can just point to them. Do you understand?"

She nodded again.

"All right," he said. "Which of these people do you know?"

She gave him an impish grin, carefully folded her small hand until just her forefinger was extended, and pointed it at him. Sarah thought her heart might burst.

He gave her an adoring smile. "Good! Who else?"

Catherine looked at Sarah and grinned again before pointing at her. Sarah rewarded her with a loving smile.

"Good girl. Now look carefully at the rest of these people. Do you know any of them?"

Obviously taking her responsibility seriously, she examined each of the other people in the room. Malloy, still holding her, helped by turning so she could see the others more easily. She frowned at Ozzie and Gilda, who returned her stare with frowns of their own, then at Lynne, who smiled tentatively. She furrowed her brow at Wilbanks, whose avid gaze had not left her since the instant they'd entered the room.

"Papa?" she whispered.

His face broke into a radiant smile. "I have something for you, little girl. Do you remember where to look?"

She nodded, then gave Malloy a questioning look. He said, "Go ahead," and set her down with the utmost care.

The distance between her and Wilbanks seemed great to Sarah. It must have seemed immense to Catherine, who also felt the focused attention of everyone in the room. Sarah took her hand and walked with her over to Wilbanks. He turned back the corner of the lap robe and shifted slightly in his chair.

Catherine smiled shyly, slipped her hand into the pocket of his suit coat, and pulled out a tin of peppermints.

"You remembered," he marveled, his voice husky with emotion.

Lynne Hicks made a strangled sound, and when Sarah looked at her, she said, "He used to bring them for Alice to find, too."

"Would you like one?" he asked Catherine.

"We'll save it for later," Sarah said.

"Are you satisfied, Mrs. Wilbanks?" Malloy asked Gilda.

"I'm not the one who needed to be satisfied," she said. "Father Wilbanks, are you sure this is the right child?"

"Gilda, really," her husband said.

"Of course I am," Wilbanks said, his ravaged face glowing.

"It's been a long time," Gilda reminded him. "And you've been ill."

"I'm ill, not senile," Wilbanks snapped. "I was afraid *she* wouldn't know *me*."

"Oh!" Catherine said, glancing back at Malloy.

"I almost forgot." She lifted her little hand and pointed at Wilbanks.

The tension in the room instantly evaporated. Even Michael Hicks chuckled. Lynne bent down and smiled at Catherine. "I'm very happy to meet you, Catherine. My name is Lynne, and I'm your . . . your aunt," she finally decided.

Gilda made an exasperated noise, but no one paid her any mind.

"Mr. Wilbanks," Sarah said, "we came today so I can assure you that Catherine is well loved. I intend to raise her as if she were my own daughter."

"I can see that, Mrs. Brandt," he said.

"I also want your family to know that we do not want or need any help or any part of your fortune, now or in the future."

"Boldly spoken, Mrs. Brandt," Michael Hicks said.

"And sincerely meant," she replied.

"I appreciate your sentiments, Mrs. Brandt," Wilbanks said, "but you cannot stop me from providing for my own child."

"I'm told that I can refuse a bequest, however, and that is what I intend to do if you insist on making one."

"Of course that's what she says now," Ozzie said.

Sarah gave him her most withering glare. "What I say *now* is to ask Mr. Wilbanks not to force me into such a situation. Sir, if you do not name Catherine in your will, then *no one* can be jealous of what she might receive."

"Thank you for your frankness, Mrs. Brandt," Wilbanks said. "Your father must be very proud to have a daughter like you."

Sarah wondered if that were true, but it didn't matter at the moment. "Are you saying you will grant my request?"

"How can I, in good conscience, refuse to keep my daughter safe?"

Relief surged through her, and Michael Hicks instinctively reached out to steady her. "Are you all right?"

"Yes, of course. *Now* I'm fine. Thank you, Mr. Wilbanks." Now Catherine was safe. No one had any reason to wish her harm again.

Wilbanks turned his attention back to Catherine and started asking her questions about herself. To Sarah's surprise, Lynne Hicks had her husband bring over a chair so she could join in the conversation. She seemed almost as taken with the child as Wilbanks. Sarah stood sentinel, half enjoying seeing Catherine interact with the only blood family she had left and half anxious lest anyone say something to distress her.

Sarah was vaguely aware of Malloy, who maintained his distance from the rest, ready in case anything untoward happened, but of course nothing did. Gilda, obviously unhappy with the outcome of this meeting, had wandered over to the front window and pretended to peer out at the street while Ozzie tried to coax her into a good humor. Hicks joined them, his voice soothing but too soft for Sarah to hear his actual words.

Sarah watched Wilbanks, savoring his joy at being reunited with his child, but she realized he was quickly tiring. "It's time for us to go now, Catherine. Would you like to give your papa a kiss?"

He leaned down, and she obediently gave him a peck on the cheek that made his eyes shine again. "Bring her back very soon," he said.

"I will," Sarah promised. "Thank you . . . for everything."

He nodded, apparently too emotional to speak.

She took Catherine's hand and headed for the door, where Malloy waited for them.

"Mr. Malloy," Michael Hicks said, "we were wondering if you could tell some details about Miss Hardy's death before you go."

Malloy frowned and met Sarah's gaze with a silent question. It was a reasonable request, but she certainly didn't want Catherine hearing anything about Emma Hardy's death. "Catherine and I will wait for you in the carriage."

"I won't be long," he promised.

The maid helped them into their coats and showed them out. Her parents' carriage sat at the curb where they had left it, the driver huddled in his coat high up on the seat.

"John, we're going to wait for Mr. Malloy. He'll be out in a few minutes," she called to him.

She had only a second to think it odd that he hadn't moved when the carriage door flew open. A dark figure sprang out and pressed a white cloth to her face. She tried to scream, tried to fight, but the sickly sweet scent engulfed her and everything went black.

Frank had no idea why Hicks wanted to hear about Emma's death again, but he was actually glad for the opportunity to speak to Ozzie, since he suspected Ozzie might have been the mysterious stranger who visited her the night she died. He gave them a brief account of finding her body, watching Ozzie's face closely. If he was indeed the killer, he was a cold one. He never even blinked.

"So it must have been her lover who killed her," he said.

"It seems that way," Frank said, happy to mislead him.

Hicks frowned but didn't remind Frank he'd voiced other theories in their previous conversation. Wilbanks started to cough, and his daughter rang for the maid. He'd kept Sarah waiting long enough.

"I'll keep you informed," he said, preparing to take his leave.

"Something's happening outside!" Gilda cried, turning Frank's blood to ice. She still stood gazing out the front window. Hicks and Ozzie hurried over to see, but Frank turned and ran, out into the hall and down the stairs. He threw open the front door and took in the scene in an instant. Sarah lay motionless on the sidewalk. The carriage stood where it had earlier, the door hanging open, empty. The driver sat slumped on his perch, dead or unconscious.

"Catherine!" he shouted, descending the front stoop in two bounds. She was nowhere in sight. *"Catherine!"*

One of the horses whickered nervously, but no other sound came in response.

He knelt down to Sarah and instantly smelled the sweet scent of chloroform. Thank God, he thought, gently rolling her over. At least they hadn't killed her. She groaned, already coming around. Relief surged through him but only for a moment. Where was Catherine?

Hicks ran out the front door and down the porch steps. "What's happened?"

"Someone's taken Catherine. They must've used chloroform on Mrs. Brandt and probably the driver, too. Check him, and call Police Headquarters and tell them to send as many men as they can."

His mind raced. Who would have done this? Where would they have gone? They would have needed a vehicle to take Catherine away. Even unconscious, she would've attracted attention. He remembered the hansom cab sitting at the corner when they arrived. It was gone now, but it had been headed west, so he ran in that direction. Maybe he could catch sight of it. When he reached the end of the street, he stopped, gasping for breath, his heart pounding in terror, and looked wildly in every direction, hoping to catch a glimpse of something. To his surprise he saw the cab not half a block away, stopped dead. He ran to it, but even before he got there, he knew. He understood it completely. They'd planned it all so very carefully. They'd had another vehicle waiting there, a vehicle no one could identify, and they'd taken Catherine away in it, and he'd never see her again.

Sarah fought her way back to consciousness, her head pounding, her eyes and nose stinging as she tried to concentrate on the voices. Someone was shouting, giving orders. Malloy? Why did he sound so angry?

"Mrs. Brandt, can you hear me?" a woman asked. "I think she's coming around."

"Sarah?" Malloy said. "Can you hear me?"

She could hear him just fine, but she couldn't answer him. She could barely manage to open her eyes a slit to find him leaning over her. Where was she? What was happening? Something terrible, she thought. Something she didn't want to remember. "Catherine?"

"They took her," he said.

Pain convulsed her heart, and she gasped in agony.

"Did you see them? Do you know who they were?" he asked.

She searched her memory, mining it for anything, anything at all. She could feel the warmth of Catherine's small hand in hers as they walked down the front steps and then . . . Nothing. She managed to whisper, "No."

Other voices were arguing, but she couldn't make sense of them. She wanted Malloy to tell her everything would be all right. She wanted him to say he'd find Catherine. But he couldn't make a promise like that, she knew. The city was large and full of evil people, and it could swallow up a small child without a trace. Tears scalded her stinging eyes.

How could she bear such pain?

"We've sent for your parents," the woman said and Sarah realized Malloy was gone. Of course he was. He'd be organizing a search and doing whatever one did when a child had been taken. But where would he start? How could he find her when they had no idea who had done it or where they might have gone? Or, she thought with another spasm of agony, how long they would keep her alive.

She couldn't bear pain like that. No one could. She would have to die herself.

She lay there while the voices around her rose and fell. Sometimes she caught a word or a phrase, but nothing made much sense. Every so often she tried opening her eyes for a few moments before the pounding in her head forced her to close them again. There was something they could do. There had to be. If she could just think . . .

Someone new was shouting now, someone who sounded like her father. He was berating someone for being reckless and foolish.

A soft hand caressed her cheek. "Sarah, are you all right?"

She opened her eyes again, and this time she saw her mother's lovely face. "They took her."

"I know, my darling." Her red-rimmed eyes flooded with tears. "We'll find her. Mr. Malloy will find her."

Sarah clung to her promise, even though she knew it for a lie. A memory niggled at her. The driver. "John?"

"He's fine," Maeve said, materializing behind her mother. Her eyes were red rimmed, too. "They have him down in the servants' hall, and they're looking after him. They used some drug on you both that put you to sleep."

"Chloroform." Sarah could still smell it. "Help me sit up."

She realized she was on a sofa in Mr. Wilbanks's parlor. Lynne Hicks hovered nearby, wringing her hands. Hicks, Malloy, and her father huddled on the other side of the room, deep in conversation. Ozzie and Gilda Wilbanks sat on the opposite side of the room, suitably solemn but offering no assistance.

To her surprise, Gino Donatelli came in and glanced around. Seeing her, he strode over. "Mrs. Brandt, how are you feeling?"

"What's going on? Have they found Catherine?"

"Not yet. Mr. Malloy has got everybody in the city looking, though. He told your father to telephone the mayor and the chief of police and everybody else he could think of. We already found the cabbie."

"What cabbie?"

"Mr. Malloy said there was a cab at the end of the street when you got here. We think they were hiding in it, waiting until you came out so they could take the little girl. We found the cabbie they stole it from."

Hope burned like a tiny ember. "Then you know they took her in a cab?"

"Only until they got around the corner and out of sight. They must've had another wagon or carriage or something. We found the cab, but they were long gone."

Who could have done this? She'd told them she didn't want their money. She'd been so certain

Catherine was safe. Dear heaven, how would they ever find her?

"There must be something I can do," her father said.

"We're already scouring the city," Malloy said.

"How do they even know where to look?" Sarah asked Gino.

His handsome face tightened, and he shook his head. No one knew where to look. No one knew anything at all.

Except that she knew no one in the Wilbanks family had done it. They'd all been right here. If only her head weren't pounding so, maybe she could figure it out.

"I could offer a reward," her father said.

"David would match it," Michael Hicks said.

"Where's Mr. Wilbanks?" Sarah asked, able to see he wasn't in the room now that she was sitting up.

"We had to put him to bed," Lynne said. "He couldn't stop coughing. He's beside himself, as you can imagine."

Sarah didn't have to imagine. She felt exactly as he did. She rubbed her head, trying to clear the fog of the chloroform. How could you find one small child in New York City? The police were looking, but Catherine could be anywhere. You'd have to tell everyone in the city to look for her. But how could you tell everyone?

"The newspapers," she said.

"What, dear?" her mother asked. She sat beside her now, holding her hand.

"The newspapers could help. Father!"

Startled, her father glanced over at her. "Sarah, are you all right?"

"Father, you must tell the newspapers."

"Tell them what?" All the men were looking at her now.

"Tell them about Catherine. Tell them she's been kidnapped, and you're offering a reward. We need everyone in the city looking for her."

"She's right," Malloy said. "The newspapers will be happy to print the story that David Wilbanks's daughter has been kidnapped."

"No," her father said. "The papers would have a field day with the scandal of his bastard child, and they'd miss the rest of the story. We'll tell them my granddaughter has been kidnapped. That will be interesting enough."

"Oh, Felix, that's a wonderful idea," her mother said.

"What time is it?" Sarah asked. "They might be able to get out an extra edition this evening."

"Some of them will, at any rate," Malloy said.

"But how can we get them the news?" her father asked.

"Down at Police Headquarters," Gino said. "There's always reporters from every paper in those flats across the street, just waiting for something to happen. I can take you down there and roust them out for you, Mr. Decker. They'll be thrilled to get a story like this."

"Malloy, what do you think?" her father asked.

Malloy nodded.

"My carriage is outside," her father said, "but I don't have anyone to drive it."

"It's faster if we take the El," Gino said.

"I've never ridden on the El," her father said, and then they were gone. Another time, she might have smiled at the image of her father squeezing onto one of the crowded cars of the elevated train.

Sarah rubbed her head again, willing away the lingering effects of the chloroform. She had to think. She had to help. They had to find Catherine.

Frank looked around the room, studying the faces, trying to read them. He had to concentrate. He had to stop thinking about Catherine. Every instinct told him to run out into the street and go after her, but he couldn't search the city by himself. Dozens of other cops were doing that already, but they had no chance at all of finding her unless he could help them. He must forget his own pain and do what he would do if he'd been called into the case as a total stranger.

How could this have happened? He turned to Hicks. "Who knew we were bringing Catherine here today?"

"I . . . I don't know. All of us, of course."

His wife immediately saw the purpose of his question. "The servants knew we were expecting guests, but not who they were."

"The maid who let us in knew who Catherine was," Sarah said. "I could tell by the way she stared."

"That's impossible," Lynne Hicks said.

"Servants know everything," Sarah's mother said.

"But they wouldn't have any reason to take Catherine," Frank said. "Who else?"

"I didn't tell anyone," Lynne said. "Not even our children."

"Nor did I," Hicks said.

Malloy looked over to where Ozzie and Gilda sat.

"Why would we have told anyone?" Ozzie said. "We hardly want our friends to know about Father's little bastard."

Frank wanted to punch the outrage right off his face, but that could wait until later. "Mrs. Wilbanks?"

"Whom would I have told? Ozzie is right, we have no reason to want anyone to know about the child."

All of which probably meant that the culprit—and most likely the killer they'd been searching for—was in this room. All he had to do was figure out which one it was. "Mr. Hicks, you were

315

the one who kept me here when Mrs. Brandt was ready to leave." And he had let Sarah and Catherine go out alone, something for which he would never forgive himself.

Michael Hicks frowned. "I simply asked you to tell us more about Miss Hardy's death."

"You already knew about her death."

The unspoken accusation shocked Hicks, but before he could respond, Gilda Wilbanks rose and moved with a stately grace to her brother-in-law's defense. "How dare you accuse him of having something to do with this."

"Gilda, really," her husband said. "I don't think—"

"Nonsense! That's exactly what he's doing. He wants someone to blame for his own failure, so he's chosen poor Michael. I won't tolerate it another moment."

"You don't really have a choice, Mrs. Wilbanks," Frank said. "Hicks, why did you stop me?"

He hesitated a second, then turned to Gilda. "Because Gilda asked me to."

"I did no such thing! I couldn't wait for him to leave."

But Hicks was nodding slowly as he remembered. "We were standing by the window, and she said she wanted to know what had happened to the actress. That's what she called Miss Hardy, *the actress*."

"Michael, how could you?" Gilda asked, her lovely cheeks flushing scarlet.

Ozzie had finally bestirred himself, and he took his place by his wife's side. "Michael, I must ask you not to upset Gilda."

Hicks ignored him. "She seemed quite concerned about your progress in finding Miss Hardy's killer."

"I can't believe you'd lie about me. Ozzie, make him stop!"

Ozzie obviously had no idea how to go about such a thing. "Really, Michael," he said, gesturing helplessly.

Frank stared at Gilda Wilbanks, at her beautiful face and her perfect hair and her expensive clothes, and wondered if it was even possible.

"It had to be a woman," Sarah said, struggling to stand. Her mother helped her, and Maeve hurried to her other side. "Remember? At the boarding-house. We thought it was Emma."

They had. They'd thought Anne Murphy would only have invited a female to her room at the boardinghouse, and that woman had to be Emma. But when a man killed Emma, they'd changed their minds. Could a woman have killed Anne and a man killed Emma?

"How did you manage to stab Anne Murphy without getting blood on you, Mrs. Wilbanks?" Frank asked.

Her eyes widened, then narrowed with loathing.

"I'm the one who told you what was happening out there." She gestured to the window, where she'd been standing when Catherine had been taken.

Frank nodded slowly. "Yes, but too late for me to stop them. You waited until they'd gotten away before you said anything, didn't you?"

"Gilda," Lynne Hicks said, and the word held wonder and disgust.

"Ozzie, are you going to allow this lout to speak to me like that?" Gilda asked.

Ozzie looked confused, but he said, "Mr. Malloy, your behavior is appalling. You can't speak to a lady like that."

"I'm not speaking to a lady, and we know she had help, Wilbanks. A man killed Emma Hardy, and it wasn't Emma's lover."

"But you said it was," Ozzie said, even more confused. "You said her lover had killed her."

"Oh, Ozzie!" Gilda cried, clutching her hands against her heart the way the heroine in a play would do. "You shouldn't have! I know you hated her, but *murder?*"

Ozzie looked at her as if she'd lost her mind, then glanced at the rest of them, probably searching for a friend. He found none.

"Was Emma happy to see you, Mr. Wilbanks?" Frank asked, willing to play his part in Gilda's little drama. "Maybe not at first, but I'll bet you offered her money to go away and not bother your father anymore. She didn't really want to marry him anyway."

"I didn't . . . I never saw her," he said.

"What did you put in the whiskey? Laudanum, maybe, or something else. A druggist will come forward to tell us what you bought when he reads about you in the newspapers. He'll want to see his name mentioned, too. It will be good for business."

Ozzie's eyes were wild. "I never bought any drugs. I'd never do that. Lynne, tell them."

"I guess you were disappointed when Emma wouldn't drink the whiskey, though," Frank said, taking a step toward him and watching him recoil in terror. "It would've been so much easier if she was unconscious, but you still had to kill her, didn't you? Gilda told you that you did, and you didn't dare leave her alive. How else were you going to make sure she didn't marry your father?"

Ozzie shook his head frantically. "No, I didn't do any of that!"

"Yes, you did, because you'd do anything for your wife, and that's what she wanted. She didn't want to share your father's money with Emma and her child, and neither did you."

"No, I didn't. I mean, I didn't want him to marry her, but I didn't *kill* her. I couldn't do that to anyone. Lynne, tell him!"

"He's right," Lynne Hicks said.

Frank looked at her, expecting outrage and seeing only disappointment.

She sighed. "I know you think I'm just defending him because he's my brother, but that's not true. I'm telling you he didn't kill that woman because he's too much of a coward to kill anyone. I told you that before, and you didn't believe me, but now you can see for yourself. He's not the one she sent to kill Emma Hardy."

"No, he's not," Sarah said. "She sent Terrance Udall."

Hicks and his wife gasped, and Gilda pretended to.

"Terrance knows nothing about this," Gilda said.

"He knows everything about this," Mrs. Decker said helpfully. "Don't you remember? He was here when we visited with you."

Gilda sent her a murderous glare, which lasted only until Frank grabbed her arm in a bruising grip. "Where is he? Where has he taken her?"

Most women of her class would have been terrified of him, but she simply lifted her chin and glared. "Take your hands off me!"

"Let her go!" Ozzie shrieked.

Frank shook her instead, shocking the arrogance out of her. "Tell me or I'll beat it out of you."

"I'll help you," Sarah said.

That made Gilda smile. "Go ahead and try. I'll tell you nothing."

Lynne Hicks made an impatient sound. "As much as I'd like to see you beat her, I know where he lives. I always wondered why he'd moved out of his parents' home and taken a flat, and now I understand. It's so you'd have a place to meet him, isn't it, Gilda?"

"I don't know what you're talking about."

Frank shoved her away from him, afraid he might snap her neck if he held on to her another moment. "Where does he live?"

Lynne gave him the address.

"He might not be there," Hicks said. "I'll go with you, and if he's not there, we can go to his family. They might know something."

Frank could only nod, grateful for his help. He went to Sarah. Her eyes were clear now, and in spite of her terror, he saw the hope she had in him. "I'll find her."

She could only nod. They both knew he might not find her alive.

"Mr. Malloy, I'll take Sarah back to our house to wait for you," Mrs. Decker said.

"And I'll wait here with Father," Lynne Hicks told her husband. "We don't want to leave him here unprotected," she added with a meaningful glance at Gilda, who simply turned her back.

Ozzie tried to comfort her, but she shook him off and stalked back to the window.

Fear and rage welled in Frank as he left the room with Hicks in his wake. He wanted nothing more than to run all the way to Udall's flat, but Hicks stopped him when they reached the front door.

"I didn't want to say anything in front of the ladies, but I don't think we'll find him at his flat."

"I know," Frank said. "But we've got to start somewhere."

"He couldn't have done this alone."

"No, he probably hired someone. That's easy enough to do if you know the right people. Do you have any idea who it could have been?"

"Yes, I do."

Frank gaped, but only for an instant. "Who?"

"He's a client of mine. He, well, as soon as Mrs. Brandt said Terrance's name, I remembered how friendly he'd been with Klink. And if I wanted to hire some kidnappers, I'd go to him myself."

Frank decided not to tell Hicks his opinion of attorneys who did business with people like this Klink. "Then take me to him."

Frank had kept a half-dozen officers with him in case he needed help. He sent two of them to Terrance Udall's flat, just in case. He and Hicks took two more and headed downtown to visit the mysterious Mr. Klink.

14

"Mrs. Hicks, would you ring for the maid? I'd like to see if our coachman is recovered enough to take us home," Sarah's mother asked.

Sarah couldn't seem to tear her gaze from Gilda Wilbanks. She stood ramrod straight with her back to them, feigning interest in something out in the street. She'd been standing like that the whole time Wilbanks had been visiting with Catherine. Had she somehow signaled the kidnappers? Of course she had. She'd planned everything.

"Shouldn't someone tell Mr. Decker about this Udall character?" Maeve asked.

"Yes," Sarah said, tearing her attention away from Gilda. "The newspapers need to say we're searching for him as well."

"That's ridiculous!" Gilda said. "You'll ruin him with your innuendos!"

"Good," Lynne Hicks said. "Should I send one of the servants?"

"I'll go," Maeve said. "I need to do something, and a servant might not be able to get to him."

"Oh, Maeve." Sarah reached out and embraced her, hugging her fiercely. "Be careful."

"We'll find her, Mrs. Brandt," she said, but it sounded more like a prayer than a promise.

"It's early, but I think we're most likely to find Klink at his saloon," Hicks said as they hurried down Avenue B in the heart of the German neighborhood known as *Kleindeutschland*. "As far as I know officially, you understand, Klink is a respectable businessman, but one hears rumors."

"I don't come to this part of the city much," Frank said, "which means there's not a lot of violence here."

"That's because men like Klink keep it out."

Even though the winter sun hadn't set yet, the bar was already crowded with workingmen enjoying a beer after their half day of work. They wouldn't be drunk enough to be rowdy for a while, though, and they showed only the usual interest in the well-dressed attorney and his companion that strangers would elicit in any neighborhood bar. Frank had left the two uniformed patrolmen out in the street. No sense alarming anyone unnecessarily.

Hicks went straight to the bartender and asked for Klink. The bartender, a portly man in a stained apron, looked Frank over with a disapproving frown, then disappeared into the back. When he returned, he led them down a short hallway and into a cramped office, where a wily German fellow sat behind a cluttered desk. He didn't stand up.

"Hicks, what are you doing here, and why have you brought a cop to my saloon?"

Hicks glanced at Frank in surprise. "How did you—"

"They always know," Frank said. "I'm not here to cause you any trouble, Klink. We need your help."

"I don't help the police."

"Not the police," Hicks said. "My family. My . . . niece has been kidnapped."

"She's four years old," Frank said.

This seemed to disturb Klink, but he said, "I don't know anything about this."

"Terrance Udall came to you for help," Hicks said. "I don't know what fairy tale he told you, but it was a lie."

Klink smiled grimly. "If you don't know what he told me, how do you know it was a lie?"

"Did he tell you he was going to murder the child?" Frank asked, glad to see Klink's shock. "Because he is. She's all that stands between him and inheriting a fortune." It wasn't quite true, but near enough, and it had the desired effect.

"Hicks, is this true?"

"He plans to kill her, yes," Hicks said. "He already killed her mother."

"What do you know about it and where can we find Udall?" Frank asked.

Klink rose and pushed past them to open the door. He hollered for Willy, and the bartender came running. Klink whispered something to him, and the man hurried off. Klink closed the door.

"He came to me," he said, going back to his seat behind the desk. "Udall. He said you had a client who needed help. A woman. Her husband had thrown her out and taken her child. He was going to help her get the girl back. No one would be hurt, he said. I don't kill children, Mr. Hicks. You did not need to bring the police."

"Mr. Malloy is here as a friend of the family and because he can call upon the resources of the police department to find Catherine."

They stared at each other for long moments, mistrustful and suspicious, waiting for whatever Klink was waiting for. Frank needed every ounce of his limited self-control to keep from diving across that desk and choking the information he needed out of Klink. The only thing stopping him was the certainty that Klink did not yet have that information.

Finally, someone tapped on the office door, and Klink said, "Come."

The door opened to reveal a nondescript little man with a ferret face wearing workingman's clothes. He hesitated when he saw the two strangers glaring at him.

"Come in, Erich, and close the door," Klink said.

He did, never taking his eyes off Frank.

"Tell them what you did today," Klink said.

"This one's a copper," he protested.

"I'm not interested in you," Frank said, although the thought that he might have put his hands on Sarah made him want to tear him limb from limb.

He must have sensed that urge because he swallowed nervously and looked questioningly at Klink.

"They say Udall is going to kill the little girl," Klink said.

"He never said nothing like that," the man protested.

"Of course he didn't," Klink said. "Tell them what happened."

"He said he needed to snatch this little girl."

"Who said it?" Frank said.

"Udall. That's what he said his name was."

"Go on."

"He said he was taking her back to her mother. Nobody got hurt. We didn't hurt anybody. He said we shouldn't."

"You stole a cab?" Frank said.

"We used chloroform on the cabbie. Then we left it. It was just around the corner from where we took the little girl."

"I know. Then what?"

"We knocked out the driver, then the woman when she came out. He thought there might be a man, too, but there wasn't. That's why he needed three of us, he said." Frank winced at the memory.

If he'd been with them . . . "He said to use it on the kid, too, in case she cried or something."

"How did you get away?"

"He'd rented a carriage."

"Where did you go?"

"We dropped him at a hotel with the kid. He said the mother was waiting for him there. Then we took the carriage back to where he rented it. That's all I know. Nobody got hurt, I swear it."

"What hotel?"

He told them. The Belvue. A dump near the East River, the perfect place to dispose of a body. He'd wait until dark. They probably had only minutes now until the sun slipped away completely.

"Thank you, Mr. Klink," Hicks was saying as Frank threw open the office door and raced out to where the two patrolmen waited in the street. He pointed at one. "You, telephone the local station and have them send as many men as they can to meet me at the Hotel Belvue. If they see a man with a child, they're to hold him. You"—he pointed at the other one—"come with me."

They fairly ran through the crowded streets, dodging pedestrians and darting through the crush of horses and wagons at every intersection. With every step, the sun seemed to sink lower, the city to grow darker, dark enough to hide a man dropping a small bundle into the river. He hadn't prayed since the night Kathleen died. When God had taken his wife, he'd turned his back on all that, but he prayed now, silently and violently, begging for Catherine's young life. It hadn't worked before, but maybe this time . . .

He thought Hicks might be somewhere behind him, but he didn't need him anymore. He knew what to do now.

If only he wasn't too late.

The gaslights cast an eerie glow in front of the Hotel Belvue. An enormously fat officer strolled up just as they reached the front door.

"You Malloy?" he asked.

"Yes, wait here. If you see a man with a child—"

"I know, I know."

Frank just hoped this fellow wouldn't have to chase anyone. He strode inside the dimly lit lobby with the other patrolman at his heels. The desk clerk jumped to his feet, obviously alarmed by the sight of the uniform and perhaps also by the sight of Frank's expression.

"I don't want no trouble!" Hotel clerks never wanted any trouble.

"Do you have a guest with a child? A man. His name's Udall, but he might be using another one."

His eyes widened with alarm. "We don't allow that kind of thing here. We allow women but not children."

Frank grabbed a fistful of his shirtfront and dragged him halfway over the counter. "What room is he in?"

"Two-twelve," he croaked.

Frank shoved him away and started for the stairs, but the clerk said, "He ain't up there, though."

"Where is he?"

"How should I know? He left a few minutes ago."

"With the child?"

"I guess."

"What do you mean, you guess?"

"He had a bundle, like she was wrapped in a blanket. It's cold out, you know?"

Dear God. He didn't let himself think what that might mean.

Frank burst out the front door to find three more patrolmen had joined the fat one. "Follow me. He's probably heading for the river. When we get there, spread out and holler if you see anything."

They raced through the shadowy streets that pointed straight to where the sunlight had disappeared behind the horizon. The stench of the river grew stronger as the chill wind carried it to them. They reached the street where the last row of warehouses squatted at the edge of the island. The men fanned out, searching the shadows for a darker shadow. A few ships lay docked farther down, but here the berths were empty. Frank scanned the skyline, willing his eyes to see in the dark, cursing Terrance Udall and praying for Catherine with alternating breaths.

"Here!" a voice called off to his left. He ran toward it. They all did.

Frank saw him then, a faintly darker silhouette standing at the edge of nothingness. His arms were empty, and Frank's heart lurched in his chest. He was too late.

"Udall!" he called.

The silhouette turned. "Who's there?"

"Malloy. Where is she?" He ran now, closing the distance between them as quickly as he could. Maybe he wasn't too late. If he'd just dropped her in, there was a chance. He could jump in the water and maybe . . .

"She's here," he said as Frank reached him, grabbing him by the lapels, ready to throw him in after her.

"Where did you drop her? Where is she?" He was already peering over the side, trying to see something, anything, in the inky blackness.

"She's here," he said again, his voice breaking as if he were weeping.

"She's *here*," one of the cops said. He'd knelt down.

That's when Frank saw it, the bundle lying at their feet. The bundle Udall had carried out of the hotel. The bundle that wasn't moving.

"What have you done to her?" Frank shouted.

"Nothing, I swear!"

The cop had unwrapped her and another struck a match. They all stared down at her sweet face, so pale and still in the flickering light.

"He's killed her," one of the cops said, and

Frank drew back his fist to smash in Udall's face, but he started screaming.

"No, no! She's just sleeping, I swear. Look at her!"

Frank pushed him away and knelt down. More matches flared as the first went out.

"She's warm," the cop who'd unwrapped her said.

Frank laid his hand on her chest and thought he detected the slightest rise and fall. "Let's get her back to the hotel," he said and lifted her small body into his arms.

Sarah's father had brought home copies of all the newspapers he'd been able to find that carried the story of Catherine's kidnapping. The single sheet "Extra" editions had been produced by the smaller newspapers, which thrived on sensation. The hastily written stories varied in accuracy, but they all contained the important information: Terrance Udall had kidnapped a four-year-old girl whose life was in danger. A two-thousand-dollar reward was offered for information leading to her safe recovery.

"That Italian fellow suggested the 'safe recovery' part," her father explained. "Very intelligent young man."

"Gino is handsome, too, isn't he, Maeve?" her mother said.

Maeve very wisely shrugged and made no comment, and Sarah smiled in spite of herself.

"How did you figure out that this Udall was involved?" her father asked.

"Mr. Malloy did it," her mother said. "I must confess, it was amazing to watch him. I wish you could have seen it. First he accused Mr. Hicks."

"Hicks? What would he have to gain?"

"I think it must have been a ploy just to throw the others off." Her mother went on, enthusiastically describing the scene and her amazement at how Malloy had finally arrived at the correct conclusion.

"I'm sure he never thought for a moment that Ozzie had really killed Miss Hardy, but he even had me believing he did," she said.

"And Gilda was actually encouraging him to," Sarah added, remembering. "She would have let her own husband be arrested for a murder her lover committed."

"But it was Mrs. Brandt who figured out that Gilda was the one who'd killed Anne Murphy," Maeve said.

"Really?" Her father's admiration warmed her for the few seconds before the truth of their situation overwhelmed her again.

"Sarah, I wish you'd drink some sherry or at least some tea," her mother said, easily reading her thoughts. "You haven't had a bite to eat all day."

The thought of food revolted her, and Sarah wasn't sure she'd ever eat again if she had to live in a world without Catherine. "Maybe some tea," she said to please her mother, although she doubted she'd be able to swallow any.

Her mother got up to ring for the maid when her father said, "Was that the doorbell?"

No one wondered who could be calling at this hour. They ran out into the hallway. Sarah reached the stairs first and leaned over the railing just as the maid opened the door to admit Malloy. He carried something but she couldn't make out what it was.

She cried out and he looked up. For one second she was so very afraid . . .

Then he smiled. "She's all right."

Sarah flew down the stairs, Maeve and her parents close behind her.

"Catherine, wake up," Malloy said, shaking the bundle in his arms. "Your mama's here."

"Mama?" she said, her eyes fluttering open.

"Yes, my darling, I'm here!" Sarah snatched the child from him, joy flooding her as she enfolded her in her arms. "Are you all right? Are you hurt?"

"She's fine," Malloy said. "She slept through most of it."

"I'm hungry," Catherine said, making everyone laugh with relief.

"We'll get you something to eat right away,"

her mother said through her tears. "You can have anything you want."

"Why is everybody crying?" Catherine asked.

"Because we're so happy to see you," Maeve said, lovingly smoothing Catherine's ratty hair. Her beautiful dress was crushed and bedraggled, some of the bows missing and others untied.

"Where did you find her? What had he done with her?" Sarah asked Malloy, who stood back a bit from the group gathered around her. Even the maid was weeping, Sarah noticed.

"It doesn't matter now," he said. "We can talk about it later. I have to go down to Headquarters and question him."

"Can't it wait until morning?" Sarah asked, wanting to share her happiness with him.

"The sooner I can talk to him, the less time he'll have to make up some story to protect Gilda. I would've done it right away, but I wanted to bring Catherine to you first."

Tears flooded Sarah's eyes, and she reached out to him. "Thank you."

He took her hand for just an instant. "I have to go."

"You'll come tomorrow and tell us everything, won't you?"

"Yes."

"We should telephone Mr. Wilbanks," her mother said. "The poor man will want to know immediately."

"Michael Hicks went to tell him," Malloy said. He reached up and touched Catherine's cheek. "Good night, little girl."

She smiled as if she understood he'd saved her.

Malloy watched Sarah carry Catherine up the stairs, with Mrs. Decker and Maeve attending her, until they were out of sight. Mr. Decker had stayed behind, and Frank braced himself for the tirade he knew was coming.

"I'm afraid I owe you an apology, Mr. Malloy."

Frank blinked, certain he'd heard wrong. "What?"

"I was hasty in my criticism of you earlier today, and I was upset, of course, although that's no excuse."

"You were right to call me reckless." Frank had called himself far worse this evening. "I should never have allowed Catherine to go to that house."

"We're all to blame for that. We'd made those plans without consulting you, and we thought it was the best way to ensure her safety."

"In any case, I should never have let them leave the house alone."

"And what if you'd been with them and hadn't been able to protect them? I berated you for not allowing me to go with them, but since then, I've had second thoughts. If I'd been there and Catherine had been kidnapped anyway . . . Well, that's what I've been considering all evening. Which would be worse, not being there at all or failing to save her?"

"I don't know."

"And now you don't have to wonder anymore. Try not to dwell on what you might have done differently. You cannot change the past, and it only spoils the future."

Frank thought of the painful regrets Felix Decker must carry and knew his wisdom had been born out of a pain even greater than the one Frank had felt today. "Thank you, sir."

"I'm afraid there will be quite a fuss from all the newspaper stories, and all for nothing."

"If I hadn't been lucky, we would've needed their help." Frank would never admit he'd sent Decker to the newspapers just to keep him occupied and away from his investigation.

"Tell me, do I owe a reward to someone?"

Frank thought of Klink and the ferret-faced man. "Somebody might think so. You can decide when I tell you the story tomorrow. I really must go now."

"Of course."

Frank stepped out into the wintry night, already thinking about the task ahead. He'd had the luxury of not worrying about Catherine ever since she'd woken up in his arms on the way back from the riverfront and asked for her mother. Since then, he'd been trying to figure out how to make

Terrance Udall and Gilda Wilbanks pay for their crimes.

Unfortunately, he hadn't come up with a single thing.

Police Headquarters was a madhouse, with mobs of people clamoring to give information about the kidnapped child so they could collect the generous reward. They didn't want to believe the child had been found and the culprit arrested. Some, he saw, had actually brought children with them, probably hoping to fool someone into believing they'd found the missing girl themselves.

"Malloy, you're going to be sorry you started this!" the harried desk sergeant called as Frank hurried through the jammed lobby. He pretended not to hear.

When Frank walked into the interrogation room downstairs, Terrance Udall looked like he'd been on a three-day bender. He'd been pretty drunk when they'd found him at the riverfront, but that didn't account for his swollen eyes and splotchy face. He'd been crying like a baby, according to the officer guarding him.

"Is the little girl all right?" he asked the moment Frank came in.

"No thanks to you."

"Thank God."

"One less murder to count against you on Judgment Day, I guess." Frank grinned at his startled look. "I know you killed Emma Hardy."

"I never—"

"Don't bother to deny it. Gilda Wilbanks told us everything."

"No! She wouldn't!"

Which, of course, meant she could have and was all the confirmation Frank needed. "To save her own skin? She would've sold out her own mother, so a distant cousin was no great loss."

"She didn't tell you anything. I know she didn't."

"If that's what you think, then let me tell you how it happened. Gilda sent for you as soon as she found out the little girl was coming to see Wilbanks today. She didn't say how long you'd been planning this, but maybe for a while, so you'd already talked to Klink—"

"Klink!"

"Yeah, he told us everything, too. You gave Klink that story about the little girl being taken from her mother and how you were going to help get her back. You must be a good liar, Udall. He believed every word, and he's no fool. It was a nice touch, telling them nobody was supposed to get hurt. Made you look like a hero instead of the kind of low-life scum who murders children."

His face was ashen. "I didn't kill her."

"Only because we got there in time. And you

did kill Emma Hardy, didn't you? What did you put in the whiskey? Laudanum?"

He shook his head but without much conviction.

"I guess you were disappointed when Emma didn't drink much of it. Is that what you were counting on? That she'd be unconscious when you choked the life out of her?"

"No! No!" He clapped his hands over his ears.

Frank grabbed his wrists and yanked his hands away. "She must've fought like a wildcat. Look at your hands." He held them up to Udall's face so they both could see the scratches. "She had your blood under her fingernails, Udall. How long did it take her to die? Two minutes? Three? Five? And you were staring right into her eyes the whole time, weren't you?"

Udall screamed and slammed his head down on the table. Frank released his hands and he clamped them over his head, as if trying to shield himself from a blow.

"Do you still see her face, Udall?"

"Yes!" he cried. "Yes, I do, every time I close my eyes! I haven't slept in days."

Frank leaned back in his chair. "Did you tell Gilda that? How did she expect you to kill a child?"

He lifted his head. "She didn't care! She said she'd stabbed that woman herself, and what did I know about killing because there wasn't even any blood when Emma died. She said it was my duty to get rid of the child. She couldn't do it because she had to be at the house with Wilbanks, so it had to be me. And then we could be together, just like we always wanted."

"Not exactly like you always wanted," Frank said, "unless you wanted to live with Gilda and her husband."

This time Udall sat back in his chair and his bloodless lips curled into a smile. "She didn't tell you that part, did she? About how she was waiting for the old man to die, and then as soon as he did, Ozzie was going to get really sick. He'd linger for a few weeks, and then he'd die. She had it all planned out. She read it in a novel, she said, just how to do it with arsenic, a little at a time."

The hairs on the back of Malloy's neck stood up. He'd had no idea. "Why didn't she hurry the old man along, too?"

"Why take a chance? He was already dying, and his doctor is there every other day. He might notice something, so she was just waiting."

Frank's mind raced. Would Wilbanks believe all this? Would he be willing to see Gilda arrested and tried for murder? But how would Frank prove any of this without Udall's testimony? And would he stick by his story when he found out Gilda hadn't betrayed him after all?

"I didn't kill the little girl," Udall reminded him.

"Only because we got to you first," Frank reminded him right back.

"No, I was supposed to kill her at the hotel. Gilda said to put a pillow over her face or something so I wouldn't have to see her. Then I was supposed to drop her in the river when it got dark. But I couldn't do it. I couldn't hurt her."

"So you were just going to drop her in the river alive and let her drown," Frank said, letting Udall see every bit of his contempt.

"I tried, but I couldn't do it! I gave her some more chloroform so she wouldn't know what was happening. I didn't want her to be afraid."

"That was kind of you."

"But I couldn't do it. I laid her down because I couldn't do it. I was still trying to figure out what to do when you found me, but I wasn't going to put her in the river, I swear to God!"

"You better hope God believes you, because I don't," Frank said, rising to his feet. "We're going to lock you up now, and tomorrow you'll go to the Tombs, where you'll stay until you're tried for killing Emma Hardy, and then you'll get to try out Old Sparky."

He frowned. "Old Sparky?"

"The electric chair where they execute murderers, Udall. So Judgment Day for you is coming a lot sooner than you thought." He started for the door, then turned back as if he'd just remembered something else. "Oh, and by the way, you were right about Gilda. She never told me anything about you. In fact, she tried to blame

Ozzie for killing Emma Hardy. So tomorrow I'm going to call on her and tell her *you* told me everything."

Frank could still hear Udall screaming when he walked out of the building.

Sarah had spent the night in the nursery, curled up beside Catherine in the bed where she herself had slept as a child. She couldn't stand the thought of being any farther away from her than that. Catherine woke up early, little the worse for her harrowing adventure the day before.

"Mama, why are you sleeping in my bed?"

"Oh, my," Sarah said, trying to act surprised. "I just lay down with you last night until you fell asleep, and I guess I never woke up!"

"I had a bad dream," she said with a frown. "A bad man took me away from you."

Sarah stroked her face. "It was only a dream, my darling. See, you're right here, safe and sound. Now let's get up and see what's for breakfast."

Mrs. Decker joined them and Maeve in the nursery for breakfast, and they had a wonderful time pretending nothing untoward had ever happened. They were debating whether to go to church that morning when the maid came up to tell them Malloy had arrived.

Catherine wanted to see him, and Sarah thought he'd want to see her as well, so they all trooped downstairs to the family parlor, where Malloy and her father were deep in a conversation that ended the instant they entered the room.

Catherine ran to him, and Sarah wished that she could, too. She followed more sedately, managing to keep her dignity. When he'd lifted Catherine into his arms and finished greeting her, he smiled at Sarah in a way that made her heart ache.

"Good morning, Mrs. Brandt."

"Good morning, Malloy. Catherine had a bad dream last night," she said quickly so he wouldn't say anything to confuse her.

"Did she?" He looked at her for confirmation.

"You were in it, too," she said. "You brought me back to my mama."

"You were the hero, Mr. Malloy," her mother said.

"I don't know about that, but I'm glad I brought you to your mama. I'm sure she was very happy about that."

"I was," Sarah said, thinking how very happy she really was.

Malloy teased Catherine a bit about how pretty she looked, and finally, Maeve said, "We need to let the grown-ups talk now. Time to go upstairs."

Catherine pretended to pout, but Malloy handed her over to Maeve, who mentioned some of the toys waiting for them upstairs, and Catherine went willingly. When they had gone, Sarah's mother had the maid bring in some coffee, and they settled into what were becoming their regular seats, with Sarah and Malloy on the sofa and her parents across from them in their chairs.

"Did you learn anything new from Udall?" Sarah asked.

"I learned we were right about most of it. Gilda is the one who planned it all."

"Gilda?" her father said. "Surely not."

"Why?" her mother asked. "Because she's a female?"

While that may well have been the true reason, her father was wise enough not to say so. "She hardly seems clever enough. Now if you'd told me Sarah had concocted an elaborate plan, or you, my dear, I would certainly believe it."

"Udall is the one who's not very clever," Malloy said diplomatically. "He said Gilda stabbed Anne Murphy."

"She must have gone to the boardinghouse looking for Catherine," Sarah said.

"But how would she have known where Miss Murphy was living?" her mother asked.

"Hicks's private investigator had found her, and Udall had access to his reports," Malloy said. "She probably didn't intend to kill Miss Murphy, but when she found out nobody else knew where Catherine was, she saw her chance. With Miss Murphy out of the way, she probably thought no one would ever find her."

"I just remembered, the girl at the Mission told us a woman had been there asking if any little girls lived there," Sarah said. "We thought it was Emma, but maybe it was Gilda."

"That's possible," Malloy said. "Gilda was the one who sent Udall to kill Emma. He'd brought the drugged whiskey for her, but she didn't drink enough of it, so killing her was a lot more difficult than he'd thought it would be. He said he hasn't slept since."

"You never told us how you found him," Sarah said.

"Are you sure you want to hear the story?"

Sarah didn't have to think about that. "Yes. I need to know."

"Michael Hicks told me they had a client who might have arranged the kidnapping for Udall, so we went to see him. Turns out he was right."

"That scoundrel," her father said. "I hope you arrested him."

Malloy gave him a sheepish grin. "Actually, he's the one you might need to pay the reward to." He explained how Udall had lied to engage Klink's help. "And he told us where to find Udall. He'd taken Catherine to a hotel, but he was so unnerved by killing Emma that he couldn't harm Catherine or at least that's what he claimed."

Sarah thought there might be more to it than he was telling her, but she said, "Thank heaven for that."

The maid knocked on the door and told Malloy that he had a telephone call.

"How did they know you were here?" Sarah asked.

"They must've sent someone to my flat. I told my mother where I was going."

He excused himself, and when he was gone, Sarah happened to remember something she'd intended to ask. "Mother, do you know what a Mickey Finn is?"

"Of course I do, dear."

Sarah smiled. She'd have to inform Malloy.

But her father said, "What is it then?"

She gave him an impatient glance. "He's one of the boys in those books that Mr. Twain wrote."

"That's *Huckleberry* Finn, my dear," he said with a smile.

"Is it? Then who is Mickey Finn?"

Sarah wouldn't tell Malloy after all.

They were still discussing Mickey Finns when Malloy returned, his expression grim.

"What is it?" her mother asked. "Not bad news, I hope."

"That was Police Headquarters. Terrance Udall hanged himself in his cell last night."

15

Frank had to get to Gilda Wilbanks before she found out about Udall, so he'd left the Deckers' house immediately and headed for Wilbanks's house. He'd asked Headquarters not to notify anyone else about Udall's death, but Gilda would have found out last night from Hicks that Catherine had been rescued and Udall arrested. She would not know he'd betrayed her, however. Still, she'd had all night to make her plans. If she loved Udall as he thought she did, she would probably try to save them both. Frank had all of that in his favor.

What he didn't know was who might still try to protect her.

The maid told him that both Mr. and Mrs. Hicks were still there, so he asked to see them. They received him in the parlor. They didn't look as if they'd slept much the night before.

"How is little Catherine?" Lynne Hicks asked when they had exchanged greetings.

"She's fine. She slept through most of her ordeal, and she thinks it was a bad dream."

"That's a blessing."

"How is Mr. Wilbanks?" Frank asked.

The two exchanged a glance. "Not well, I'm afraid," Hicks said. "The shock made him very ill."

"He was greatly relieved to hear you'd found Catherine, of course," Lynne said, "but he's so weak. We don't know how well he can recover from this, if he can at all."

"I was afraid of that, but I must speak with him. I need to know how he wants me to handle the situation with Gilda."

"Was she really involved in Catherine's kidnapping?" Lynne asked.

"According to Udall, she was the one who planned everything, and she actually killed Anne Murphy herself."

Frank had expected shock, but Lynne Hicks was merely furious. "Then you must arrest her like the common criminal she is."

"I'd like nothing better, but it's not that simple."

Michael Hicks nodded. "You're concerned about who might want to protect her."

"When Mr. Wilbanks dies, Ozzie will be a very rich man, and Gilda is his wife," Frank said. "He can use his money to make sure she never even goes to trial. And if he won't protect her, her own family probably would, if only to spare themselves from the scandal."

"Her family no longer has any great wealth, but

they can probably marshal enough influence to accomplish the same thing," Michael said. "They'll also want to see Udall released."

Frank wasn't going to tell them about Udall yet. "Your father might want to protect his family from scandal as well, but I know something that will change his mind. May I speak with him?"

"I'll ask him if he feels up to it," Lynne said.

When she was gone, Frank said, "Thank you for your help yesterday, Mr. Hicks."

"I'm just glad I guessed correctly. Klink might have had nothing to do with it."

"I guess we're lucky Udall didn't have any other criminal friends."

"I've never liked Gilda, but it's hard to believe a woman could be so cold-blooded, especially about a child," Hicks mused.

"We often underestimate the female of the species, Mr. Hicks. What she lacks in physical strength, she often makes up for in intelligence. We should be grateful that most of them use their talents for good."

Lynne returned. "Father is quite anxious to see you. He wants to hear everything that happened yesterday. But please, you can't stay long. He tires very easily."

Frank asked Michael and Lynne to accompany him. He wanted them to know exactly what he said to Wilbanks and what Wilbanks said to him.

Wilbanks lay in his bed, his face white against

the pile of pillows supporting him. His valet had placed a chair beside the bed, and Frank sat down. Michael and Lynne stood at the foot of the bed.

Frank saw the pad of paper lying in his lap and the pencil grasped loosely in his fingers.

"Speaking makes him cough," Lynne said. "So if he needs to tell you anything, he'll write it down."

Frank assured Wilbanks that Catherine was perfectly all right, then told him everything that had happened yesterday, how Hicks had taken him to Klink and how they'd found Udall with Catherine at the river's edge. He spared none of the details he'd glossed over for Sarah's benefit. He wanted Wilbanks to know exactly how close they had come to losing the child. Then he told him what Udall had confessed and how Gilda had killed Anne Murphy and Udall had killed Emma Hardy.

"The only thing he told me that I didn't already suspect was Gilda's plan to kill Ozzie," Frank said finally.

Lynne Hicks gasped, but Frank's gaze never left Wilbanks's face. Pain flickered in his eyes before igniting into fury.

"She wasn't going to be satisfied being the wife of a wealthy man," Frank continued. "She wanted all the money for herself and Udall, so as soon as you die, Gilda plans to slowly poison Ozzie.

Then she and Udall will have your money and each other."

"We must tell Ozzie," Lynne said. "He's been defending her, insisting she couldn't possibly have been involved."

"He won't believe it," Hicks said. "He'll just defend her more vigorously."

"Mr. Wilbanks, what I need to know is whether you want to shield your family from scandal by protecting her."

Fury blazed in his eyes, and the words he scratched out on his pad reflected it. "Let her hang."

Gilda refused to see him alone. Ozzie sat beside her on the parlor sofa, and Frank wondered why she'd insisted on his presence. Frank couldn't believe she wanted her husband to hear her accused of murder, but maybe she did. Maybe she had a plan he couldn't even imagine.

Frank sat down in the chair across from them. "Mrs. Wilbanks, your cousin Terrance told me some very disturbing things last night."

"I doubt that very much."

Frank had seen that expression before. Rich women used it when they wanted to intimidate someone. He'd even seen Sarah use it on occasion, and it could be very effective on servants and people who felt powerless. Frank did not feel powerless. "I can understand why you don't believe me. Udall told me how you've been in love for years and weren't allowed to marry because you're cousins. You must've thought he'd never betray you, but I'm afraid I lied to him to get him to cooperate. I told him you'd betrayed him first. You see, I'd figured out almost all of your plans, and I knew you'd killed Anne Murphy—"

"That's ridiculous!" she said.

"Really, Mr. Malloy," Ozzie said.

Frank just smiled. "And I knew he'd killed Emma Hardy—"

"How dare you!"

"And he'd hired some of Mr. Klink's men to help him kidnap Catherine. Mr. Hicks was the one who guessed that, so it was just luck we found him, but he didn't know it. He thought you'd told me everything. He believed me when I said you'd betrayed him to save your own skin."

She didn't want to believe him. He could see it in her eyes, but she was no longer as certain as she had been. "Terrance would never . . ."

"Would never what? Would never think the worst of you? He knew you'd stabbed a woman to death. He knew you'd ordered him to kill another woman and her child." Frank paused and looked meaningfully at Ozzie. "He knew you planned to kill your own husband."

That was it, the one piece of information that could only have come from Udall.

"No!" she cried, raising a trembling hand to her lips.

"He told me how you were going to poison Ozzie slowly with arsenic so it would just seem like he was sick. He said you'd read about it in a novel," Frank continued relentlessly.

She shook her head, trying to deny it, but her eyes held the terror of a cornered animal. She hadn't made a plan for this, for how she'd deal with Udall turning on her. She glanced at Ozzie, but his shocked expression told her she'd lost him, at least for the moment.

"Terrance would never . . . He loves me!"

"Maybe he doesn't love you as much as you love him," Frank said. "He turned on you in a moment when he thought you'd betrayed him. What kind of love is that?"

"He does! He loves me!"

"Does he love you or the money you were going to bring him? That was the plan, wasn't it? You'd marry a rich man and get all his money. Did you think of that or did he?"

She jumped to her feet. "It wasn't like that!"

"What was it like, Mrs. Wilbanks? Which one of you came up with the plan for you to marry a rich man and murder him?"

"No, no, that was never the plan!"

"Are you saying you married Ozzie out of love?"

354

"They made me marry him! They said it was a brilliant match!"

"But it wasn't, was it?" Frank said, glancing speculatively at Ozzie and thinking about what marriage to him must be like. "He's boring and stupid, and he's not even rich."

"I say, Malloy!" Ozzie said, but he was too boring and stupid to know what else he should say.

"That was the final insult, wasn't it? Ozzie didn't even have any money of his own," Frank said. "At least not until his father died. Lucky for you, that wasn't going to be much longer. But even after the old man died, you'd still have to put up with Ozzie, so you'd have to kill him. Slowly. With arsenic. Like in the novel."

She was thinking now. He could see it, and she'd realized she needed to win Ozzie back. "It's not true, darling. None of it is true," she said, sitting back down and trying to take his hand.

He let her, but he watched her warily, as one would a poisonous snake.

"Was money really that important to you, Mrs. Wilbanks?" Frank asked. "Important enough to kill for it?"

"Of course not!" she said, managing some of her usual hauteur. "I'm a Van Horn."

"But you were a poor relation," Ozzie said, still watching her intently and pulling his hand from her grasp. "You told me how you hated it. You hated the hand-me-down clothes and the second-best schools and the pity from your friends. You told me all about it."

"And Terrance hated it, too, didn't he?" Frank said. "So you hatched this plan and started killing everyone who stood in your way."

"No, you're wrong. Terrance never betrayed me. He would never do that. He loves me too much."

"Well, he did betray you," Frank said, "but I'm afraid it doesn't matter now. You see, I wanted to watch him being executed in the electric chair for killing Emma Hardy, but I would've been willing to give him life in prison instead in exchange for testifying against you."

Gilda had blanched at the mention of execution, but she lifted her chin.

"I knew it. He won't say a word against me, will he?"

"He won't say a word against anyone anymore. He's dead."

She stared back at him, stunned. "Wh . . . what?"

"He's *dead*."

"You're lying!"

"No, I'm not."

The color rose in her face. "What did you do to him? You killed him, didn't you?"

"No, as much as I might have wanted to, I didn't. He killed himself."

She shook her head. "He'd never do that!"

"I blame myself. I should have seen it coming.

After I got him to tell me everything, I admitted that I'd lied to him and you hadn't betrayed him at all. I guess he couldn't stand the thought of you finding out what he'd done, so he hanged himself in his cell last night."

The pain in her eyes was so raw, for a moment Frank almost pitied her, but only for a moment. Then she started to wail, a primal cry of agony and loss. At the sound, the parlor doors burst open and Lynne and Michael Hicks rushed in.

Gilda had slumped to the floor, and Ozzie was backing away from her in horror.

"Are you going to arrest her?" Lynne asked, eyeing Gilda with disgust.

"Yes. Her family will probably have her released by tomorrow, but at least Ozzie won't be defending her anymore."

"I'm going to speak with her family, so they understand what she and Udall have done," Michael said.

"It probably won't make any difference. They still won't want one of their own tried for murder, and quite frankly, I doubt I can prove anything against her if she did stand trial. The only witnesses against her are dead."

"I doubt her family will want a murderess living with them, though, so I imagine they'll make some arrangements for her," Michael said.

Frank knew about those "arrangements." "Just so long as she can't hurt anyone else."

• • •

David Wilbanks's funeral was held on a beautiful spring day almost two months later. Fortunately, he'd recovered enough after Catherine's kidnapping to enjoy a few more visits from his daughter, but eventually, he'd asked Sarah not to bring her anymore. He didn't want Catherine to see him and be frightened by his condition, and Sarah couldn't blame him.

Malloy had accompanied Sarah and her parents to the funeral. Michael Hicks took her and Malloy aside for a moment after the graveside ceremony and asked them to come to his office the next day.

"It has to do with Mr. Wilbanks's estate," he said.

Remembering they were in a cemetery, Sarah fought to control her outrage. "Mr. Wilbanks left Catherine something in his will after all, didn't he?"

But Michael Hicks merely smiled. "I assure you, he did not. It's something else entirely."

"Can't you just tell us what it is?" she asked.

"Sarah, this is a funeral," Malloy said.

"Besides," Hicks said, still smiling, "I'm an attorney, and we must do everything in a proper way."

So the next afternoon, Malloy came by, and they took a cab uptown to Michael Hicks's office.

Sarah had to admit she could understand why

he'd wanted them to meet him there. The rich furnishings were probably meant to intimidate people into doing whatever their attorney advised. Well, she wasn't feeling the least bit intimidated, and she had no intention of allowing David Wilbanks to dictate to her from his grave.

"I've asked you both to come here today because the terms of Mr. Wilbanks's will affect both of you. I know what you're thinking, Mrs. Brandt," Hicks said, "but David was very careful to follow your wishes. He left nothing to Catherine or to you."

"Then why are we here?" Sarah asked.

Hicks cleared his throat. "In view of what happened, Mr. Wilbanks was extremely concerned about his son's future."

"His *son?*" Malloy said.

"Yes, Ozzie had been taken in by an adventuress who apparently intended to murder him for his money. David was already concerned about Ozzie's ability to manage his inheritance before any of this happened, and he wanted to ensure Ozzie's happiness and security for as long as he lives. To accomplish this, he created a trust to benefit Ozzie. A trust is a legal entity into which a sum of money is invested. The beneficiary receives the income earned from the invested funds but cannot spend any of the principal. This ensures that the income lasts for life, and David invested just enough to allow Ozzie to live comfortably but not enough to make him attractive to someone like Gilda again."

"I saw the announcement of their divorce in the newspaper," Sarah said.

"Yes, her family was furious, of course. They assumed Ozzie would continue to pay for her care in that place they put her."

"It's in Switzerland, isn't it?" Sarah asked.

"Yes, and I understand she isn't doing well at all. Udall's suicide completely unhinged her. But Ozzie has chosen to cut all ties to her, so she's their problem now."

Sarah probably should feel sorry for the woman, but she decided that was asking too much.

"All of this is very interesting, Mr. Hicks," Malloy said, "but you still haven't told us why we're here."

"I'm getting to that. I just wanted you to understand Mr. Wilbanks's concern for his son. As I said, he only put a portion of his estate into the trust for Ozzie. The rest he has left to you, Mr. Malloy."

Sarah thought she had misunderstood him, and apparently, Malloy did, too.

"I don't understand."

"Mr. Wilbanks was very impressed with the way you handled the entire situation with Catherine, Mr. Malloy. He could also see how much you genuinely care for his daughter, and he wanted to leave her in safe hands. Obviously, Ozzie is in no position to take on the care of a young child, and he did not want to burden Mrs. Hicks and myself with his illegitimate child, whose very existence is painful for my wife. Mr. Malloy, he has named you as Catherine's guardian until she turns twenty-one or marries, whichever comes first, and he has left you the balance of his estate so you can provide her with the life he would have given her had he been able to raise her himself."

Malloy sat there a full minute before he replied, obviously as stunned by this news as she. "But Mrs. Brandt is Catherine's guardian," was all he could manage.

"Not any longer, I'm afraid."

Malloy turned to her as if expecting her to have some explanation. She stared back, completely dumbfounded. She felt as if the earth had tipped on its axis. Nothing made sense anymore, but she knew what Hicks was telling her would change her life. She just couldn't figure out how yet.

"But Mrs. Brandt is the one who's raising Catherine," Malloy said. "Why didn't he leave Catherine to her?"

"Mr. Wilbanks was old-fashioned. He'd want a man to be looking after his daughter's well-being. Besides, Mrs. Brandt has already said she would refuse any inheritance."

Sarah was still trying to make sense of this. "What does this mean for Catherine? Will she have to go live with Mr. Malloy?"

"Mr. Malloy is her guardian, and he can make whatever arrangements for her that he feels are suitable."

"So she can continue to live with me?"

"If Mr. Malloy agrees, yes."

She could see Malloy was getting angry, and she didn't blame him. She was pretty angry herself. How dare Wilbanks do this to them?

"You said he left me some money," Malloy said. "If Mrs. Brandt could refuse it, I can, too, can't I?"

"Yes, you certainly may refuse it, but please understand, if you do, it will go to Ozzie. This would violate the intent of Mr. Wilbanks's plans to protect his son and would leave Ozzie vulnerable to every gold digger in the city. He is also an inveterate gambler, so perhaps my fears are unfounded. Perhaps he will lose the entire fortune at cards before he falls prey to another wicked woman. In any event, you would also be denying Mr. Wilbanks the right to provide for Catherine."

"A girl doesn't need a lot of money to grow up happy," Malloy said.

"No, but money can prevent a lot of misery."

Sarah had a hundred questions, but she decided they should get one thing settled first. "You said Mr. Wilbanks left his son part of his estate and Mr. Malloy the other part. How much money will Mr. Malloy inherit?" After all, a few thousand dollars was nothing to get upset about. How much could be left after he set up the trust for Ozzie?

"I won't have an exact figure for several months, of course, but when everything is settled, it should be approximately five million dollars."

"*Five million dollars!*" Malloy fairly shouted.

"Give or take a few hundred thousand."

Malloy shot up out of his chair and was gone, leaving the office door hanging open behind him.

Sarah and Hicks stared after him for a long moment.

"I don't believe I've ever had anyone react like that to being told he'd inherited five million dollars."

"And I don't believe I've ever seen Mr. Malloy quite so angry," Sarah said.

"Do you think he'll refuse to accept it?"

"I have no idea." Sarah realized she had no idea about anything at all. She felt as if someone had bashed her in the head and left her reeling. "Mr. Hicks, why on earth did Mr. Wilbanks do this?"

"For exactly the reason I told you. He saw how much you and Mr. Malloy care for Catherine, and he wanted her to remain with you."

"But I intended to raise Catherine anyway."

Hicks leaned back in his chair and folded his hands on his shiny desktop. "May I be frank with you, Mrs. Brandt?"

"I hope you will."

"Mr. Wilbanks did not want Catherine raised by a single woman alone. He wanted her to have the family that had been denied her."

"But she still doesn't have a family."

"Not yet."

"What does that mean?"

"I'm sure you'll figure it out, Mrs. Brandt. Do you have any more questions?"

None that she wanted to ask now, she realized. "I should try to find Mr. Malloy." And find out what he was thinking and what he was going to do and how it would affect the rest of her life.

"Please tell him I am at his disposal to answer any questions he may have, and I'm sure he'll have many. And Mrs. Brandt, please encourage him to accept the money. Making these arrangements gave Mr. Wilbanks great peace in his final days, knowing Catherine would be well taken care of."

Sarah stepped out onto the sidewalk and looked up and down the street, but she saw no sign of Malloy. Where would he go? What would he do? She tried to think of someone whose counsel he might seek, but no one came to mind except herself. Maybe she'd find him waiting for her at her house. She started walking, heading in the general direction of home and scanning the sidewalk on both sides of the street for a glimpse of Malloy. Eventually, she got all the way home without finding him.

The next morning, Frank knocked on Sarah's door, then wiped his damp palm on his pant leg.

This shouldn't be so hard, not after all they'd been through together. Not after the conversations they'd had about matters of life and death, the things they'd talked about, the times they'd saved each other's lives. In spite of all that, they'd never discussed really important things, though. He'd never told her how he felt about her, and he had no idea how she felt about him. Well, that wasn't strictly true. He knew she was fond of him. But that was all he'd allowed himself to know.

She opened the door, which he hadn't expected. He'd thought the girls would open it, as they usually did, and he'd have a minute or two to adjust to seeing her. But there she was, and she smiled the way she always smiled at him, the smile that haunted his dreams.

"Malloy. I've been so worried about you. Come in."

"Where are the girls?"

"They went to the market with Mrs. Ellsworth." She took his hat and hung it up. "Would you like some coffee? Mrs. Ellsworth brought over a cake."

"Yes, thanks."

He followed her into the kitchen the way he'd done so many times, but this time he really let himself see her, the gold of her hair and the shape of her body. She was beautiful. Too beautiful for the likes of him. That was what people would say, and it would be true.

To his surprise, she didn't ask him any

questions. She served him coffee and a piece of cake he didn't want, and she sat down across from him and waited.

"I'm sorry I left like that yesterday."

She gave him her kind smile, the one she gave Catherine when she was upset. "I probably would've done the same thing in your place. That was quite a shock."

"Yes, it was, and I don't think I'll get over it for quite a while."

"Mr. Hicks said to tell you he'll be happy to answer any questions you have."

"I saw him this morning."

"You did?"

"Yes. Like he thought, I had some questions." If she only knew.

"Have you decided what you're going to do?"

Frank leaned back in his chair. "I've decided what I *want* to do."

"Oh, Malloy, I know how angry you must be at Mr. Wilbanks, but I'm sure he thought he was doing this for the best. Men like that always think they know what's best for other people."

"Lots of people think that," he said.

"Yes, especially when those people are their children. He wanted a good life for Catherine, and heaven knows, she's had a hard time of it until now, so she deserves it. I just hope you'll let me continue to keep her, at least for the time being. She's lost so much, and another change would be upsetting to her. You'll always be welcome to visit her, of course. You are her guardian, after all, and—"

"Sarah."

She stopped, flushing, and he realized she was as nervous as he. Did she really think he'd take Catherine away from her?

"What?" Her voice was like a child's, soft and uncertain.

"Don't you want to know where I went when I ran off and left you yesterday?"

"Of course I do." That was better, more like the Sarah he knew.

"I can't believe you didn't ask me right away. I went to see your father."

"My father?"

"Yeah, well, I have to admit, the reason I went was because I thought he might've been the one who convinced Wilbanks to do this in the first place."

"Why would he have done that?"

Good, she didn't know. "I'll explain that later. I went to your father's office and scared his poor secretary out of his wits, and then I started shouting at your father, but it didn't take long to realize he had no idea what I was talking about."

"What did he say?"

"He gave me some good advice."

"He did?"

"Your father is a wise man."

"A wise man who likes to tell other people what to do. Did he tell you what to do?"

"He tried." That made her smile, as he'd intended.

"What did he tell you to do?"

"He told me to take the money."

"That's probably good advice."

"Sarah, I want you to understand some things. First of all, I never wanted to be rich."

"Of course not."

"There's no 'of course' about it. I'm not a fool. I've dreamed about being rich. All men do. We think about what we'd do and where we'd go and how nice it would be to never have to worry about supporting our families. I've done that. But I never wanted to have the kind of life where all you worried about were what clothes to wear and who invited you to dinner and which gentleman's club to join."

"I never wanted that life either. That's why I left my parents' home and never went back."

"I know. That's why . . . Well, that's why I was so angry. But your father pointed out that I don't have to have that kind of life, even if I take the money. I can live however I want."

"He said that?"

"Yes. And he also solved another problem for me, one that's been bothering me for a while."

"And what problem was that?"

"Well, you see, I'd been sure that nothing could

make an Irish Catholic cop socially acceptable in this city."

"Since when did you want to be socially acceptable?"

"Oh, for about two years now. And your father explained it to me. He said there are two ways to be accepted in this city. You can be born into an old, respected family, like the Deckers."

"Or the Van Horns," she reminded him.

"Or you can have lots of money, like Wilbanks or the Vanderbilts."

"And if you have *enough* money, the Van Horns will want to marry you."

"Will the Deckers want to marry me, too?"

"What?"

"Well, I'm really only interested in one of the Deckers."

"Which one?" She still didn't understand.

"Definitely not your father, and your mother is already married."

"Malloy, what are you talking about?"

He really hadn't expected this to be easy, but he was making it harder than it needed to be, he knew. "Sarah, maybe you already know this, but I've been in love with you since . . . Well, I can't remember even knowing you when I wasn't in love with you, so almost from the very beginning. Two years ago." He watched the color bloom in her cheeks for a moment. "The trouble was, I couldn't imagine any way that I could

369

offer you a proper kind of life, but now . . ."

"Now?"

"Now I'm asking you to be my wife."

He didn't know what he'd expected but not the frown she was giving him. "Did you think I wouldn't marry you before, when you were just an ordinary policeman?"

"I didn't know, but I thought you might, and that's why I never asked you."

She gaped at him. "You didn't ask me to marry you because you thought I would say yes?"

"Yes, and I couldn't ask you to live that kind of life."

"I wouldn't have cared!"

"*I* would have cared. You'd have my Irish name, and you'd live off the money I got from bribes, and people would feel sorry for you because you'd settled for a crooked cop, and your family would try to put a good face on it, but their friends would laugh at them behind their back, and someday maybe you'd be sorry but I'd be sorry for sure that I did that to you."

"Am I supposed to accept that explanation?"

"No, I'm just answering your question."

She glared at him for another long moment, but slowly, the anger died out of her eyes. "So now you think you're good enough to marry me?"

"No, but at least I don't have to be a cop anymore and people won't feel sorry for you because you married me."

"That's right. They'll think I'm a gold digger instead."

"I hadn't thought of that."

"Don't let it go to your head."

"No danger of that. I'm still trying to figure out why you're so mad I proposed to you."

She seemed surprised. "I'm not mad you proposed!"

"I told you I love you and I asked you to be my wife, and all you've done is complain because I didn't ask you sooner."

"Oh, Malloy, I did, didn't I? I'm so sorry! That's not what I meant at all."

"What *did* you mean?"

"I just wanted you to know that I'm not just willing to marry you because of the money and because you're Catherine's guardian and all of that."

"Then you *are* willing to marry me?"

"Yes, of course!"

"Why?"

"Why what?"

"Why are you willing to marry me?"

"Oh! Because I love you, too. I can't say I loved you from the very beginning, because you were quite unpleasant to me in the very beginning, but it wasn't long before I began to appreciate your finer qualities and—"

"Sarah?"

"Yes?"

"That's good enough." He took her hand and stood up, and she rose and stepped into his arms as if she'd been waiting to do it all her life. He kissed her long and deeply, the way he'd wanted to kiss her every day since he'd met her, and when they were both breathless, she said, "That was much better than the first time."

"You remember?"

"Of course."

She pulled his face to hers for another kiss, and when they paused again for breath, he said, "It won't be easy. People will still talk about you behind your back and make fun or pity you."

She smiled and shook her head. "But I'll be the luckiest woman in the world, and nothing else will matter."

AUTHOR'S NOTE

Like many of you, I have been hoping Frank and Sarah would find a way to get together and live happily ever after. Well, maybe not completely happily, since they'd continue to deal with many tragic murders as they move on with their lives, but at least they'd be together. The problem, of course, was that I had placed so many barriers between them, I couldn't figure out how to overcome them all.

Luckily for Frank and Sarah (and those of us who love them), I expressed my frustration one day to my classmates in the Seton Hill University Master's of Fine Arts program. I even mentioned that I was considering having a contest to ask for help from my fans in solving this difficult problem. One of my classmates, David Wilbanks, decided to "enter" the proposed contest by offering a list of suggestions. Since Dave had never read the series and knew practically nothing about it, he was not hindered by any of the facts that prevented me from seeing a solution, and he sent me a list of suggestions. None of them were exactly right, but one of them triggered the idea I eventually chose. Dave suggested that Frank inherit a fortune from a rich relative he didn't know existed. I thought, "Frank is Irish. He's never had a rich relative in his whole family tree!" and skipped to the next suggestion on his list, but then I thought, "Wait a minute, it doesn't have to be a relative!" I had already plotted this book, and I knew immediately that Catherine's father would want to take care of her. So thanks to Dave, Frank and Sarah will be starting a new chapter in their lives. They'll have a lot of things to work out. Where will they live? What will they do with Frank's mother? Will Sarah continue to work as a midwife? How will Frank adapt to being a wealthy man? But one thing will not change: People will still ask them to solve mysteries, hopefully for many years to come.

Dave's reward was to have a character named for him in this book. The fan contest became a test to see who could guess how I would finally get Frank and Sarah together. Many people guessed that Sarah's father would somehow intervene. Believe me, that was always a possibility, but I'm afraid Frank would never have accepted anything from Felix Decker. The solution had to be something Frank earned on his own and which did not leave him in anyone's debt. The clever Ingrid Cordova is the fan who came closest to guessing the real solution, so she also has a character named for her as well.

Please let me know how you liked this book by contacting me through my website www.victoriathompson.com or "like" me at www.facebook.com/Victoria.Thompson.Author. I'll put you on my e-mail list and send you a reminder when the next book in the series comes out.